P9-CDA-428

THE PRESIDENT'S DAUGHTER

ALSO BY JACK HIGGINS

Year of the Tiger
Drink with the Devil
Angel of Death
Sheba
On Dangerous Ground
Thunder Point
Eye of the Storm
The Eagle Has Flown
Cold Harbor
Memories of a Dance-Hall Romeo
A Season in Hell
Night of the Fox
Confessional
Exocet
Touch the Devil
Luciano's Luck
Solo
Day of Judgement
Storm Warning
The Last Place God Made
A Prayer for the Dying
The Eagle Has Landed
The Run to Morning
Dillinger
To Catch a King
The Valhalla Exchange

JACK HIGGINS

THE PRESIDENT'S DAUGHTER

G. P. PUTNAM'S SONS

NEW YORK

G. P. PUTNAM'S SONS
Publishers Since 1838
a member of
Penguin Putnam Inc.
200 Madison Avenue
New York, NY 10016

Published simultaneously in Canada

Library of Congress Cataloging-in-Publication Data

Higgins, Jack, date.
The president's daughter / by Jack Higgins.
p. cm.
ISBN 0-399-14239-8
I. Title.
PR6058.I343P76 1997 96-48654 CIP
823'.914—dc21

Printed in the United States of America
4 6 8 10 9 7 5 3

This book is printed on acid-free paper. ♾

Book design by Julie Duquet

In fond memory
of my dear friend George Coleman

There is more truth in one sword
than in ten thousand words.

—THE KORAN

VIETNAM

1 9 6 9

Jake Cazalet was twenty-six years old when it happened, the incident that was to have such a profound effect on the rest of his life.

His family were Boston Brahmins, well respected, his mother hugely wealthy, his father a successful attorney and Senator, which meant that the law seemed the natural way to go for young Jake. Harvard and the privileged life, and as a college student it was possible to avoid the draft and Vietnam seemed far away.

And Jake did well, a brilliant student who got an excellent degree and moved on to Harvard Law School with enormous success. A great future was predicted. He started on a doctorate, and then a strange thing happened.

For some time, he had been disturbed by the scenes from Vietnam, the way he saw that brutal war portrayed on television each night. Sometimes it seemed like a vision from hell. A sea change took place as he contrasted his comfortable life with what life seemed like over there. The ironic thing was that he could actually get by in Vietnamese, because at the age of thirteen he had lived in Vietnam, when his father had spent a year at the U.S. Embassy.

And then came the day in the cafeteria at college. People were lining up for the lunch counter, lots of new students, and amongst them one who was no more than twenty, dressed in white tee shirt and jeans like anyone else, books under one arm, the difference being that where his right arm had been there was now only a small stump. Most people ignored him, but one guy, a swaggering bully whose last name was Kimberley, turned to look at him.

"Hey, what's your name?"

"Teddy Grant."

"You lose that over there in 'Nam?"

"That's about the size of it."

"Serves you right." Kimberley patted his face. "How many kids did you butcher?"

It was the pain on Grant's face that got to Cazalet and he pulled Kimberley away. "This man served his country. What have you ever done?"

"So what about you, rich boy?" Kimberley sneered. "I don't see you over there. Only over here." He turned and patted Grant's face again. "If I come in anywhere, you step out."

Jake Cazalet's only sport was boxing and he was on the team. Kimberley had twenty pounds on him, but it didn't matter. Spurred on by rage and deep shame, he gave Kimberley a double punch in the stomach that doubled him over. A boxing club he went to in downtown Boston was run by an old Englishman called Wally Short.

"If you're ever in a real punch-up, here's a useful extra. In England, we call it nutting somebody. Over here it's head-butting. So, use your skull, nine inches of movement, nice and short, right into his forehead."

Which was exactly what Cazalet did as Kimberley came up to grapple with him, and the big man went crashing back over a table.

Pandemonium followed, girls screaming, and then security arrived and the paramedics.

Cazalet felt good, better than he had in years. As he turned, Grant said, "You damn fool, you don't even know me."

"Oh, yes, I do," Jake Cazalet said.

Later, in the Dean's office, he stood at the desk and listened to the lecture. The Dean said, "I've heard the facts and it would seem that Kimberley was out of line. However, I can't tolerate violence, not on campus. I'll have to suspend you for a month."

"Thank you, sir, but I'll make it easy for you. I'm dropping out."

The Dean was truly shocked. "Dropping out? But why? What will your father say? I mean, what are you going to do?"

"I'm going to go right down to that recruiting office downtown and I'm going to join the army."

The Dean looked devastated. "Jake, think about this, I beg you."

"Good-bye, sir," Jake Cazalet told him and went out.

SO HERE HE was eighteen months later, a lieutenant in Special Forces by way of the paratroops—his knowledge of Vietnamese had seen to that—and halfway through his second tour, decorated, twice wounded, a combat veteran who felt about a thousand years old.

The Medevac helicopter drifted across the Delta at a thousand feet. Cazalet had hitched a lift because it was calling at a fortified camp at Katum and they needed him there to interrogate a high-ranking Vietnamese regular officer.

Cazalet was only five feet six or seven, with the kind of hair that had red highlights. His eyes were brown, his broken nose a legacy of boxing days and, in spite of the tan, the bayonet scar that bisected his right cheek was white. It was to become his trademark in the years ahead.

Sitting there now in his camouflaged uniform, sleeves rolled up, the Special Forces beret tilted forward, he looked like what war had made him, a thoroughly dangerous man. The young medic-cum-air gunner, Harvey, and Hedley, the black crew chief, watched him and approved.

"He's been everywhere, or so they say," Hedley whispered. "Paratroops, Airborne Rangers, and now Special Forces. His old man's a Senator."

"Well, excuse me," Harvey said. "So what do you get for the man who has everything?" He turned to toss his cigarette out of the door and stiffened. "Hey, what gives down there?"

Hedley glanced out, then reached for the heavy machine gun. "We got trouble, right here in River City, Lieutenant."

Cazalet joined him. There were paddy fields below and banks of reeds stretching into infinity. A cart was blocking the causeway that crossed the area and a local bus of some sort had stopped, unable to continue.

Harvey peered over his shoulder. "Look, sir, it's pajama night at the Ritz again."

There were Vietcong down there, at least twenty, in their conical straw hats and black pajamas. A man got out of the bus, there was the distinctive crack of an AK47, and he fell. Two or three women emerged and ran, screaming, until the rifle fire cut them down.

Cazalet went to the pilot and leaned over. "Take us down and I'll drop out and see what I can do."

"You must be crazy," the pilot said.

"Just do it. Go down, drop me off, and then get the hell out of here and fetch the cavalry, just like good old John Wayne."

He turned, found himself an M16 and several pouches of magazines, and slung them around his neck. He clipped half a dozen grenades to his belt and stuck some signaling flares in the pockets of his camouflage jacket. They were going down fast and the V.C. were shooting at them, Hedley returning the fire with the heavy machine gun.

He turned, grinning. "You got a death wish or something?"

"Or something," Cazalet said, and as the helicopter hovered just above the ground, he jumped.

There was a call. "Wait for me." When he turned, Harvey was following him, his medical bag over one shoulder.

"Crazy man," Cazalet said.

"Aren't we all?" Harvey replied, and they ran through the paddy field to the causeway as the helicopter lifted and turned away.

There were more bodies now and the bus was under heavy rifle fire, windows shattering. Screams came from inside, and then several more women emerged, two of them running for the reeds, and three Vietcong emerged on the road farther along, rifles ready.

Cazalet raised his M16 and fired several short bursts, knocking two of them down. There was silence for a moment and Harvey knelt beside one of the women and tried for a pulse.

"She's had it, for a start," he said, turning to Cazalet, and then his eyes widened. "Behind you."

In the same moment, a bullet took Harvey in the heart, lifting him onto his back. Cazalet swung, firing from the hip at the two who had emerged on the causeway behind him. He caught one and the other slipped back into the reeds. Now there was only silence.

THERE WERE FIVE people left alive in the bus, three Vietnamese women, an old man traveling to the next village, and a dark-haired, pretty young woman who looked badly frightened. She wore a khaki shirt and pants and the shirt was stained with blood, someone else's, not hers.

She'd been speaking in French to the old man earlier, and now he turned to her as a single bullet hit the fuel tank of the bus and flames erupted.

"Not good staying here, we must hide in the reeds." He repeated what was presumably the same message in Vietnamese to the women.

They shouted something back to him and he shrugged and said to the young woman, "They are afraid. You come with me now."

She responded instantly to the urgency in his voice, sliding out of the door after him, crouching, then starting to move. A bullet took him in the back and she ran for her life down the side of the causeway and plunged into the great banks of reeds. Cazalet, who was in their shelter a little farther along the causeway, saw her go.

She forced her way through the water and mud, pushing the reeds aside, ploughing straight out into a dark pool to find two Vietcong confronting her on the other side, AKs at the ready. Fifteen yards away, no more, so that she could see every feature of these young faces, mere boys, not much more.

They raised their weapons, she braced herself for death, and then there was a terrible cry and Cazalet erupted from the reeds on her left, firing from the hip, blasting them both back into the water.

Voices called nearby and he said, "No talking." He stepped back into the reeds and she followed.

They seemed to move several hundred yards until he said, "This will do." They were on the edge of the paddy fields protected by a final curtain of reeds. A small knoll rose above the water. He pulled her down beside him. "That's a lot of blood. Where are you hit?"

"It's not mine. I was trying to help the woman sitting next to me."

"You're French."

"That's right. Jacqueline de Brissac," she said.

"Jake Cazalet, and I wish I could say it was a pleasure to meet you," he replied in French.

"That's good," she said. "You didn't learn that at school."

"No, a year in Paris when I was sixteen. My dad was at the Embassy." He grinned. "I learned all my languages that way. He moved around a lot."

Her face was spotted with mud, hair tangled as she tried to straighten it. "I must look a mess," she said and smiled.

Jake Cazalet fell instantly and gloriously in love. What was it the French called it, the thunderclap? It was everything he'd ever heard. What the poets wrote about.

"Have we had it?" she said, aware of voices calling nearby.

"No, the Medevac helicopter I was going to Katum in cleared off to call up the cavalry. If we keep our heads down, we stand a good chance."

"But that's strange. I've just been to Katum," she said.

"Good God, what for? That really is the war zone."

She was silent for a moment. "I was searching for my husband."

Cazalet was aware of an unbelievably hollow feeling. He swallowed. "Your husband?"

"Yes. Captain Jean de Brissac of the French Foreign Legion. He was in the Katum area with a United Nations fact-finding mission three months ago. There were twenty of them."

What a strange sensation. Sorrow, sympathy . . . was that almost relief? "I remember hearing that," he said slowly. "Weren't they all . . . ?"

"Yes," she said quietly. "Caught in an attack. The Vietcong used hand grenades. The bodies were not recognizable, but I found my husband's bloodstained field jacket, and his papers. There's no doubt."

"So why are you here?"

"A pilgrimage, if you like. And I had to be sure."

"I'm surprised they let you come."

She gave a small smile. "Oh, my family has a great deal of political influence. My husband was Comte de Brissac, a very old military family. Lots of connections in Washington. Lots of connections everywhere."

"So you're a countess?"

"I'm afraid so."

He smiled. "Well, I don't mind if you don't."

She was about to say something when they heard voices nearby, shouting to each other, and Cazalet called out in Vietnamese.

She was alarmed. "Why did you do that?"

"They're beating through the reeds. I told them there was no sign of us over here."

"Very clever."

"Don't thank me, thank my dad for a year at the Embassy in Saigon."

"There, too?" she said, smiling despite herself.

"Yes, there, too."

She shook her head. "You are a most unusual man, Lieutenant

Cazalet." She paused. "I suppose, if we get out of this, that I owe you something. Would you have dinner with me?"

Jake grinned. "Countess, it would be my pleasure."

There was the distant thud of rotors rapidly approaching and several Huey Cobra gunships came in, line astern. Cazalet took two recognition flares from his pocket, a red and a green, and fired them up into the sky. The sound of the Vietcong voices faded as they retreated and Cazalet took her hand.

"The cavalry arriving in the nick of time, just like the movies. You'll be okay now."

Her hand tightened in his as they waded out into the paddy field and one of the gunships landed.

THE EXCELSIOR WAS French Colonial from the old days and the restaurant on the first floor was a delight, a haven from the war, white tablecloths, linen napkins, silverware, candles on the tables. Cazalet had waited in the bar, a striking figure in his tropical uniform, the medal ribbons a brave splash of color. He was excited in a way he hadn't been for years. There had been women in his life, but never anyone who had moved him enough to contemplate a serious relationship.

When she entered the bar, his heart turned over. She wore a very simple beaded white shift, her hair tied back with a velvet bow, not much makeup, a couple of gold bracelets, a diamond ring next to her wedding ring. Everything was elegance and understatement, and the Vietnamese head waiter descended on her at once, speaking fluent French.

"A great pleasure, Countess." He kissed her hand. "Lieutenant Cazalet is waiting at the bar. Would you care to sit down straight away?"

She smiled and waved to Jake, who approached. "Oh, yes, I think so. We'll have a bottle of Dom Perignon. A celebration."

"May I ask the occasion, Countess?"

"Yes, Pierre, we're celebrating being alive."

He laughed and led the way to the corner table on the outside veranda, seated them, and smiled. "The champagne will be here directly."

"Do you mind if I smoke?" she asked Cazalet.

"Only if I can have one as well."

As he leaned across to give her a light, he said, "You look wonderful."

She stopped smiling, very serious, then smiled again. "And you look very handsome. Tell me about yourself. You are a regular soldier?"

"No, a volunteer on a two-year hitch."

"You mean, you chose to come here? But why?"

"Shame, I think. I avoided the draft because I was at college. Then I went to law school at Harvard. I was working on a doctorate." He shrugged. "Certain things happened, so I decided to enlist."

The champagne arrived, and menus. She sat back. "What were these things?"

So he told her everything, exactly what had happened in the cafeteria and its consequences. "So here I am."

"And the boy who lost an arm?"

"Teddy Grant? He's fine. Working his way through law school. I saw him when I went home on leave. In fact, he works for my father now during his vacation. He's bright, Teddy, very bright."

"And your father is some sort of diplomat?"

"In a way. A brilliant lawyer who used to work for the State Department. He's a Senator now."

She raised her eyebrows. "And what did he think of your enlisting?"

"Took it on the chin. Told me to come back in one piece and start again. When I was last on leave, he was campaigning. To be honest, it rather suited him to have a son in uniform."

"And a hero?"

"I didn't say that."

"No, but your medals do. But we're forgetting the champagne." She picked up her glass. "What shall we drink to?"

"Like you said, to being alive."

"To life, then."

"And the pursuit of happiness."

They clinked glasses. "When do you go back?" he asked.

"To Paris?" She shook her head. "I'm in no hurry now. I don't really know what I'm going to do next."

"Now that you've laid the ghosts?"

"Something like that. Come on," she said, "let's order."

Jake Cazalet was deliriously happy, and afterwards couldn't even remember what he had for dinner except that some sort of steak featured in there. A small band started to play, and they moved inside and danced. She was so light in his arms, he was always to remember that, and the smell of her perfume.

And how they talked. He could never recall having such a conversation with anyone in his life. She wanted to know everything. They had a second bottle of champagne, and ice cream and coffee.

He gave her a cigarette and sat back. "We shouldn't be here. We should be up there in the mud."

A shadow crossed her face. "Like Jean?"

"I'm sorry." He was instantly contrite and reached for her hand.

She smiled. "No, I'm the one who should be sorry. I told you I was through with ghosts, and then. . . . Listen, I'd like to do a ride 'round in one of those horse-drawn carriages. Will you take me?"

"I thought you'd never ask," he said and pushed his chair back.

The streets of Saigon were as noisy as usual and crowded with cars, scooters and cyclists, people everywhere, girls propping up the wall outside the bars, looking for custom.

"I wonder what they'll all do when we go?" Cazalet asked.

"They managed after we left, the French," she said. "Life always goes on in one way or another."

"You should remember that," he said and took her hand.

She didn't resist, simply returned the pressure and peered out. "I love cities, all cities, and particularly at night. Paris, by night, for example, and the feeling of excitement, that anything might happen just up there around the next corner."

"And usually doesn't."

"You are not a true romantic."

"Teach me, then." She turned her face toward him in the shadows and he kissed her very gently, an arm sliding around her shoulder.

"Oh, Jake Cazalet, what a lovely man you are," she said and laid her head against his shoulder.

AT THE EXCELSIOR, she got the key to her suite from reception, handed it to him without a word, and went up the broad carpeted stairway. She paused at the door of the suite, waiting, and Cazalet unlocked the door and opened it. He stood to one side, then followed her in.

She crossed to the open French window and stood on the terrace looking down at the crowded street. Cazalet slipped his arms around her waist.

"Are you sure about this?"

"Oh, yes," she said. "As we were saying, life is for living. Give me a few moments, then come in."

AFTERWARDS, CAZALET LAY propped up against pillows, smoking. It had been the most wonderful experience of his entire life, and now she slept quietly beside him. He checked his watch and sighed. Four o'clock and he was due at base for a briefing at eight.

He eased out of bed gently and started to dress. A muffled voice said, "You're leaving, Jake?"

"Sure, I'm on duty. Important briefing. Can we meet for lunch?"

"That would be wonderful."

He leaned down and kissed her forehead. "I'll see you later, my love," he said and went out.

THE BRIEFING WAS at general staff level and couldn't be avoided. His colonel, Arch Prosser, caught him over coffee and said, "General Arlington wants words. You've been covering yourself with glory again."

The general, a small energetic man with white hair, took his hand. "Damn proud of you, Lieutenant Cazalet, and your regiment is proud of you. What you did out there was sterling stuff. You'll be interested to know that others share my view. It seems I've been authorized to promote you to captain." He raised a hand. "Yes, I know you're young for the rank, but never mind that. I've also put you in for the Distinguished Service Cross."

"I'm overwhelmed, sir."

"Don't be. You deserve it. I had the pleasure of meeting your father three weeks ago at a White House function. He was in tiptop form."

"That's good to know, General."

"And very proud, and so he should be. A young man of your background could have avoided Vietnam and yet you left Harvard and volunteered. You're a credit to your country."

He shook hands vigorously and walked away. Cazalet turned to Colonel Prosser. "Can I get off now?"

"I don't see why not, Captain." Prosser grinned. "But you don't leave this base until you call in at the quartermaster's and get fitted with proper rank insignia."

HE PARKED HIS jeep outside the Excelsior, went in and ran up the stairs, excited as a schoolboy. He knocked on the door of her suite and she opened it, her face wet with tears, and flung her arms around his neck.

"Oh, Jake, thank God you're here. I was just leaving. I didn't know if I'd see you."

"Leaving? But—but what happened?"

"They've found Jean. He's not dead, Jake! A patrol picked him up in the bush, he's badly wounded; they flew him down this morning. He's at Mitchell Military Hospital. Will you take me?"

Jake felt the room spinning around him, but he spoke carefully. "Of course I will. I've got my jeep outside. Is there anything you need?"

"No, Jake, just get me there."

Already, she was slipping away from him, like a boat making for different waters and not his.

At the hospital, he peered through the window in the door of the private room and saw the man who was Captain Comte Jean de Brissac lying there, his head heavily bandaged, Jacqueline at his side with a doctor. They came out together.

Jake said, "How is he?"

It was the doctor who answered. "A bullet creased his skull and he was half-starved when they found him, but he'll live. You're both very lucky."

He walked away, and Jacqueline de Brissac smiled through her tears. "Yes, aren't we?" Her voice caught. "Oh, God. What do I do?"

He felt incredibly calm, knowing that she needed his strength. The tears were streaming down her face, and he took out his handkerchief and wiped them away gently. "Why, you go to your husband, of course."

She stood there looking at him, then turned and opened the door into the private room. Cazalet went down the corridor to the main entrance. He stood on the top step and lit a cigarette.

"You know what, Jake, I'm damn proud of you," he said softly and then he marched very fast toward the car, trying to hold back the tears that were springing to his eyes.

. . .

When his time was up, he returned to Harvard and completed his doctorate. He joined his father's law firm, but politics beckoned inevitably, Congressman first and then he married Alice Beadle when he was thirty-five, a pleasant, decent woman for whom he had a great affection. His father had pushed for it, feeling it was time for children, but there weren't any. Alice's health was poor and she developed leukemia, which lasted for years.

Over the years, Jake was aware of Jean de Brissac's rise to the rank of full general in the French Army. Jacqueline was a memory so distant that what had happened seemed like a dream, and then de Brissac died of a heart attack. There was an obituary in the *New York Times,* a photo of the general with Jacqueline. On reading it, Cazalet discovered there was only one child, a daughter named Marie. He considered writing but then thought better of it. Jacqueline didn't need an embarrassing echo of the past. What would be the point?

No, best to leave well enough alone . . .

Once elected Senator and regarded as a coming man, he had to take trips abroad on government business, usually on his own, for Alice simply wasn't up to it. So it was that in Paris in 1989, on government business, he was once again on his own, except for his faithful aide and private secretary, a one-armed lawyer named Teddy Grant. Amongst other things, there was an invitation to the Presidential Ball. Cazalet was seated at the desk in the sitting room of his suite at the Ritz when Teddy dropped it in front of him.

"You can't say no, it's a command performance like the White House or Buckingham Palace, only this is the Élysée Palace."

"I haven't the slightest intention of saying no," Cazalet told him. "And I'd like to point out it says Senator Jacob Cazalet and companion. For tonight, that means you, Teddy, so go find your black tie."

"Oh, I don't mind," Teddy told him. "Free champagne, strawberries, good-looking women. For you, anyway."

"Good-looking *French* women, Teddy. But I'm not in the market anymore, remember? Now get out of here."

The ball was everything one could have hoped for, held in an incredible salon, an orchestra playing at one end. All the world seemed to be there, handsome men, beautiful women, uniforms everywhere, church dignitaries in purple or scarlet cassocks. Teddy had departed to procure some more champagne, and Cazalet stood alone on the edge of the dance floor.

A voice said, "Jake?"

He turned around and found her standing there, wearing a small diamond tiara and a black silk ballgown. "My God, it's you, Jacqueline."

The heart turned over in him as he took her hands. She was still so beautiful it was as if time had stood still. She said, "Senator Cazalet now. I've followed your career with such interest. A future President, they say."

"And pigs might fly." He hesitated. "I was sorry to hear of your husband's death last year."

"Yes. It was quick, though. I suppose one can't ask for more than that."

Teddy Grant approached with a tray holding two glasses of champagne. Cazalet said, "Teddy, the Comtesse de Brissac . . . an old friend."

"Not *the* Teddy Grant from that Harvard cafeteria?" She smiled. "Oh, I truly am pleased to meet you, Mr. Grant."

"Hey, what is this?" Teddy asked.

"It's okay, Teddy. Go and get another glass of champagne and I'll explain later."

Teddy left, looking slightly flummoxed, and he and Jacqueline sat down at the nearest table. "Your wife isn't with you?" she asked.

"Alice has been fighting leukemia for years."

"Oh, I'm sorry."

"She's a brave woman, but it dominates her life. That's why we didn't have any kids. You know, it's ironic. My father, who died last year, too, urged me to marry Alice because he thought I should have a family. People worry about politicians who don't."

"Didn't you love her?"

"Oh, I have a great deal of affection for Alice, but love?" He shook his head. "I've only known love once."

She touched his arm. "I'm sorry, Jake."

"So am I. We all lost—Alice, you, and me. I sometimes think I came off worst, having no kids."

"But you do, Jake," she said gently.

Time seemed to stop for Jake. "What do you mean?" he said at last.

"Look over there, just at the French window to the terrace," Jacqueline said.

The girl's hair was long, the white dress very simple. For a heart-stopping moment, it might have been her mother.

"You wouldn't kid a guy," he whispered.

"No, Jake, that would be too cruel. She was conceived that one night in Saigon, and born in Paris in nineteen-seventy. Her name is Marie and she is halfway through her first year at Oxford."

Jake couldn't take his eyes off the girl. "Did the general know?"

"He assumed she was his, or so I thought, until the end, when the doctors told him just how bad his heart was."

"And?"

"It seems that while he was in the hospital in Vietnam after being found up-country, that someone sent him a letter. It told him that his wife had been seen with an American officer, who had not left her suite until four o'clock in the morning."

"But who—?"

"A member of staff, we think. The maliciousness of it! Sometimes I despair of human beings. But he had known, all that time, my dear Jean. Before he died, he signed a declaration under the provisions of the Code Napoléon, stating that he was Marie's titular father. It was to preserve her position and title legally."

"And she doesn't know?"

"No, and I don't want her to, and neither do you, Jake. You're a good man, an honorable man, but a politician. The great American public doesn't take kindly to politicians who have illegitimate daughters."

"But it wasn't like that. Dammit, everyone thought your husband was dead."

"Jake, listen to me. You could be President one day, everybody says that, but not with this sort of scandal hanging over you. And what about Marie? Isn't it better if she just lives with her memory of her father, the general? No, if Marie isn't told, that leaves only two people in the world who know—you and me. Are we agreed?"

Jake gazed at the lovely girl by the window, and then back at her mother. "Yes," he said. "Yes, you're right."

She took his hand. "I know. Now . . . would you care to meet her?"

"My God, yes!"

She led the way to the French windows. "She has your eyes, Jake, and your smile. You'll see."

Marie de Brissac turned from speaking to a handsome young officer. "Mama," she smiled. "I've said it before, but you look incredible in that dress."

Jacqueline kissed her on both cheeks. "Thank you, cherie."

Marie said, "This is Lieutenant Maurice Guyon of the French Foreign Legion, just back from the campaign in Chad."

Guyon, very military, very correct, clicked his heels and kissed Jacqueline's hand. "A pleasure, Countess."

"And now allow me to introduce Senator Jacob Cazalet from Washington. We're good friends."

Guyon responded with enthusiasm. "A pleasure, Senator! I read the article about you last year in *Paris Soir.* Your exploits in Vietnam were admirable, sir. A remarkable career."

"Well, thank you, Lieutenant," Jake Cazalet said. "That means a lot, coming from someone like you." He turned and took his daughter's hand. "May I say that, like your mother, you look wonderful."

"Senator." She had been smiling, but now it faded and there was only puzzlement there. "Are you sure we haven't met before?"

"Absolutely." Jake smiled. "How could I have possibly forgotten?" He kissed her hand. "Now, if you'll excuse me, I'd like to dance with your mother."

As they circled the floor, he said to Jacqueline, "Everything you said—everything—is true. She's wonderful."

"With such a father, she would be."

He looked down at her with enormous tenderness. "You know, I think I never stopped loving you, Jacqueline," he said. "If only—"

"Hush," she said, putting her fingers to his lips. "I know, Jake, I know. But we can be happy with what we have." She smiled. "Now, let's put some life into those feet, Senator!"

HE NEVER SAW her again, the years rolled on, his wife finally died from the leukemia that had plagued her for years, and it was a chance meeting with the French ambassador at a function in Washington three years after the Gulf War that brought him up to date. He and Teddy were standing with him on the lawn at the White House.

The ambassador said, "Congratulations would seem in order. I understand the Presidential nomination is yours for the asking."

"A little premature," Jake said. "There's still Senator Freeman, if he decides to run."

"Don't listen to him, Mr. Ambassador, he can't fail," Teddy said.

"And I must believe you." The ambassador turned to Cazalet. "After all, as everyone knows, Teddy is your *éminence grise.*"

"I suppose so." Jake smiled. Then, he didn't know why—was it the music?—he said, "Tell me, Ambassador, there's a friend of mine I haven't seen in many years, the Comtesse de Brissac—do you know her?"

An odd expression came over the ambassador's face, then he said, "*Mon Dieu,* I was forgetting. You saved her life in Vietnam."

"Hell, I'd forgotten that one," Teddy said. "That's how you got your D.S.C."

"You are not in touch?" the ambassador said.

"Not really."

"The daughter was engaged to a Captain Guyon, a fine boy. I knew the family. Unfortunately, he was killed in the Gulf."

"I am very sorry to hear that. And the Countess?"

"Cancer, my friend, at death's door, as I understand it. A great pity."

CAZALET SAID TO Teddy, "I've got to get out of here, and fast. Two things." He was walking rapidly along a White House corridor. "Get in touch with our Embassy in Paris and check on the present condition of the Comtesse de Brissac, then phone the airport and tell them to get the Gulfstream ready for a flight to Paris."

His mother's death a couple of years before had left him very wealthy, although with his interest in politics, he was content to put it all in a blind trust and leave the finances to others. However, it did give him the privileges of rank, and the Gulfstream private jet was one of them.

Teddy was already speaking over his mobile phone, and as they reached the limousine, said, "They'll call me." They got in the rear and he closed the glass partition between them and the driver. "Jake, is there trouble? Anything I should know about?"

Cazalet did an unusual thing for him during the day. He reached for the bar and selected a crystal glass. "Pour me a Scotch, Teddy."

"Jake, are you okay?" Teddy said anxiously.

"Sure I am. The only woman I ever truly loved is dying of cancer and my daughter is all alone, so give me a Scotch."

Teddy Grant's eyes widened and he poured. "Daughter, Jake?"

Cazalet took the Scotch down in one swallow.

"That was good," he said, and then he told him everything.

IN THE END, the mad dash across the Atlantic proved fruitless. Jacqueline de Brissac had died two weeks before. They had missed the funeral by five days. Cazalet seemed to find himself moving in slow motion and it was Teddy who saw to everything.

"She was laid to rest in the de Brissac family mausoleum. That's in a cemetery at Valency," he said, turning from the phone in their suite at the Ritz.

"Thanks, Teddy. We'll pay our respects."

Cazalet looked ten years older as they settled in the limousine, and Teddy Grant cared for him more than any other person on this earth, more even than he cared for his long-term partner, who was a professor of physics at Yale.

Cazalet was the brother he'd never had, who'd taken interest in his career ever since the cafeteria incident at Harvard, had given him a job with the family law firm, had given him the totally unique job of being his personal assistant, and Teddy had grabbed it.

Once, at a Senate committee meeting, he'd sat at Cazalet's shoulder, monitoring and advising on the proceedings. Afterwards, a senior White House liaison had come up to Cazalet, fuming.

"Hell, Senator, I truly object to this little cocksucker constantly appearing at these proceedings. I didn't ask for fags on this committee."

The room went quiet. Jake Cazalet said, "Teddy Grant graduated magna cum laude from Harvard Law school. He was awarded the Bronze Star for bravery in the field in Vietnam and the Vietnamese Cross of Valor. He also gave an arm for his country." His face was terrible to see. "But more than that, he is my friend and his sexual orientation is his own affair."

"Now, look here," the other man said.

"No, you look here. I'm off the committee," and Cazalet had turned to Grant. "Let's go, Teddy."

In the end, when the President had heard, it was the White House staffer who got moved, not Jake Cazalet, and Teddy had never forgotten that.

It was raining at the cemetery and slightly misty. There was a small records office, with a clerk on duty, and Teddy went in to find the location. He returned with a piece of paper and a single rose in a cellophane holder, got in the limousine, and spoke to the driver.

"Take the road north, then left at the top. We'll get out there."

He didn't say anything to Cazalet, who sat there looking tired and tense. The cemetery was old and crowded with a forest of Gothic monuments and gravestones. When they got out, Teddy raised a black umbrella.

"This way." They followed a narrow path. He checked the instructions on the paper again. "There it is, Senator," he said, strangely formal.

The mausoleum was ornate, with an angel of death on top. There was an arched entrance to an oaken door banded with iron and the name de Brissac.

"I'd like to be alone, Teddy," Cazalet told him.

"Of course." Teddy gave him the rose and got back into the limousine.

Jake went into the porch at the door. There was a tablet listing the names of members of the family laid to rest there, but there was a separate one for the general. Jacqueline de Brissac's name was in gold beneath it and newly inscribed.

There were some flower holders and Jake took the rose from its wrapping, kissed it, and slipped it into one of the holders, then he sat down on the stone bench and wept as he had never wept in his life before.

A little while later—he didn't know how long—there was a footstep on the gravel, and he looked up. Marie de Brissac stood there, wearing a Burberry trenchcoat and a headscarf. She held a rose just like his own, and Teddy Grant stood behind her, his umbrella raised.

"Forgive me, Senator, this is my doing, but I thought she should know."

"That's all right, Teddy." Cazalet was filled with emotion, his heart beating.

Teddy went back to the limousine and the two of them were left staring at each other. "Don't be mad at him," she said. "You see—I already know. My mother told me a year or two after we met at the Ball, when she was first ill. It was time, she said."

She put her rose into one of the other holders. "There you are,

Mama," she said softly. "One from each of us, the two people in the world who loved you best." She turned and smiled. "So here we are, Father."

As Cazalet wept again, she put her arms around his neck and held him close.

Afterwards, sitting on the bench, holding hands, he said, "I must put things right. You must allow me to acknowledge you."

"No," she said. "My mother was adamant about that, and so am I. You are a great Senator, and as President of the United States of America you could achieve remarkable things. Nothing must spoil that. An illegitimate daughter is the last thing you need. Your political opponents would have a field day."

"Screw them."

She laughed. "Such language from a future President. No, my way is best. Only you and I know, the perfect cover."

"And Teddy."

"Ah, yes, lovely Teddy. Such a good man and your true friend. My mother told me about him. You mustn't be annoyed that he spoke to me."

"I'm not."

She raised her voice. "Teddy, come here."

Teddy Grant got out of the limousine and joined them. "I'm sorry, Jake."

"You did right, Teddy. I'm grateful, but she won't allow me to go public. Tell her she's wrong."

"No, I'm afraid she's right. You could cripple your chances. The opposition would make it look real dirty. That's politics."

Jake's heart churned, but in his head, he knew they were both right. Damn it! "All right." Cazalet turned to her, still holding her hand. "But we must see each other on a regular basis."

She smiled gently and raised her eyebrows to Teddy, who said, "I'm sorry, Jake, but there would be talk. Hell, the press would jump on it. They'd think you'd found yourself a new girlfriend."

Cazalet's shoulders sagged. She touched his face gently. "Perhaps the odd occasion, some public function. You know the kind of thing."

"God, but this is painful," he said.

"You are my father and I love you, and not because you were that glorious young war hero who saved my mother in some godforsaken swamp. It's the decency of a man who nursed his wife through an appalling illness to the very end and never wavered that I admire. I love you, Jake Cazalet, for yourself, and I'm truly glad to be your daughter." She held him close and turned to Teddy, who had tears in his eyes. "Look after him, Teddy. I'm going now." She stepped out into the rain and walked away.

"God help me, Teddy, what am I going to do?" Jake Cazalet said brokenly.

"You're going to make her proud of you, Senator. You're going to be the best damn President our country has ever seen. Now let's go."

As they walked to the limousine, Cazalet said, "Kennedy was right. Anyone who believes in fairness in this life has been seriously misinformed."

"Sure, Senator, life's a bitch, but it's all we've got," Teddy said as they got into the limousine. "Oh, and by the way, I just had a call on my mobile. Senator Freeman's decided not to run. The nomination is yours. We're on our way."

LONDON • SICILY
CORFU
EASTERN MEDITERRANEAN

---

1 9 9 7

RAIN SWEPT IN ACROSS LONDON FROM THE WEST DURING THE night, driven by a cold wind, hard and relentless. By morning, the wind had dropped, but when the prison officer in a navy blue mackintosh opened the gate to the exercise yard at Wandsworth Prison, the rain itself was more relentless than ever. The officer was called Jackson and sported a clipped military moustache, which was hardly surprising as he was a former Grenadier Guard.

He pushed Dermot Riley forward. "On your way."

Riley, dressed only in prison denims, peered out. The yard, surrounded by high brick walls, was empty.

"I'll get soaked," he said in a hard Ulster accent.

"No, you won't. I'm being good to you." Jackson held out a small folding umbrella.

"I'd rather go back to my cell," Riley said morosely.

"One hour's exercise a day, that's what it says in regulations, then we bang you up for the other twenty-three. Can't have you associating with honest crooks, can we? You know how much they'd like to get their hands on a piece of IRA scum like you. That bomb in the West End last week killed sixteen people and God knows how many injured. You're not popular, Riley, not popular at all. Now get on with it."

He shoved Riley into the rain and locked the door behind him. Riley pressed the button on the folding umbrella and it opened. He took a tin of cigarettes from a pocket, lit one with a cheap plastic lighter, and started.

Funny how walking in the rain gave him a lift and the cigarette tasted good. On the other hand, anything was better than the solitary life he led for twenty-three hours a day in that cell. So far he had endured six months of it, which only left fourteen and a half years to go. Sometimes he thought he was going mad when he considered the prospect of those years stretching into infinity. It wouldn't have been so bad if they'd sent him back home to a prison in Ulster. At least he'd have been serving his time with old comrades, but here at Wandsworth . . .

At that moment the door opened and Jackson appeared. "Get over here, Riley, you've got a visitor."

"A visitor?" Riley said.

"Yes, your brief." Riley stood there in the rain, the umbrella over his head, and Jackson added impatiently, "Your brief, your lawyer, you stupid Irish git. Now move it."

JACKSON DIDN'T TAKE him to the general visiting hall but opened a door at the end of a side corridor. There was a table, a chair at each end, and a large barred window. The man who stood there peering out of it wore a fawn Burberry trenchcoat over a dark brown suit. The white shirt was set off by a college-type striped tie. He had black curling hair, a pleasant, open face and horn-rimmed spectacles. He looked around forty.

"Ah, Mr. Riley. I don't know whether you will remember me. I was in court the day you were sentenced. George Brown."

Riley played it very cool indeed. "Oh, yes."

"I've been retained by the Defense League to go into the question of an appeal on your case. There were certain irregularities, statements by witnesses which might well have been tainted." He turned to Jackson, who stood by the door. "I wonder if you'd mind stepping outside, Mr. . . . ?"

"Jackson, sir."

"I think you'll find if you check Section Three regulations, that where a question of appeal is being considered, a lawyer and his client are entitled to privacy."

"Suit yourself," Jackson said.

The door closed behind him, and Riley said, "What the hell is going on? I've never seen you in my life before, and I've already had any hope of an appeal turned down by the Public Defender."

Brown took a leather cigarette case from his inside pocket and offered him one. "Fifteen years," he said as he gave Riley a light. "That's a long time. Bad enough here, but they'll be sending you to Parkhurst on the Isle of Wight soon. Toughest nick in Britain and the hardest cons. Like the coffin lid closing when they get you in there. I know about these things. I am a lawyer, although naturally, my name isn't Brown."

"What's your game, fella?" Riley demanded.

"Sit down and I'll tell you." Riley did as he was told and Brown carried on. "I'd like to make you an offer you can't refuse, just like the Godfather."

"And what might that be? A fresh appeal?"

"No." Brown walked to the window and peered out. "How would you like to be free?"

"Escape, you mean?" Riley said.

"No, I mean really free. Slate wiped clean."

Riley was stunned and his voice was hoarse as he said, "I'd do anything for that—anything."

"Yes, somehow I thought you might, but there's even more to it. Do as I tell you and you'll not only be a free man once more, you'll have twenty thousand pounds in your hand to start fresh again."

"My God," Riley whispered. "And who would I have to kill?"

Brown smiled. "No one, I assure you, but let me ask you a question. Do you know Brigadier Charles Ferguson?"

"Not personally, no," Riley said, "but I know of him. He runs an intelligence unit specializing in antiterrorism. They call it the Prime Minister's private army. It's got nothing to do with the SIS or MI5. I know one thing; it's given the IRA a bad time in the last few years."

"And Sean Dillon?"

"Jesus, is that bowser in this?" Riley laughed. "Sure and I know Sean like my own self. We fought the bloody war together in Derry back in the seventies, and little more than boys. Led those Brit soldiers a right old dance through the sewers, but the word is Sean works for Ferguson these days."

"Tell me about him."

"His mother died giving birth to him and he and his dad went to London. Sean had a genius for acting. He could change himself even without makeup. I've seen him do it. The Man of a Thousand Faces, that's what Brit Intelligence called him, and they never managed to put a finger on him in twenty years."

"His father was killed by British soldiers on a visit to Belfast, I understand," Brown said.

"That's right. Sean was nineteen, as I remember. He went home, joined the Movement, and never looked back. At one time he was the most feared enforcer the Provisional IRA had."

"So what went wrong?"

"He never liked the bombing, though they say he was behind that mortar attack on Ten Downing Street during the Gulf War. After that, he cleared off to Europe and offered himself as a sort of gun for hire to anybody who'd pay, and he was even-handed. One minute he'd be working for the PLO, the next blowing up Palestinian gunboats in Beirut."

"And where did Ferguson come in? I've heard the story, but I'd like it confirmed."

"Well, among his other talents, our Sean can fly just about anything that *can* fly. He was running medicine for children into Bosnia and got shot down. It seems the Serbs were going to shoot him and Ferguson turned up and did a deal of some sort, blackmailed Sean into going to work for him."

"Set a thief to catch a thief," Brown said.

"That's about it. It hasn't made him too popular with the Provos back home."

"Well, it wouldn't, would it?"

There was a pause. Finally, Riley said, "Look, what do you want?"

"Sean Dillon, actually." Brown smiled and offered him another cigarette. "Or to put it another way, the people I represent want him."

"And who might they be?"

"None of your business, Mr. Riley, but I think I can guarantee that if you do exactly as I say, you'll have your freedom and we'll have Dillon. Does that give you a problem?"

"Not in the slightest." Riley smiled. "What do I have to do?"

"To start, you apply to see the Governor and ask for Ferguson. Say you have important information for his ears only."

"Then what?"

"Ferguson is certain to want to see you. There's been a series of small doorstep bombs in Hampstead and Camden during the past two weeks. It's a known fact that the IRA have at least three Active Service Units operating in London at the moment." He took a piece of paper from a wallet and passed it across. "You tell Ferguson he'll find an Active Service Unit at that address plus a supply of Semtex and fuses and so forth."

Riley looked at the paper. "Holland Park." He looked up. "Is this kosher?"

"No ASU, just the Semtex and timers, enough to show you were telling the truth. Not your fault if there's no one there."

"And you expect Ferguson to get my sentence squashed for that?"

Riley shook his head. "Maybe if he'd been able to nick an ASU." He shrugged. "It won't do."

"Yes, he'll want more and you're going to give it to him. Two years ago, an Arab terrorist group called the Army of God blew up a Jumbo as it was lifting off from Manchester. More than two hundred people killed."

"So."

"Their leader was a man called Hakim al Sharif. I know where he's been hiding. I'll tell you and you tell Ferguson. There's nothing he'd like better than to get his hands on that bastard, and he's certain to use Dillon to pull the job off."

"And what do I do?"

"You offer to go with him, to prove you're genuine in this thing." Brown smiled. "It will work, Mr. Riley, but only if you do exactly as I tell you, so listen carefully."

BRIGADIER CHARLES FERGUSON'S office was on the third floor of the Ministry of Defense overlooking Horse Guards Avenue. He sat at his desk, a large, untidy man with a shock of gray hair, wearing a crumpled fawn suit and a Guards Brigade tie. He was frowning slightly as he pressed his intercom.

"Brigadier?"

"Is Dillon there, Chief Inspector?"

"Just arrived."

"I'll see the both of you. Something's come up."

The woman who led the way was around thirty and wore a fawn Armani trouser suit. She had close-cropped red hair and black horn-rimmed spectacles. She was not so much beautiful as someone you would look at twice. She could have been a top secretary, a company director, and yet this was Detective Chief Inspector Hannah Bernstein, product of an orthodox Jewish family, M.A. in Psychology from Cambridge, father a professor of surgery, grandfather a rabbi, both hugely shocked when she had elected to join the police. A fast-track career had taken her to Special Branch, from where Ferguson had procured her secondment as his assistant. In spite of her appearance and the crisp English upper-class voice, she had killed in the line of duty on three occasions to his knowledge, had taken a bullet herself.

The man behind her, Sean Dillon, was small, no more than five feet five, with the kind of fair hair that was almost white. He wore dark cords and an old black leather flying jacket, a white scarf at his throat. His eyes seemed to lack any kind of color and were very clear and he was handsome enough, a restless, animal vitality to him. The left corner of his mouth was permanently lifted into the kind of smile that said he didn't take life too seriously, perhaps never had.

"God save the good work, Brigadier," he said cheerfully in the distinctive accent that was Ulster Irish.

Ferguson laid down his pen and removed his reading glasses. "Dermot Riley. He ring a bell for you, Dillon?"

Dillon took out an old silver case, selected a cigarette, and lit it with a Zippo lighter. "You could say that. We were not much more than boys fighting together in the hard days in the seventies in the Derry Brigade of the Provisional IRA."

"Shooting British soldiers," Hannah Bernstein said.

"Well, they shouldn't have joined," Dillon told her cheerfully and turned back to Ferguson. "He was lifted last year by Scotland Yard's Antiterrorist Squad right here in London. Supposed to have been a member of one of the Active Service Units."

"As I recall, they found Semtex at his lodgings and assorted weaponry."

"True," Dillon said, "but when they stood him up at the Old Bailey, he wouldn't cough. They sent him down for fifteen years."

"And good riddance," Hannah said.

"Ah, well, now, everyone has their own point of view," Dillon told her. "To you he's a terrorist, whereas Dermot sees himself as a gallant soldier fighting a just cause."

"Not anymore he doesn't," Ferguson said. "I've just had a call from the Governor at Wandsworth Prison. Riley wants to do a deal."

"Really?" Dillon had stopped smiling, a slight frown on his face. "Now why would he want to do that?"

"Have you ever been inside Wandsworth, Dillon? If you had, you'd know why. Hell on earth, and Riley's had six months to sample it and another fourteen and a half years to go, so let's see what he's got to say."

"And you want me?" Dillon said.

"Of course. After all, you knew the damn man. You, too, Chief Inspector. I'd like your input." He pushed back his chair and stood. "The Daimler is waiting, so let's be off," and he led the way out.

THEY WAITED IN the interview room at Wandsworth, and after a while, the door opened and Jackson pushed Riley into the room and closed the door.

Riley said, "Sean, is that you?"

"As ever was, Dermot." Dillon lit a cigarette, inhaled, and passed it to him.

Riley grinned. "You used to do that in the old days in Derry. Remember when we ran rings round the Brits?"

"We did indeed, old son, but times change."

"Well, you've certainly changed," Riley said. "And from one side to the other."

"All right," Ferguson broke in. "So you've had the old pals act. Now let's get down to business. What do you want, Riley?"

"Out, Brigadier." Riley sat on one of the chairs at the table. "Six months is enough. I can't face anymore, I'd rather be dead."

"Like all those people you killed," Hannah said.

"And who might you be?"

"A Detective Chief Inspector, Special Branch," Dillon told him, "so mind your manners."

"I was fighting a war, woman," Riley began, and Ferguson cut in.

"And now you've had enough of the glorious cause," Ferguson said. "So what have you got for me?"

Riley appeared to hesitate and Dillon said, "Hard as nails this old bugger, Dermot, but very old-fashioned. A man of honor, so tell him."

"All right." Riley raised a hand. "You people always thought there were three Active Service Units operating in London. There was a fourth and a different kind of setup. Nice house in Holland Park. Three guys and a woman, all with good jobs in the City. Another thing—all handpicked because they'd been born in England or raised here. Perfect for deep cover."

"Names?" Ferguson demanded.

"It won't do you any good. Not one of them has a police record of any kind, but here goes."

He rattled off four names, which Hannah Bernstein wrote down in her notebook. Dillon watched impassively.

Ferguson said, "Address?"

"Park Villa, Palace Square. It's on old Victoria Place in a nice garden."

"So you had dealings with them?" Dillon asked.

"No, but a friend of mine, Ed Murphy, was their supplier. He got a little indiscreet one night. You know how it is with the drink taken. Anyway, he told me all about them."

"And where's Murphy now?"

"Rotated back to Ireland last year."

Dillon turned to Ferguson and shrugged. "If it was me, I'd be long gone, especially after Dermot was lifted."

"But why?" Hannah demanded. "There's no connection."

"But there always is," Dillon said.

"Stop this bickering," Ferguson told them. "It's worth a try."

He banged on the door, and when it opened and Jackson appeared, took an envelope from his pocket. "Take that to the Governor and get it countersigned. It's a warrant for this man's release into my custody. Afterwards, take him back to his cell to collect his things. We'll be waiting in my Daimler in the courtyard."

"Very well, Brigadier." Jackson stamped his booted feet as if back on the parade ground and stood to one side as they filed past.

. . .

A NUMBER OF PEOPLE were waiting in the rain outside the main gate for prisoners on release. Among them was the lawyer who had called himself George Brown, standing beside a London black cab, an umbrella over his head. The driver looked like your average London cabbie, which he was, a very special breed, dark curly hair flecked with gray, a nose that had at some stage been broken.

"Do you think it's going to work?" he asked.

At that moment, the gates opened and several men emerged, the Daimler following.

"I do now," Brown said.

As the Daimler passed, Riley, sitting beside Dillon and opposite Ferguson and Hannah, glanced out and recognized Brown at once. He looked away.

Brown waved to a Ford sedan on the other side of the road and pointed as it moved away from the curb and went after the Daimler.

Brown got into the cab. "Now what?" the driver asked.

"They'll follow them. Ferguson's got to keep him somewhere."

"A safehouse?"

"Perhaps, but what would be safer than having him stay at Dillon's place in Stable Mews, very convenient, for Ferguson's flat is just round the corner in Cavendish Square. That's why I've made the arrangements I have. We'll see if I'm right. In the meantime, we wait here. I chose visiting day because I was just one of two or three hundred people and no one at reception will remember me, but the prison officer who took me to Riley will. Jackson is his name." He glanced at his watch. "The present shift should have just finished. We'll wait and see if he comes out."

Which Jackson did twenty minutes later and hurried away along the street to the nearest tube station. A keen snooker player he was, in a tournament at the British Legion that evening, and wanted to get home to shower and change.

The tube was as busy as usual, and as he entered, the black cab pulled in at the curb and Brown got out and went after him. Jackson went down the escalator and hurried along the tunnel, Brown close behind, but keeping a few people between them. The platform was crowded and Jackson pushed his way through and waited on the edge. There was the sound of the train in the distance, and Brown slipped in closer as the crowd surged forward. There was a rush of air, a roaring now as the train appeared, and Jackson was aware of a hand against his back, the last thing he remembered in this life as he plunged headfirst onto the track and directly into the path of the train.

The black cab driver waited anxiously. He'd already had to turn down several fares, was sweating a little, and then Brown emerged from the tube entrance, hurried along the pavement, and got in the back.

"Taken care of?" the driver asked and switched on his engine.

"As the coffin lid closing," Brown told him and they drove away.

FERGUSON SAID, "YOU'LL stay with Dillon at his place. Only five minutes' walk from my flat."

"Very convenient," Riley said.

"And try and be sensible, there's a good chap. Don't try playing silly buggers and making a run for it."

"And why would I do that?" Riley said. "I want to walk away from this clean, Brigadier. I don't want to have to look over my shoulder for the rest of my life."

"Good man."

At that moment, the Daimler turned into Stable Mews, negotiating a gray BT van parked on the pavement, a manhole cover raised behind a small barrier. A telephone engineer wearing a hard hat and a distinctive yellow oilskin jacket with the BT logo printed across the back worked in the manhole.

Ferguson said, "Right, out you get, you two. The Chief Inspector and I have work to do."

"When will we make the hit?" Dillon asked.

"Sometime tonight. Sooner rather than later."

The Daimler moved away and Dillon unlocked the door of the cottage and led the way in. It was small and very Victorian, with a scarlet and blue Turkish carpet runner up the hall. A door stood open to a living room, polished wood block floor, a three-piece suite in black leather, oriental rugs scattered here and there. Above the fireplace was an oil painting, a scene of the Thames River by night in Victorian times.

"Jesus," Riley said, "that's an Atkinson Grimshaw and worth a powerful lot of money, Sean."

"And how would you be knowing that?" Dillon asked.

"Oh, once I had to visit Liam Devlin at his cottage at Kilrea outside Dublin. He had at least six Grimshaws on the walls."

"Five now," Dillon said and splashed Bushmills whiskey into two glasses on the sideboard. "He gave that one to me."

"So the old bugger is still alive."

"He certainly is. Eighty-five and still claiming seventy."

"The living legend of the IRA."

"The best," Dillon said. "On my best day and his worst, the best. To Liam." He raised his glass.

Outside on the corner of the mews, the man working in the manhole got out, opened the door of the van, and went inside. Another man dressed as a BT engineer sat on a stool manipulating a refractive directional microphone, a tape recorder turning beside it.

He turned and smiled. "Perfect. Heard everything they said."

AND AT NINE o'clock that evening, Palace Square in Holland Park was sealed off by the police. Ferguson, Dillon, and Riley sat in the Daimler at the gate of Park Villa and watched armed police of the antiterrorist squad smash the front door down with their hammers and flood inside.

"So far so good," Ferguson said.

Dillon took the car umbrella, got out and lit a cigarette, and stood there in the pouring rain. Hannah Bernstein emerged from the front door and came toward them. She wore a black jump suit and flak jacket, a holstered Smith & Wesson pistol on her left hip.

Ferguson opened the door. "Any luck?"

"A stack of Semtex, sir, and lots of timers. Looks as if we've really nipped some sort of bombing campaign in the bud."

"But no Active Service Unit?"

"I'm afraid not, Brigadier."

"I told you," Dillon said. "Probably long gone."

"Sod it!" Ferguson told him. "I wanted them, Dillon."

Riley said, "Well, I kept my side of the bargain. Not my fault."

"Yes, but not enough," Ferguson told him.

Riley was really working very well. He added a little anxiety to his voice. "Here, you won't send me back, not to Wandsworth?"

"I don't really have much choice."

Riley switched to panic. "No, not that. I'll do anything. Lots of things I could tell you and not just about the IRA."

"Such as?"

"Two years ago. The Jumbo from Manchester that blew up over the Irish Sea. Two hundred and twenty dead. That Arab fundamentalist lot, the Army of God, was behind that, and you know who was in charge."

Ferguson's face had gone very pale. "Hakim al Sharif."

"I can get him for you."

"You mean you know where that murderous bastard is?"

"I spoke with him last year. He was also supplying arms for the IRA."

Ferguson raised a hand. "That's enough." He looked up at Hannah. "Get in, Chief Inspector. We'll go to Dillon's cottage and pursue this further."

. . .

THE KETTLE IN Dillon's kitchen was the old-fashioned kind that whistled when it boiled. Ferguson was on the telephone checking in to the office and Riley was on the couch by the fireplace, Hannah Bernstein at the window.

She got up as the kettle sounded, and Dillon said, "None of that. It wouldn't be politically correct. I'll make the tea."

"Fool, Dillon," she told him.

He made a large pot, put it on a tray with milk and sugar and four mugs, and took it in. "Barry's Tea, Dermot," he said, naming Ireland's favorite brand. "You'll feel right at home."

Hannah poured and Ferguson put the phone down. He took the tea Hannah offered and said, "All right, let's start again."

Riley said, "Before I was lifted here in London last year, I was pulled in by the Chief of Staff in Dublin as a courier. I had to fly to Paris, visit a certain bank where there was a briefcase in a safe deposit. All I know is it was a lot of money in American dollars. I never knew how much. I understood it was a down payment against an arms shipment to Ireland."

"And then?"

"I had exact instructions and I followed them. Flew to Palermo in Sicily where I hired a car and drove across to the south coast of the island, a fishing port called Salinas, a real nothing of a place. I was told to phone a certain number and simply say: 'The Irishman is here.' "

"Go on," Ferguson urged.

"Then I was to wait at this bar on the waterfront called the English Café."

The story was so good that Riley was almost believing it himself, and it was Dillon who said, "And they came?"

"Two men in a Range Rover. Arabs. They took me to this villa by the sea about six or seven miles out of Salinas. Nothing else around. There was a jetty, some sort of motorboat."

"And Hakim al Sharif?" Hannah asked.

"Oh, yes. Very hospitable. He checked out the cash, gave me a sealed letter for the Chief of Staff in Dublin, and made me stay the night."

"How many people?" Dillon asked.

"The two fellas that picked me up were obviously his minders, then there was an Arab couple in a small cottage next door. The woman cooked and her husband was a general handyman. It seemed as if they looked after the place when he was away." He drank some of his tea. "Oh, and there was a younger Arab woman who lived with them. I think she was there to make Hakim happy on occasions. That's how it seemed, anyway."

"Anything else of interest?" Ferguson asked.

"Well, he wasn't your ordinary Muslim. Drank a great deal of Scotch whiskey."

"So he opened up?" Dillon said.

"Only to the extent that his tongue loosened. Kept going on about the jobs he'd pulled and how he'd made fools of the intelligence services of a dozen countries. Oh, and he told me he'd had the villa for six years. Said it was the safest base he'd ever had, because all the local Sicilians were crooks of one sort or another and everybody minded their own business."

"And he's still there?" Hannah asked.

Riley managed to sound reluctant. "I don't see why not, but I couldn't swear to it."

There was silence. Ferguson said, "God, I'd love to get my hands on him."

"Well, if he *is* there, and I think there's a fair chance he is," Riley said, "you could get what you want. I mean, it's another country, but you knock people off from other countries all the time, don't tell me you don't."

"It's certainly a thought." Ferguson nodded.

"Look, send Dillon," Riley said. "Send whoever you want and I'll go with them, put myself on the line every step of the way."

"And make a run for it first chance you get, Dermot boy," Dillon said.

"Jesus, Sean, how many times do I have to tell you? I want out of this clean. I don't want to be on the run for the rest of my life." He turned to Ferguson. "Brigadier?"

Ferguson made his decision. "Take him out for a meal or something, Dillon. I'll phone you in two hours." He turned to Hannah. "Right, Chief Inspector, we have work to do."

He went out, she raised her eyebrows at Dillon, and followed.

Dillon went to a drawer in the sideboard, opened it and took out a silenced Walther, which he tucked into the waistband of his cords at the rear under his coat.

"Like they say in those bad movies, Dermot, one false move and I'll kill you."

"No, you won't, Sean, because I'm not going to make one."

"Good, then it's the King's Head on the other side of the square. Great pub grub. They do a shepherd's pie like your mother used to make, and after six months in Wandsworth I'd say you could do with."

Riley groaned. "Just show me the way."

THEY HADN'T BEEN back at the cottage for more than five minutes when the phone rang. Dillon picked it up.

"Ferguson," the Brigadier said. "This is the way of it."

Dillon listened intently, then nodded. "Fine. We'll expect you at nine o'clock in the morning."

He put the phone down and lit a cigarette. Riley said, "Is it on?"

Dillon nodded. "Ferguson's been in touch with the Marine Commando Special Boat Squadron at Akrotiri, the British sovereign base area in Cyprus. A Captain Carter and four men have been given the job. They'll leave for Sicily by boat posing as fishermen. Weather permitting, they should make it to Salinas by early evening tomorrow."

"And you and me?"

"Ferguson will pick us up at nine with Hannah Bernstein and take us out to Farley Field. That's an RAF proving ground. You and I, plus Bernstein, fly in the department's Lear jet to Sicily. We drive to Salinas. Carter will make himself known on arrival. The Lear will fly on to Malta."

"Why Malta?"

"Because that's where we go after Carter and his boys snatch Hakim. You and I go in with them, by the way."

"Just like old times."

"Short sea voyage. Do you good after Wandsworth."

Riley nodded. "Would you anticipate any problem with Hakim at Malta?"

"None at all. They're on our side. I mean, it isn't Bosnia. A shot of something to subdue him, and the Lear, after all, bears RAF rondels. By the time Hakim has stopped being sick, he'll be in London."

IN THE BT van, the man at the directional microphone nodded to his friend, then turned off the tape recorder.

"I got everything. You close the manhole cover and clear up while I call in."

A moment later, he was speaking to the man called Brown. "Right, see you soon."

He switched off the phone and got out of the van and went round to the driver's seat. A moment later, his friend joined him.

"Perfect," the one behind the wheel said. "Couldn't be better. Our people are already waiting in Salinas, and Riley and Dillon will be there tomorrow evening."

"What happened?"

The driver eased out into the square and told him. When he was finished, his friend said, "Special Boat Squadron. They're hot stuff."

"It will be taken care of. All in the plan, exactly as Judas envisaged. He's a genius, that man—a genius."

He turned out of the square into the main stream of traffic and drove away.

CHAPTER 3

THE LEAR JET THEY WERE USING STOOD ON THE APRON IN front of one of the hangars. It was very official-looking, with RAF rondels, and the two pilots who stood waiting by the cabin door wore RAF overalls with rank insignia.

As the Daimler stopped, Ferguson said, "All nice and official. It should make things easy at Malta." He took a small leather case from his pocket and gave it to Hannah Bernstein. "You'll find a hypodermic in there, ready charged. Just give our friend Hakim a shot in the arm. He'll stay on his feet, but he won't know what time of day it is, and here's a passport I got Forgery to make up for him. Abdul Krym, British citizen." He took another from his inside pocket and passed it to Riley. "There's yours, Irish variety. I thought it would go better with the accent. Thomas O'Malley."

"Now isn't that the strange thing," Riley told him. "And me with a cousin once removed called Bridget O'Malley."

"I haven't the slightest interest in your family connections," Ferguson told him. "Just get on board, there's a good chap, and try doing as you're told."

They all got out and approached the Lear. Flight Lieutenant Lacey, in command, was an old hand and had been attached to Ferguson's section for two years now. He introduced his fellow pilot, a Flight Lieutenant Parry.

Ferguson said, "How long to Sicily, then, Flight Lieutenant?"

"Headwinds all the way today, Brigadier. Can't see it taking less than a good five hours."

"Do your best." Ferguson turned to the others. "Right, on you go and good luck."

They went up the steps, one by one, the door closed. Ferguson stepped back as the engines started and the Lear taxied away to the far end of the field. It thundered along the runway and lifted.

"Up to you now, Dillon," he said softly, turned, and walked back to the Daimler.

IT WAS ALL a dream, Riley decided, and he might wake up in his cell at Wandsworth instead of sitting here on the leather club seat in the quiet elegance of the Lear. It had all worked out as Brown had promised.

He watched Hannah Bernstein, glasses removed, take some papers from her briefcase and start to read them. A strange one, but a hell of a copper from what he had heard, and hadn't she shot dead that Protestant bitch, Norah Bell, when she and Michael Ahern had tried to assassinate the American President on his London visit?

Dillon came through from the cockpit area, slid into the chair opposite. He opened the bar cupboard. "Would you fancy a drink, Dermot? Scotch whiskey, not Irish, I'm afraid."

"It'll do to take along."

Dillon found a half bottle of Bell's and splashed some into a couple of glasses. He passed one to Riley and offered him a cigarette.

"Cigarettes and whiskey and wild, wild women, isn't that what the song says, only not for the Chief Inspector. She thinks I'm taking years off my life."

She glanced up. "And so you are, Dillon, but you go to hell in your own way."

She went back to her work and Dillon turned to Riley. "The hard woman, but she loves me dearly. Tell me, was that a fact about you having a cousin called O'Malley?"

"Jesus, yes," Riley said. "Didn't I ever mention her? My mother died when I was five. Derry, that was, and I had a ten-year-old sister, Kathleen. My old man couldn't cope, so he sent for my mother's niece, Bridget O'Malley, from a village called Tullamore between the Blackwater River and the Knockmealdown Mountains. A drop of the real old Ireland that place, I can tell you."

"And she raised you?"

"Until I was eighteen."

"And never married?"

"She couldn't have children, so she could never see the point."

"What happened to her?"

"Her father was a widower. Her eldest brother had died fighting for the Brit army in the Far East somewhere, so when her father passed away, she inherited the farm outside Tullamore."

"So she went back?"

"A small place, but her own."

"Did you keep in touch?"

"She put me up more than once when I was on the run, Sean, though she doesn't approve of the IRA. Mass three times a week, that's Bridget. It's only a small farm, forty cows, a few pigs, goats, a small herd of sheep on the mountainside."

"And you liked it when you were laying low there?"

"Liked it?" Riley's face was pale. "She always said she'd leave it to me. She only has a couple of retired old boys from the village to help out, so there was plenty to do. There I was, the stench of the war zone still in my nose, up the mountain to see to the sheep in the rain with that Alsatian of hers, Karl, snapping at my heels. And you know what, Sean? I loved it, every minute of it. Isn't that the strange thing?"

"Not really. Roots, Dermot, that's what we all need, and your roots are in her."

"And what about you, Sean, where are your roots?"

"Maybe nowhere, nowhere at all. A few cousins scattered here and there that I haven't seen in years and probably frightened to death of me." He smiled. "Take my advice, old son. Once out of this, get back to Ireland and that farm outside Tullamore. You've been offered a miracle. From death in life at Wandsworth Prison to your present situation."

"I know," Riley said. "It's like the stone being rolled aside from the mouth of the grave on the third day."

"Exactly." Dillon yawned. "I'll have a little snooze now. Give me a push in an hour," and he closed his eyes.

Riley watched him for a while. A good stick, Sean, one hell of a comrade in the old days fighting the Brits in Derry. On one memorable occasion when Riley had taken a bullet in the left leg, Dillon had refused to leave him, had hauled him to safety through the sewers of the city.

He glanced at Dillon, sleeping now. Sorry, Sean, he wanted to say, but what would have been the point? He couldn't face going back to Wandsworth and another fourteen and a half years of living hell, so he closed his eyes and tried to sleep himself.

AT AROUND TWO o'clock in the afternoon they came in over the sea, Palermo to one side, and landed at Punta Raisi. Lacey obeyed orders from the tower and taxied to a remote area at the far end of the airport, where a number of private planes were parked. There was a small man in a cloth cap and old flying jacket standing in front of the hangar, and a Peugeot was parked to one side.

"And who might he be?" Riley asked.

"Don't let appearances deceive you, Mr. Riley," Hannah said.

"That's Colonel Paolo Gagini of the Italian Secret Intelligence Service. He's put more Mafia godfathers inside than anyone I know, and he's an old friend of ours."

Parry got the door open and Lacey went after him, the rest of them following.

Gagini came forward. "Chief Inspector, nice to see you again, and you, Dillon. Still around and still in one piece? Amazing."

Dillon took his hand. "This is Tom O'Malley, a colleague."

Gagini looked Riley over and laughed out loud. "A colleague, you say? Ah, well, it takes all sorts."

"Stop playing policeman, Paolo," Hannah told him.

"Anything for you, Chief Inspector. I've always found beauty with brains more exciting than beauty on its own, and anything for my old friend Charles Ferguson. I don't know why you're here and I don't want to know, only try to keep it out of the papers." He turned to Lacey. "And what can I do for you, Flight Lieutenant?"

"I need to refuel and then it's Malta next stop."

"Good. Let me dispose of my friends here first." He turned and led the way to the Peugeot. The driver got out, a small, eager dark-haired man in a check shirt and jeans.

"Colonel?"

Gagini put a hand on the man's head. "Luigi, I made you a sergeant because I thought you had a certain intelligence. This lady is a Chief Inspector, so treat her accordingly. Mr. Dillon and Mr. O'Malley are colleagues. You drive them across the island and drop them at Salinas. Afterwards, you return."

"Yes, my Colonel."

"And if you cock this up in any way, I'll have your balls."

Luigi smiled and held open the rear door. There was a bank of two seats. "Chief Inspector."

Hannah kissed Gagini on the cheek and got into the rear seat. Dillon and Riley sat in the other. Gagini smiled through the open window. "Good hunting, my friends."

He stepped back and Luigi drove away.

. . .

IT WAS SOME saint's day or other, and as they passed through Palermo they slowed to a crawl as the traffic became snarled up with various religious processions. There was an enormous catafalque being carried by hooded men in robes, an ornate statue of the Virgin standing on top.

"Would you look at that?" Riley said. "A religious lot, these people."

"Yes," Hannah Bernstein said. "But no ordinary Virgin. Haven't you noticed the knife in her heart?"

"That's Sicily for you," Dillon said. "Death is like a cult here. I don't think your cousin Bridget would like it at all, Dermot."

"She would not," Riley said forcefully but looked out of the open window all the same, fascinated.

They moved out of Palermo into the heart of the island, following the route usually taken by tourists driving across to Agrigento on the south coast, and the scenery was spectacular.

They passed peasants on donkeys, vegetables for market in panniers, old men in tweed caps and patched suits, usually with a *lupara,* the short-barrelled shotgun favored by Sicilians, slung from a shoulder.

There were women in black, working in the fields or walking in a line at the side of the road, baskets on their heads, seemingly impervious to the sun and the villages, buildings that were centuries old, open drains down the center of the street, the smell of urine strong in the sun.

"Jesus, Mary, and Joseph, but give me Ireland any day of the week. This is a poor sort of place," Riley said.

"Still very medieval," Hannah Bernstein observed.

Luigi spoke for the first time and in excellent English. "These are poor people ground down by poverty. Great landowners and the Mafia have sucked them dry for years, and in Sicily there is only the land. Olive groves, vineyards and, these days, the tourists."

"Soaked in blood over the years," Dillon said. "Everybody's had a piece, from the Arabs to the Normans. Did you know Richard the First of England was once king here?" he asked Hannah.

She showed surprise. "No, I didn't. You learn something new every day."

"Isn't that a fact?" Dillon said and lit a cigarette.

AT THE SAME moment in Corfu, Marie de Brissac was walking down the cliff path from the small cottage she had rented on the northeast coast of the island of Corfu.

She was a slim woman, twenty-seven at the time and looked younger. She wore a tee shirt and khaki shorts, and a straw hat shadowed a calm, intelligent face with high cheekbones. Her fair hair was tied into a ponytail, and she carried a cold box in one hand, her easel under the arm, and in the other hand was her paint box.

The horseshoe beach was delightful and gave her views across to Albania on one hand and to Greece on the other. A folding chair was where she had left it behind a rock, and an umbrella. She positioned them to her satisfaction, then set up her easel and started.

Watercolors were her favorite, much more than oils. She did a quick charcoal sketch of the scene before her, catching a fishing boat as it passed, then faded it down and started to paint.

She still hadn't got over the death of her beloved mother. The cottage had been a refuge, at least in her mind. No staff, just a peasant woman who arrived on a donkey three times a week with fresh bread and milk and firewood. Time to reflect on the meaning of life and its purpose and to paint, of course.

She opened the cold box. Amongst the other things in there was a bottle of Chablis, ice-cold. She uncorked it and poured a glass.

"Strange," she said softly, "but everyone seems to die on me. First Maurice in that stupid Gulf War, then the general, and now Maman. I wonder what I've done?"

She was not aware of any sound of approach, only the voice saying, "Excellent, I particularly admire that blue color wash and the way you soak it in to the shoreline."

She glanced up and found him standing there. Probably about her own age, with blond hair and a strong, tanned face. He wore jeans and an old reefer jacket. His English had a slight accent that she couldn't place.

She said, "I don't want to sound unwelcoming, but this is a private beach."

"Yes, I'm aware of that, just as I'm aware that you are the Comtesse de Brissac."

She knew then, of course, that this was no casual interloper, that there was purpose here. "Who are you?"

"What's in a name." He smiled. "Let's say David Braun." He took the bottle of Chablis from the cold box and examined the label. "Interesting." He poured a glass and sampled it. "Not bad, not bad at all."

"I'm glad you're enjoying it." Strange, but she felt no sense of fear. This was no casual encounter, no threat of rape.

He whistled and called out, not in English this time, and a young man came down the path to join him and she recognized the language at once.

"Hebrew," she said. "You spoke in Hebrew. I've been to Israel. I recognize the language."

"Good." He finished his wine. "Now, then," he said in English, "pack up the lady's things and follow us up to the cottage."

"What's this all about?" she asked calmly.

"All in good time, Comtesse." He gestured with one hand. "After you, if you please."

A Ford station wagon was parked outside the cottage. The other young man put her painting things in the rear and she saw that it was also filled with her suitcases.

"This is Moshe, by the way," David Braun told her. "He started packing up the moment you left. The cupboard, as they say, is bare. I know you've only been using taxis while you've been here, so the old woman, when she turns up on her donkey, will think you've just up and left."

"To where?"

He opened the rear door. "Your carriage awaits, and an interesting plane ride. What could be better?"

She hesitated, then did as she was told, and he got in beside her. As Moshe drove away, she said, "And the final destination?"

"Ah, now you're expecting too much. Just enjoy the ride. The view over there, for example."

She turned automatically, was aware of a prick in her bare right arm, turned and saw a plastic medical hypo in his hand.

"Damn you!" she said, "What was it?"

"Does it matter?" He tossed the hypo out of the open window. "You'll sleep now—a nice long sleep. You'll actually feel better when you waken."

She tried to reply, but her eyes felt heavy, and suddenly he just wasn't there anymore and she plunged into darkness.

IN SICILY, THE Peugeot was really into the high country, Monte Cammarata rising six thousand feet to one side.

"That looks like rough country," Riley said.

Luigi nodded. "Salvatore Guiliano made his home up there for years. The army and the police couldn't catch him. A great man, a true Sicilian."

"A great bandit, he means," Hannah said to Riley, "who paid the rent for some poor old woman now and then and liked to see himself as Robin Hood."

"God, but you take a hard line, woman," Dillon said. "Guiliano wasn't such a bad ould stick."

"Just the kind of man you would approve of."

"I know, it's wicked I am." At that moment, they entered a village and he added, "A pit stop, Luigi. I could do with the necessary and so could all of us, I suspect."

"Of course, signor."

They paused outside a *trattoria* with a few rough wooden tables and chairs under an awning. The proprietor, an old, gray-haired man wearing a soiled apron, greeted them. Luigi whispered to him, then turned.

"The toilet is at the back, Chief Inspector."

"On your way," Dillon told her cheerfully. "We'll take turns."

She followed Luigi, who went to the bar area to order the drinks. It was dark in there and the smell of the toilet was unmistakable. Dillon and Riley lit cigarettes as some kind of compensation. The only concession to modern living was an espresso machine.

Luigi turned. "Coffee okay?"

"Why not," Dillon said.

Hannah emerged from the shadows and made a face. "I wouldn't linger, gentlemen. I'll wait outside."

Dillon and Riley found the back room, which was in an appalling state. Dillon went first and shuddered when he came out. "Make it quick, Dermot. A man could die in there."

Luigi was still getting the coffees and Dillon moved to the beaded entrance, pausing to light another cigarette. There was a cry of indignation from Hannah. He stepped outside and dropped the cigarette.

She was seated at one of the tables and two young men had joined her, poverty-stricken agricultural workers from the look of it, in patched jackets, scuffed leather leggings, and cloth caps. One sat on the table, a shotgun slung over one shoulder, laughing, the other was stroking the back of Hannah's neck.

"I said stop it!" She was truly angry now and spoke in Italian.

The man laughed and ran his hand down her back. Dillon punched him in the kidneys, grabbed him by the collar, and ran him headlong to one side so that he stumbled over a chair and fell. In virtually the same movement, he turned and gave the one sitting on the edge of the table the heel of his hand, feeling the nose go, knocking him to the ground.

Dermot called, "I'm with you, Sean," and came out through the bead curtain on the run. The one who had gone down first sprang a knife in his right hand as he came up, and Dermot grabbed for the wrist, twisted, and made him drop it. The other pulled the sling of the *lupara* over his head and stood, his face a mask of blood. As he tried to cock it, Dillon knocked it to one side and gave him a savage punch to the stomach, and the man dropped the *lupara.*

There was a single shot as Luigi arrived and fired into the air. He suddenly seemed a different man, the pistol in one hand, the warrant card in the other.

"Police," he said. "Now leave the *lupara* and clear off."

They shambled away. The old man appeared, strangely unconcerned, four espressos on a tray. He placed it in the center of the table.

"Sorry for the fuss, grandad," Dillon said in excellent Italian.

"My nephew and his friend." The old man shrugged. "Bad boys." He picked up the *lupara.* "I'll see he gets this back and there will be no charge. I'm sorry the signorina was molested in this way. It shames me."

He went inside and Dillon took one of the coffees. "He's ashamed. It was his nephew and a friend . . ."

"I heard what he said," Hannah told him. "My Italian is as good as yours."

Dillon turned to Riley. "Thanks, Dermot."

"Nothing to it," Riley said. "Just like the old days."

"You move quick, signor," Luigi said.

"Oh, he does that all right," Hannah said as she drank her coffee. "Boot and fist, that's our Dillon, and you should see him with a gun."

Dillon smiled amiably. "You have a way with the words, girl dear. Now drink up and let's be moving."

AS THEY MOVED down toward the south coast, things changed, the landscape became softer.

"During the war, the Americans came through here on their way through the Cammarata to Palermo. The Italian soldiers fled after receiving a Mafia directive to support the Americans against the Germans," Luigi told them.

"And why would they do that?" Dillon asked.

"The Americans released from jail in New York the great Mafia don, Lucky Luciano."

"Another gangster," Hannah said.

"Perhaps, signorina, but he got the job done and the people believed in him. He went back to prison in America, but was released in nineteen forty-six. On the pardon, it said: For services to his country."

"And you believe in such fantasy?" she asked.

"During the campaign, my own father saw him in the village of Corleone."

Dillon laughed out loud. "Now that's a showstopper if ever I heard one."

As the landscape softened, there were flowers everywhere, on the slopes knapweed with yellow heads, bee orchids, ragwort and gentians.

"So beautiful." Hannah sighed. "Yet centuries of violence and killing. Such a pity."

"I know," Dillon said. "Just like the Bible. As for me, I'm just passing through."

He closed his eyes and Riley glanced at him and it was the plane all over again and he felt as guilty as hell, but there was nothing he could do after all. Salinas soon, and it would all be over. Some comfort in that.

MARIE DE BRISSAC SURFACED in a kind of instant moment, one second nothing, dark as the grave, the next pale evening light. The first thing she was aware of was that she felt fine in herself, no headache, no heaviness, and that seemed strange.

She was lying on a large four-poster bed in a room with a vaulted ceiling and paneled walls of dark oak. There was oaken furniture, heavy and old, and a tapestry on the far wall with some sort of medieval scene on it. What seemed to be the outer door was also oak and studded with iron bands. There was another door beside the bed itself.

There was a large window, barred, of course, a table, and three chairs beside it. The man who had called himself David Braun sat there reading a book. He glanced up.

"Ah, there you are. How do you feel?"

"Fine." She sat up. "Where am I?"

"Oh, in another country, that's all you need to know. I'll get you some coffee, or tea if you prefer it."

"No, coffee would be fine, strong, black, and two sugars."

"I shan't be long. Look around."

He opened the door and went out and she heard a key turn in the lock. She got up, crossed to the other door, opened it, and found herself in a large old-fashioned bathroom. The toilet, basin and bath with a stand-in shower looked straight out of the nineteenth century, but on the shelf beside the wash basin there was a range of toiletries. Soaps, shampoos, talcum powder, deodorants, a selection of sanitary napkins. There was even an electric hairdryer, combs and hairbrushes, and it occurred to her that all this had very probably been procured for her.

Her belief was further reinforced by her discovery on the desk in the bedroom of a carton of Gitanes, her favorite cigarette, and a couple of plastic lighters. She opened a pack, took a cigarette and lit it, then went to the window and peered out through the bars.

The building, whatever it was, was situated on the edge of a cliff. There was a bay below with an old jetty, a speedboat moored there. Beyond that was only a very blue sea, the light fading as dusk fell. The key turned in the door behind her, it opened, and Braun entered carrying a tray.

"So you've settled in?"

"You could call it that. When do I get some answers?"

"My boss will be along in a few minutes. It's up to him." He poured coffee for her.

She picked up the book he had been reading. It was in English, an edition of T. S. Eliot's *The Four Quartets.* "You like poetry?" she asked.

"I like Eliot." He misquoted: "In our end is our beginning and all that. He says so much so simply." He walked to the door and paused. "He won't want you to see his face, so don't be alarmed."

He went out and she finished her coffee, poured a second cup, and lit another cigarette. She paced up and down for a while, trying to make sense of it all, but the truth was that there wasn't any sense to it. Behind her, the key rattled in the lock, and as she turned the door opened.

DAVID BRAUN CAME in and stood to one side, and it was the man following him who shocked her. He seemed about six feet tall, with good shoulders, and wore a black jump suit. The shock was the black knitted ski mask he wore, through which his eyes seemed to glitter. All in all, as sinister-looking a creature as she had ever seen in her life.

His voice, when he spoke, was good Boston American. "A pleasure, Countess, and I'm sorry for the inconvenience."

"My God, you're American, and I thought you were Israelis when I heard Hebrew spoken."

"My dear Countess, half the men in Israel speak English with an American accent. That's where most of us received our education. Best in the world."

"Really?" she said. "A matter of opinion."

"Yes, I was forgetting. You went to Oxford and the University of Paris."

"You're well informed."

"I know everything about you, Countess—everything. No secrets."

"And I know nothing about you. Your name, for example."

She could see his teeth through the slot for his mouth and it was as if he smiled. "Judas," he said. "Call me Judas."

"Very biblical," she said, "but, alas, an unfortunate connotation."

"Oh, yes, I know what you mean, Judas betraying Christ in the Garden." He shrugged. "But there were sound political reasons. Judas Iscariot was a Zealot. He wanted his country free of the Romans."

"And you?"

"I just want my country free of everybody."

"But how does that concern me, for God's sake?"

"Later, Countess, later. In the meantime, David will see to your every need. You'll have to eat in here, naturally, but if there's anything special you'd like, just ask him. Plenty of books on the shelves, and you've got your painting. I'll speak to you again."

Braun opened the door for him and followed him out. Judas pulled off the hood and ran his fingers through close-cropped, copper-colored hair. He had a strong face, high cheekbones, blue eyes, and there was a restless vitality to him. He looked around fifty years of age.

"See to her, David," he said. "Anything she wants for the moment."

"Consider it done." Braun hesitated. "She's a nice woman. Do you really intend to go through with it if you don't get what you want?"

"Certainly," Judas said. "Why, are you weakening on me, David?"

"Of course not. Our cause is just."

"Well, keep that in the front of your mind. I'll see you later."

As he turned, Braun said, "Any news from Aaron and the other two?"

"He called in from Salinas on his ship's radio. It marches, David." The man who called himself Judas smiled. "It's going to work. Just keep the faith."

He walked away along the stone-flagged corridor, and Braun unlocked the door and went in. She turned from the window.

"There you are. So the big bad wolf has gone?"

He ignored the remark. "I know you're not a vegetarian. On the menu tonight is vichyssoise, followed by fresh sea bass, grilled, potatoes, a mixed salad, and an assortment of fruit to follow. If you don't care for the fish, there are lamb chops."

"You sound like a waiter, but no, it will suit very well indeed."

"Actually, I'm the cook. Would you care for a white wine?"

"No, claret would calm my nerves, and I've never subscribed to the idea that you should drink red or white because the food dictates it. I drink to suit me."

"But, of course, Countess." He half-bowed in a slightly mocking way and moved to the door.

As he opened it, she said, "And David?"

He turned. "Yes, Countess."

"As you like Eliot so much, here's a quote from *The Waste Land* for you."

"And what would that be, Countess?"

"I think we are in rats' alley where the dead men lost their bones."

He stopped smiling, turned, opened the door, and went out, closing it. The key clicked in the lock, and suddenly she was afraid.

SALINAS WAS A SCATTERING OF HOUSES, A HARBOR ENCLOSED by two jetties and jammed with small fishing boats. Luigi drove along the waterfront and stopped outside the establishment with the sign over the door that said *English Café.*

"God knows why it has this name," Luigi said.

"Perhaps they serve a full English breakfast," Dillon said. "English tourists like that."

"What tourists?" Luigi said and shrugged. "Anyway, here you are. I'll just turn round and drive back to Palermo."

They got out and Hannah shook his hand. "Grateful thanks, Sergeant. One cop to another." She smiled and kissed him on the cheek and he drove away.

Dillon led the way up the steps. The night was warm, and as darkness fell, there were lights on some of the boats out there in the harbor. He opened the door and went in. Half a dozen fishermen were at the bar, and it was a poor sort of place, very hot, and the ceiling fan didn't seem to be working.

He waved to the barman and turned to the others. "It's a dump. Let's sit outside."

They did just that, taking a table by the veranda rail, and the barman appeared. "What have you got to eat?" Hannah asked him in Italian.

"We only do one main dish each day, signorina. Tonight it's cannelloni ripieni. The way our chef does it, there's a special stuffing of savory meat and onions. You could have a salad with it."

"Good, and bring us a bottle of wine," Dillon told him. "Something cold."

He explained the meal prospects to Riley, and the barman appeared with three glasses and an ice-cold bottle. He splashed some into a glass and Dillon sniffed it.

"This is the stuff. Passito. Strong, very strong. Three glasses and you're on your back." He grinned at Hannah. "I'd make it lemonade if I were you, girl dear."

"Go stuff yourself, Dillon."

At that moment, the barman came out, followed by a stout lady who carried a tray with three plates on it and a basket of bread. He deposited all this on the table and he and the woman departed.

The meal was, in fact, excellent, and Riley cleaned his plate. "God help me, but that bread was the best since I last tasted my cousin Bridget's baking."

"It was good, I've got to admit that," Dillon said, "although I'm not too certain that it was strictly kosher."

"Don't be stupid, Dillon," Hannah told him coldly. "The Bible doesn't tell me to starve myself in difficult circumstances. Now I'll take another glass of wine."

As Dillon poured, a quiet voice said in good public-school English, "Chief Inspector Bernstein?" They all turned and looked at the man who stood at the bottom of the steps. "Jack Carter."

He was of medium height and wore a salt-stained sailor's cap, reefer coat with tarnished brass buckles, and jeans. His face was tanned and he was younger than Dillon had thought he would be. Perhaps twenty-five and certainly no more.

Hannah made the introductions. "This is Sean Dillon and Thomas O'Malley. They're . . ."

"I know very well who they are, Chief Inspector. I've been well briefed."

He joined them on the veranda and Dillon offered him a glass of wine, but Carter shook his head. "I've already made inquiries about our friend Hakim's villa when we first arrived, discreetly, of course. There's not much like it in this area, so it was easy to find. We took a run past it."

"Was that wise?" Hannah asked.

"No problem. A lot of fishing boats around here, and the motor launch we're using doesn't look much different, not with a few nets draped around it. Further discreet inquiries at the village store indicate that Hakim is in residence. His two goons were in for supplies this morning."

"Very efficient," Dillon said. "So when do we go in?"

"Tonight around midnight. No sense in hanging about, and the Lear's waiting at Malta. We'll go down to the boat and I'll show you how I intend to make our move. Needless to say, I'm going to need Mr. Riley's input . . ."

"Mr. O'Malley," Dillon said.

"Yes, of course. Then I'll need Mr. O'Malley's input. He, after all, has actually been inside the place." He turned to Hannah. "You'll hold the fort here until we return, Chief Inspector. They do have rooms upstairs."

She nodded. "I'll walk down to the boat with you, just to see for myself. Then I'll come back and book in."

IT WAS QUIET on the waterfront, water lapping against the breakwater, music playing from somewhere, cooking smells. The boat was a forty-foot cruiser festooned with nets, as Carter had indicated. Two men in knitted caps and reefer coats worked on deck forward of the wheelhouse.

"I know it doesn't look much, but she can do twenty-five knots," he said, and called, "Only me," and added to Hannah, "I've two more with me, but they're ashore at the moment. This way."

He went down the companionway and into the main saloon. There were a couple of charts spread across the table.

"Here you are," he said. "Salinas, and there's the villa to the east. I've circled it in red."

They all leaned over the table, and Riley found that he was sweating and felt a distinct need to throw up. It was Hannah who broke the tension.

"Nothing more for me here, so I'll go back to the English Café, book a room, then I'll phone Ferguson on my mobile just to bring him up to date."

She went up the companionway, the others following. When they reached the deck, Dillon said, "Grand legs you've got on you, girl, and well shaped. Must come from pounding the beat when you were a constable."

"Mind your manners, Dillon," she said severely, but put a hand on his arm. "Try and stay in one piece. You're a bastard, but for some reason I can never fathom, I like you."

"You mean there's still a chance for me?"

"Oh, go to hell," she said and walked away along the jetty.

"We'd better go and have a look at that chart again," Carter said and led the way below. Dermot followed, his heart pounding, for he knew this must be it.

Dillon leaned over the table, and Carter said, "By the way, are you carrying, Mr. Dillon?"

"Of course."

"Your usual Walther?"

It was then, as some instinct, the product of twenty years of the wrong kind of living, told Dillon he was in very bad trouble indeed, that Carter produced a Browning.

"Hands on head, old chap, nothing silly." He felt in Dillon's pockets and found the Walther in one of them. "There we are. Hands behind your back."

Dillon did as he was told, and Carter took some handcuffs from the table drawer and handed them to Riley. "Cuff him."

Dillon shook his head. "Naughty, Dermot, very naughty."

"Arnold, get down here," Carter called in Hebrew.

Dillon, having once worked for Israeli intelligence, recognized the language at once. It was not one of his best, but he knew enough to get by.

One of the seamen appeared in the entrance. "I'm here, Aaron. You've got him, then?"

"What does it look like? You and Raphael make ready for sea. I've got to go after the woman."

"Will you kill her?"

"Of course not. We need her to communicate to Ferguson in London. Go on, get moving." He turned to Riley. "You stay here and watch him."

"What about my money?" Riley asked thickly.

"You'll get it when we get there."

"Get where?"

"Just shut up and do as you're told," and he went up the companionway.

DILLON SAID, "YOU might as well tell me, Dermot."

Which Riley did in finest detail, Brown and the visit to Wandsworth, details of the plot as it had been put to him—everything.

"So good old Hakim isn't up the coast at his villa?"

"I wouldn't know. I never even heard of him till Brown told me his name." He shook his head. "You've got to realize, Sean, it was

Brown who came up with everything, the false ASU arms dump in London, this bloody Hakim fella."

"And you never communicated with him once after leaving Wandsworth?"

"He said there was no need; that he'd always be on my case."

"So how did he know we were coming?"

"I asked him about that. He said directional microphones were a wonderful invention. He said you could be in the street and still hear what went on in a house."

"The BT van in the mews," Dillon said. "The clever bastards."

"I'm sorry, Sean, but you've got to see it from my point of view. All those years facing me in prison. Brown's offer was something I couldn't refuse."

"Oh, shut up," Dillon told him, "and get out my wallet."

Dermot did as he was told. "And what am I supposed to do with this?"

"You'll find five thousand dollars in assorted bills in there and you're going to need it, old son. It was my operating money."

"But they're paying me twenty thousand pounds," Riley said. "I don't need it."

"Oh, yes, you do, you poor bloody fool," Dillon told him.

HANNAH WAS SHOWN to a bedroom by the woman who had brought the food on the tray. It was small and simple, a window open to the night so that she could see the harbor. There was a single bed, and a toilet and shower in what was little more than a cupboard. She put her overnight bag on the bed. She was wearing a traveler's purse on a belt around her waist. It carried her operating money and a Walther, which she took out and checked expertly. Then she went downstairs.

She felt restless and strangely unsure of herself, thinking of Dillon and the job in hand. She didn't approve of Dillon, never had. All that killing for the IRA and the work he'd done for just about every terrorist group there was. Of course since working for Ferguson, he'd compensated. But her knowledge of his earlier misdeeds simply wouldn't go away.

She did an unusual thing for her, went to the bar and ordered a cognac, then she went outside and sat at the small corner table.

"Damn you, Dillon!" she said softly.

Something cold nudged her in the nape of the neck and the man who had called himself Carter said softly, "Don't turn around, Chief Inspector. I should imagine you're carrying, so take the weapon from your bag in your left hand and hold it up."

She did as she was told. "What is this?"

He took the gun from her. "Let's say all is not what it seems. By the way, we got Hakim for you. Consider that a bonus, but everything else was a means to an end. Poor Dermot, his conscience is killing him, but he did as he was told simply to get out of Wandsworth."

"But to what purpose?"

"We needed Dillon. Oh, we'll send him back quite soon and all will be revealed. Tell Ferguson we'll be in touch and he'll have to manage without him for a while. Now put your hands on your head."

There was a short silence. She said, "But why? And what happened to the real Carter and his men?"

There was no reply, and when she turned cautiously he had gone. She went down the steps and hurried along the waterfront, but as she reached the jetty she heard an engine start and then the boat eased away. There was one man in the wheelhouse, another coiling lines in the stern. Nothing to be done, and she turned and hurried along the waterfront.

CARTER WENT DOWN the companionway and found Dillon seated on a bench seat, Riley with a glass in his hand, sitting morosely on the other side of the table.

"Ah, you found the whiskey," Carter said.

"You saw the Chief Inspector?"

"Yes, and gave her a message for Ferguson."

"That was kind of you. You were talking Hebrew earlier. I don't speak it, but I recognize the language. If you're Israeli, that's the grand English public-school accent you've got."

"My father was a diplomat in London. I went to St. Paul's."

"Not bad. Dermot has revealed all, by the way. So Hakim was just a fantasy?"

"Not at all. The villa exists and Hakim was in residence."

"You say *was?"*

"We did you a favor. I dropped in with my boys last night and knocked him off."

"Just him?"

At that moment, the engines rumbled into life. "Oh, no, we killed all of them."

"Including the two women?"

Carter shrugged. "No choice, it had to be all of them. The Arab nations are at war with us, Dillon, so it's all or nothing. As an old IRA hand, I'd have thought you'd appreciate that."

Dillon said, "What about the real Carter and his men? Did you kill them, too?"

"No need. They got in this afternoon and tied up on the other side of the jetty. Moshe swam across and waited until they all went below for a meal or perhaps a conference. He boarded with a canister of Calsane and released it down the companionway. It's a nerve gas that knocks you out for twelve hours. Only temporary, no ill effects afterwards."

"As far as you know."

Carter smiled. "Got to go. We'll have words later."

He went out and Dillon turned to Riley. The boat wasn't moving very fast, obviously easing out through the small fleet of fishing boats. Riley poured another whiskey, looking hunted.

Dillon said, "So you don't know who they are?"

"I swear on the Virgin, Sean. I don't know and I don't want to know. I want my money and I want out."

"Really? And when do you go over the side with a bullet in the head?"

Riley looked shocked. "Why in the hell would they do that?"

"Because they don't need you anymore. You've served your purpose. Christ, Dermot, are you thick or something? You heard Carter. You're dealing with thoroughly ruthless people." Dillon was actually feeling angry. "They not only stiffed Hakim and his two goons, they also killed the caretaker and his wife and the daughter. They simply don't take prisoners, and I don't care what they say, Calsane gas is still experimental and there's a high chance of permanent brain damage."

"Holy Mother of God!" Riley moaned.

"So who needs you, Dermot?"

"Sean, what do I do?"

"It's staring you in the face. You've got my five thousand dollars operating money, you've got a passport. Over the side with you before we're out of the harbor, but be quick about it."

Riley seemed galvanized into action. "By Christ, and I will." He hesitated. "I can't take you with me, Sean, the handcuffs."

"Oh, get on with it," Dillon told him.

Riley opened the door at the top of the companionway cautiously and peered out. One of the men was on the prow. Carter and the one he had called Arnold were in the wheelhouse. The boat was edging forward, threading its way between the little ships of the fishing fleet. Riley dodged across the deck, went over the rail, hung there for a moment, then eased into the water. It was surprisingly warm and he swam under the stern of a fishing boat, turned and watched the lights of the boat move out of the harbor entrance.

"Good luck, Dillon, you're going to need it," he said softly, turned and swam to some steps, then hurried along the jetty. He had the money and the passport. Palermo next stop and a plane to Paris and from there to Ireland and safe amongst his own people again. He couldn't get there fast enough.

. . .

As THE BOAT moved out to sea, Carter went down the companionway and found Dillon still in place on the bench seat. He frowned. "Where's Riley?"

"Long gone," Dillon told him. "After hearing how you dealt with Hakim and company, it occurred to him that you might just find him as disposable."

"Oh, you persuaded him? I'm surprised, Mr. Dillon, after the way he betrayed you."

"Come off it, old son, he didn't have much choice. I'd have done the same faced with that kind of prison sentence, and Dermot and I go back a long way."

Carter called in English, "Arnold, get down here."

He opened a drawer and found a leather case, removed a hypodermic, and filled it from a small bottle.

"What do I call you?" Dillon asked.

Carter smiled. "Why not? It's Aaron, Mr. Dillon, and this is Arnold," he added, as the other man entered. "Turn Mr. Dillon over, Arnold."

Arnold did as he was told. Dillon felt a hard finger tap on the back of his right hand, then the needle.

"I hope this one isn't as experimental as Calsane."

"A derivative of Pethidine, but it lasts longer."

"No sense in asking where we're going?"

"None at all." Aaron nodded to Arnold. "Take him to the cabin and lock him in."

Dillon managed to make it along the corridor, was aware of the door being opened, the bunk bed, but after that, nothing.

HANNAH GOT THROUGH to Ferguson with no trouble at all, using her satellite-linked mobile phone. He was at his flat in Cavendish Square, sitting beside the fire in the drawing room, and he listened patiently while she filled him in.

"My God, but they really shafted us on this one, whoever they are."

"But what would they want with Dillon, sir? And what about the real Carter?"

"God knows, but we'll know soon enough. They said they'd be in touch and they also said Dillon would be back. We'll just have to wait."

"Yes, sir."

"I'll contact Lacey at Malta and tell him to fly back to Palermo to pick you up in the morning, and I'll ask Gagini to send the car back for you."

"I'd be grateful," she said.

"Just come home, Chief Inspector, nothing else to be done at the moment."

Ferguson sat there thinking about it for a while, then phoned Wandsworth Prison and asked to speak to the head of security.

DILLON CAME HALF-AWAKE in the darkness of the cabin. His handcuffs had been taken off and it was very dark. He tried to make sense of the luminous dial of his watch, which appeared to indicate that he had been out for about eight hours. The motion of the ship indicated a reasonably fast speed and he stood up, felt by the door, and found the light switch.

The porthole was bolted tight and painted black. His mouth was bone dry, but there was a small corner basin and a plastic cup, which he filled with water several times, sitting on the edge of the bed. A key turned in the door, it opened, and Aaron came in. A different man was behind him carrying a tray.

"I thought you'd be up and about by now," Aaron said. "This is Raphael, by the way, bearing gifts. There's a razor and shaving cream and shampoo. You'll find a little shower room through that door. More importantly, a flask of tea, milk and ham sandwiches."

"Ham?" Dillon said. "And you a nice Jewish boy?"

"Yes, disgraceful, isn't it, but then, as I told you, I went to St. Paul's. We'll see you later."

They left and Dillon started on the sandwiches, which were excellent, then had a cup of tea. He felt surprisingly good considering the drug, and afterwards, stripped, had a shower and a shave and dressed again. Afterwards, he got his cigarettes from his jacket pocket and lit one. There were books on a shelf. He glanced through them and found an old copy of *From Russia with Love* by Ian Fleming. *James Bond.* Somehow it seemed appropriate, and he got on the bunk bed and started to read.

It was a couple of hours later when the key turned and the door opened. Aaron came in, with Arnold at his back.

Dillon held up the book. "Did you know this is a first edition? They're bringing a fat price at the auctions these days."

"I'll remember that," Aaron said. "Sorry to be a bore, but it's time for bed again, Mr. Dillon. Hand out, please."

And as there wasn't much Dillon could do about that, he complied. Aaron tapped the back of the hand and applied the needle.

"You're sure I won't end up a vegetable?" Dillon asked.

"No chance, Mr. Dillon. You're a very important man. In fact, you'd be surprised at how important a man you are."

But Dillon was already falling back against the pillow, the sounds fading.

AT THAT MOMENT, Marie de Brissac, seated by the window of her room, painting, glanced up as the door opened and David Braun came in carrying a tray. He placed it on the table. There were cakes and a jug of coffee, and he stood back to look at the painting.

"Excellent. My sister used to paint in watercolors. It's a difficult medium."

"You say she used to?"

"She's dead, Countess. I had two sisters. They were killed when an Arab terrorist blew up a student bus in Jerusalem."

She was shocked and it showed. "I'm very sorry, David, truly sorry," and she reached for one of his hands.

His reaction was electric and most disturbing, particularly the realization of the effect this wonderful woman had on him. He pulled away hastily.

"It's all right. Five years ago. I've learned to cope. It's my mother I'm sorry for. She never got over it. She's in a psychiatric unit." He managed a ghastly smile. "I'll see you later."

He went out and Marie de Brissac sat there, wondering, and not for the first time, whether God had had an off-day when he'd decided to create the world.

THIS TIME WHEN Dillon surfaced he was in a room very similar to Marie de Brissac's, paneled walls, four-poster bed, a vaulted ceiling. He felt surprisingly clear-headed and checked his watch, which indicated a time lapse of some twelve hours since leaving Sicily.

He got up and went to the barred window, saw very much the same view Marie had—the cliffs, the beach, the jetty—the only difference being that the motor launch was now tied up on the other side from the speedboat. He visited the bathroom, and it was on the return that the door opened and Aaron entered.

"Ah, up and about."

He stood to one side and Judas entered in the black hood and jump suit. He was smoking a cigar and his teeth gleamed as he smiled. "So, Sean Dillon. They tell me you were the best the IRA had. Why did you change?"

"Well, as a great man once said, as the times change, all men change with them."

"A point, but a man like you would need a better reason than that."

"Let's say it seemed like a good idea at the time."

"Afterwards, you worked everyone. ETA in Spain, the PLO, then the Israelis. You blew up Palestinian gunboats in Beirut harbor."

"Ah, yes," Dillon agreed, "but for that I was very well paid."

"You certainly don't take sides."

Dillon shrugged. "Now that really doesn't pay."

"Well, this time you're going to take my side, old buddy."

"Go stuff yourself," Dillon told him. "Let's face it, I don't even know you."

"Just call me Judas."

"Jesus, son, and now you must be joking."

Aaron said in Hebrew, "Why waste time?"

Judas replied in the same language. "We need him, and don't worry, I know how to handle him." He turned to Dillon and said in Hebrew, "And I really do know how to handle you, don't I?"

Although Dillon's Hebrew was far from perfect, he understood but decided not to advertise the fact.

"Look, I don't understand a word."

Judas laughed. "Of course not, just trying you out. I've seen your record in Mossad files, and they're thorough. That account of the job you did for them in Beirut. Fair Arabic, but no Hebrew."

"I know what *shalom* means."

"Well, *shalom* to you, and now you can follow me."

"Just one more thing," Dillon said. "Excuse my insatiable curiosity, but are you a Yank?"

Judas laughed. "I'm really getting tired of being asked that. Why do you all assume that an Israeli can't be an Israeli if he speaks good American English?"

He turned and went out, and Aaron gestured with one hand. "This way, Mr. Dillon."

The study was huge and spacious, with an enormous stone fireplace and tapestries on the walls. Leaded windows stood open, the scent of flowers from some gardens beyond. Judas sat down behind a large cluttered desk and gestured to a chair opposite.

"Sit down. You'll find cigarettes in the silver box."

Aaron leaned against the wall beside the door. Dillon took a cigarette and lit it from a desk lighter. "When the boy here spoke Hebrew to his chums on the boat, I at least recognized the language."

"Yes, I noticed that on your Mossad file. A talent for languages. Everything from Irish to Russian."

"It's a kink in my brain, languages," Dillon told him, "like some people can calculate quicker than a computer."

"Then why not Hebrew?"

"I don't speak Japanese, either. I only worked for Mossad the once, as you know, and if you know as much as you say, you'll be aware that the Beirut operation was an in-and-out job. Three days and I was away with the check on a Swiss bank clutched in one greedy hand. Anyway, who in the hell are you and what's this all about?"

"Well, you know we're Israelis, but we're patriotic Israelis willing to go to any lengths to preserve the integrity of our country."

"Like shoot Prime Minister Rabin?"

"That was none of our affair. Frankly, we have more important things to do."

"So what are you, some sort of latter-day Zealots?"

"Not really, old buddy," Judas said cheerfully. "They wanted the Romans out and were strong patriots, but we go back to an earlier tradition. My country under Syrian domination, the Temple defiled, our religion, our whole way of life threatened."

"Just like today, is that what you think?"

"We are constantly under threat. I've lost relatives to Hamas bombs, Aaron there had a brother, a pilot, shot down over Iran. He was tortured to death. Another of my men lost two sisters in the bombing of a student bus. We all have our stories." He relit his cigar, which had gone out.

"So what's this earlier tradition you mentioned?"

"The Syrians were defeated by Judas called Maccabeus, which means the Hammer."

"Ah, light dawns."

"His followers were known as Maccabees, ardent nationalists who wished for national independence for our country. Under the leadership of Judas, they fought a guerrilla war with such success that they defeated Syrian armies much larger than their own, took Jerusalem, cleansed and reconsecrated the Temple."

"I know the story," Dillon said.

"From the redoubtable Chief Inspector Hannah Bernstein?"

"Now she does speak Hebrew," Dillon said. "Anyway, she told me once what Chanukah was about."

"Celebrated every year in memory of what the Maccabees achieved. A small country became independent again."

"Until the Romans came."

"True, but we will not allow that to happen this time around."

Dillon nodded. "So you see yourself as Judas Maccabeus, and your followers, the fellas who knocked me off, for example, are twentieth-century Maccabees?"

"Why not? In your game, codenames are a necessity, so Judas Maccabeus does very well."

"Leading an army of Maccabees."

"I don't need an army, just a small group of dedicated followers." Judas raised a hand. "No, believers, and a few hundred scattered around the world, Jews like myself who believe above everything else that the State of Israel must survive and are prepared to go to any lengths to ensure it."

"I'd have thought Israel has done a pretty good job of that. When the U.N. withdrew in nineteen forty-eight, you defeated six Arab countries. In the Six-Day War in nineteen sixty-seven, you defeated Egypt, Syria, and Jordan."

"True, but before my time. Yom Kippur was my war, in seventy-three, and we'd have lost it if the Americans hadn't poured in fighter planes and weaponry for us. Since then, nothing but trouble. We live on the edge. Our settlers in the north never know when they're going to come under attack, Hamas constantly wages bombing campaigns. Scud missiles in the Gulf War showed our vulnerability. It can't go on."

Almost reluctantly, Dillon said, "I can see that."

"Even in Britain there are Muslims who call for the annihilation of Jews. Syria, Iran, and Iraq will never be happy until we are crushed. Saddam Hussein proceeds with the further development of chemical weapons, the mullahs in Iran call for war against America, the Great Satan. The bombing attack on the U.S. barracks in Dharan was only the start. It is a known fact that Iran is working on the production of a nuclear bomb. They have numerous training camps for terrorists. There are also nuclear research establishments in Syria."

"Common knowledge for years," Dillon said. "So what else is new?"

"Missiles purchased from Eastern Europe since the breakup of the Soviet Union, and as we saw in the Gulf War, Israel is vulnerable to such weapons."

Dillon reached for another cigarette, and Judas picked up the lighter near his right hand, leaned across, and gave him a light. It was tarnished silver, a black bird of some kind in bas-relief, with jagged lightning in its claws, obviously some military motif.

Dillon said, "So—you've made your case. What's the solution?"

"It's time to bring a stop to it, once and for all. Iraq, Syria, and Iran brought to heel for all time."

"And how in the hell do you achieve that?"

"We don't. The Americans will achieve it for us, under the inspired guidance of their President."

"Jake Cazalet?" Dillon shook his head. "Sure, and the good old U.S. of A. has always been willing to retaliate when pushed—the Gulf War proved that—but to take out three countries?" He shook his head. "I don't see it."

"What I'm talking about are surgical airstrikes," Judas said. "Total destruction of nuclear research sites for a start, and all chemical weaponry sites. Also nuclear power stations, and so on. Total destruction of the infrastructure. Ballistic missiles with nuclear warheads can also take out targets such as the Iranian Navy at Bandar Abbas. Army headquarters in all three countries are known targets. No need for a ground war."

"A holocaust?" Dillon said. "That's what you mean? You'd be willing to go that far?"

"For the State of Israel?" Judas nodded. "I can do no other."

"But the Yanks would never go for it."

"Now there you may be wrong. In fact, such a plan *has* existed at the Pentagon since the Gulf War. They call it Nemesis," Judas told him. "There has never been any shortage of people in high command in the American military who would love to put it into action."

"So why haven't they?"

"Because as Commander-in-Chief, the President must sign the operational order, and he's always rejected it. It's been presented every year since the Gulf War to the President's secret committee—the Future Projects Committee, they call it. Bizarre, isn't it? It meets again next week. And this time, something tells me the result will be a little different."

"You think Jake Cazalet will sign?" Dillon shook his head. "You must be crazy."

"Special Forces in Vietnam," Judas said. "Distinguished Service Cross, Silver Star, two Purple Hearts."

"So what?" Dillon said. "He's worked harder for peace than any President in years. The kind of Democrat that even Republicans love. He'll never sign a thing like Nemesis."

"Oh, I think he could when he hears what I have to say, and that's where you come in, old buddy. Brigadier Ferguson has access to the President, courtesy of the British Prime Minister. You've actually met the President. Foiled a bomb plot by Protestant para-militaries to assassinate him when he was in London, and you've been of great assistance in helping out over one or two tricky bits as regards the Irish peace process or lack of it."

"So what?"

"You can go and see him for me, you and Ferguson, if you like. All very hush-hush, of course. It has to be that way."

"Like hell I will," Dillon told him.

"Oh, I think you could be persuaded." Judas got up and nodded to Aaron, who took a Beretta from the pocket of his reefer coat. "Let me show you."

"And what's that come down to? Do you wire up what my old aunty Eileen would have called my extremities to a very large battery?"

"No need. Time for you to reflect, that's all. Now if you'd be kind enough to follow me?"

He opened the door and went out, and Dillon shrugged and followed, Aaron bringing up the rear.

They went along the corridor and down a series of wide stone steps, three levels in all. Dillon could hear someone calling out, high and shrill, a woman's voice filled with terror.

As they reached a lower level, Arnold and Raphael appeared from another corridor holding Marie de Brissac between them. She was struggling madly, obviously badly frightened, and David Braun came up behind and tried to soothe her.

"There's nothing to worry about."

"Listen to him, Countess," Judas said. "He's telling the truth. This is Mr. Dillon, by the way. I've brought him down here to show I mean business, and I always keep my word. Watch and learn, then you can go back to your nice warm room."

Aaron unbarred a great oaken door, opened it, and led the way in, switching on a light. It was an ancient cellar, stone block walls wet with moisture. There was a well in the center, a low, round brick wall and a bucket on a rope suspended from some kind of lifting mechanism.

Judas picked up a stone and dropped it down. There was a hollow splashing. "Forty feet and only four or five feet of water and mud," he said. "Hasn't been used in years. Kind of smelly and pretty cold, but you can't have everything. Let the countess take a look."

She was shivering uncontrollably as Raphael and Arnold tried to pull her forward, and Dillon said to Judas, "What are you, a sadist or something?"

The eyes glittered in the black hood and there was a pause that was broken by David Braun. "I'll take her." Arnold and Raphael stepped back and he put an arm around her shoulders. "It's all right, I'm here. Trust me."

He moved her to the well and Judas picked up another stone and dropped it. “There you go.” There was a splash and then a kind of eerie whining. He laughed. “That must be the rats. They love it on account of the lower sewer that runs through. Isn’t this fun?” He turned to Dillon. “Or it will be when you stand in the bucket and we put you down.”

In that one single moment, Dillon knew that he was facing madness, for Judas was enjoying himself too much, but he kept his cool.

“I’ll tell you one thing. You obviously don’t know the first thing about sewers.”

“And what’s that supposed to mean?”

“If you swallow human pathogens, you stand a great chance of dying, and if a rat bites you down there, you stand an even better chance of catching Weil’s disease. Only a fifty-fifty chance of dying from that when your liver packs in, so it strikes me you aren’t too concerned about keeping me around.”

Judas exploded in rage. “Fuck you, you clever bastard. Now stand in the bucket or I’ll blow your head off.”

He snatched the Beretta from Aaron and leveled it, and Marie de Brissac cried out, “No!”

Dillon smiled at her. “I don’t know who you are, girl dear, but don’t worry. He needs me too much.”

He got his feet into the bucket, and Raphael and Arnold lowered him down. He glanced up, saw Judas peering down at him, and then a few moments later he hit the water. His feet sank into a foot of mud and the water was to his chest. A moment later and the bucket was raised. He looked up at the circle of light and suddenly it went dark, and he was alone.

The smell was terrible and the water very cold. He remembered a similar situation in Beirut once. He’d thought himself in the hands of Arab terrorists, had been put down a rather similar well with a Protestant terrorist from Ulster, who was trying to get into the uranium business. It had turned out to be an Israeli intelligence scam with the aim of breaking the other man down. It had still taken four baths for Dillon to get rid of the stink.

He found a ledge in the brickwork and sat on it, arms folded against the cold, wondering who the woman was. Mystery piled on mystery here. Only one thing was certain. Judas was not only a fanatic, he was truly mad, and Dillon had never been so convinced of anything in his life.

Something brushed across his thighs and swam away and he knew what it was.

MARIE DE BRISSAC, IN her room, was crying and David Braun held her close and suddenly found he was stroking her hair as he might that of a child.

"You're all right now," he said softly. "I'm here."

"Oh, David." She looked up, tears on her face. "I was so afraid, and Judas." She shuddered. "He terrified me."

"He carries a great weight," Braun said. "Many burdens."

"That man, the one he called Dillon, who is he?"

"You mustn't concern yourself. I know what would be good for you, a nice bath. I'll turn the water on and then I'll go and check on your dinner."

"Not tonight, David, I couldn't eat a thing. But wine, David! God help me, I'm no drinker as a rule, but I need it tonight."

"I'll see you later."

He opened the door, went out and locked it and stood for a moment in the corridor, aware that his hands were shaking.

"What's happening to me?" he said softly and hurried away.

UP TO HER neck in suds, Marie de Brissac smoked a cigarette and tried to relax. It was a bad dream, the whole thing, and the explosion of rage from Judas had been terrifying. But the man Dillon. She frowned, remembering the strange ironic smile on his face as they lowered him down. It was as if he didn't give a damn and that didn't make sense. And then there was David. She was woman enough to know what was happening. So be it. In her present situation, she would have to use every possible advantage.

IN LONDON, IT was raining, driving hard against the windows of Charles Ferguson's flat in Cavendish Square. Hannah Bernstein peered out through the window and Kim, Ferguson's Ghurka batman, came in from the kitchen with a pot of coffee and cups on a tray.

Ferguson, sitting by the fire, called, "Come on, Chief Inspector, no point in fretting. Have some coffee."

She joined him, sitting in the chair opposite, and Kim poured. "No news, sir."

"I know that," he said. "But there will be. I mean, there has to be a meaning to all this."

"I suppose so."

"You like Dillon, don't you?"

"If you mean do I fancy him, no. I don't approve and never have. His past damns him."

"And still you like him?"

"I know. It's an absolute bastard, isn't it, sir? But never mind."

"So how did you get on at Wandsworth?"

"I saw Dunkerley, the head of security, and he told me pretty much what he told you when you phoned him. The prison is like a souk on visiting day. No way anyone in reception remembers Brown amongst several hundred people. As Mr. Dunkerley said, it was rather unfortunate that the prison officer, Jackson, the only one who handled Brown personally, was killed in that accident."

"Accident, my backside," Ferguson said.

"That's what the police report says, sir. All available witnesses say he just fell forward."

"Too damn convenient. What about the Law Society?"

"They have three George Browns on their books, or did. One died a month ago, the second is black, and the third is famous for going to court in a wheelchair."

"I see."

"I've got a copy of the reception-area surveillance tape, but only one person could identify Brown from it."

"Riley?"

"Exactly, sir."

"Oh dear," Ferguson said. "And one more piece of news for you. Captain Carter has been in touch on the way back to Cyprus. He and his team were having a conference in the saloon of their boat when it appears they were gassed. They all passed out for several hours."

"Are they all right, sir?"

"He's not happy about two of them. They'll book into the military hospital when they get in. We'll keep our fingers crossed."

DILLON, COLDER THAN ever now, leaned back against the brick wall. "Jesus," he said softly. "A fella could tire of this in no time at all."

There was a sudden flurry in the water and a rat slipped across his right leg. He brushed it away. "So there you are, you little rascal. Now behave yourself."

CHAPTER 5

As they'd allowed him to keep his watch, Dillon was aware of the time, although whether that was a good thing or not, he wasn't sure, for time seemed to stretch into eternity.

He remembered noticing that it was four o'clock in the morning and then, in spite of the circumstances, he must have dozed because he came awake with a start, a rat leaping from his shoulder, and when he checked the time again, he found that it was seven-thirty.

Not long after that, a light appeared up above and Judas leaned over. "You still in one piece, Dillon?"

"In a manner of speaking."

"Good. We'll take you up."

The bucket came down, Dillon scrambled his feet into the bucket and was hauled up slowly. As his head passed the brick wall, he saw Judas, Aaron, and Arnold standing there.

"My God, but you stink, Dillon, you really do." Judas laughed. "Get him out of here, Aaron, and carry on as I suggested."

He ran up the stairs ahead of them and Aaron said, "I'll take you back to your room. I think you need a shower."

"Or three or four," Dillon said.

He stripped in the bathroom and put the contaminated clothing into a black plastic bag Aaron had provided. Halfway through the second shower Arnold appeared and took the bag away. Dillon tried another shower and then a fourth. As he reached for a towel, Aaron glanced in.

"Fresh clothes on the bed, Mr. Dillon."

"The right size, I trust."

"We know everything about you."

"Shoes? What about shoes?"

"Those, too. I'll be back when you're dressed."

Dillon dried his hair, shaved, then went into the bedroom to discover fresh underwear, a checked shirt, jeans and socks, and a pair of sneakers. He dressed quickly and was combing his hair when the door opened and Aaron appeared.

"That's better. Are you ready for breakfast?"

"You could say that."

"Then come this way."

He opened the door, led the way out and along the corridor, and stopped at another door. He opened it and stepped to one side.

"This way, Mr. Dillon."

Marie de Brissac, at her easel, turned. She hesitated, paintbrush in hand, and Aaron said, "I've brought you some company. I'll bring breakfast in a moment." The door closed and the key turned.

"Sean Dillon." He held out his hand. "Countess, is it?"

"Never mind that. Marie will do—Marie de Brissac. Did you have a bad time?"

"A bad night, certainly. I'll pinch one of those cigarettes if you don't mind."

"Of course not."

He lit one and blew out a plume of smoke. "Do you by any chance know where we are?"

"I haven't the slightest idea. And you?"

"I'm afraid not. Last I recall, I was in a fishing port called Salinas in Sicily. I know by my watch that I was at least twelve hours at sea, but I was unconscious most of the time."

"The same with me. I was in Corfu when they kidnapped me. A plane ride was mentioned and then a needle in the arm, and I knew nothing until I woke up here."

"But what in the hell is it all about?" Dillon asked, and the door opened and Braun, not Aaron, came in with a tray.

"Good morning, Mr. Dillon—Countess." He put the tray down. "Scrambled eggs, toast, marmalade, and English breakfast tea. Much better for you than coffee. I'll be back."

He went out and Dillon said, "I don't know about you, but I'm starving. Let's eat it while it's hot."

"I agree," she said.

They sat on either side of the table and talked as they ate. Dillon said, "So we don't know where we are. Could be Italy or Greece, maybe even Turkey or Crete. Egypt would be a possibility."

"A wide choice, but who are you, Mr. Dillon, and why are you here?"

"I work for a branch of British intelligence. I was in Sicily to arrest in a highly illegal manner a much-wanted Arab terrorist. My partner was with me, Chief Inspector Hannah Bernstein of Special Branch at Scotland Yard. The whole thing turned out to be a setup. They took me but left Hannah to report back to my boss, Brigadier Ferguson. What about you?"

"I was on a painting holiday in northeast Corfu on the coast, and on my own because I prefer it that way at the moment."

"You're French," Dillon said.

"That's right. I was painting at the beach when the one called David, David Braun, appeared, with another called Moshe. They packed up my clothes, and picked me up with no explanation. The rest you know."

"There's got to be a reason," Dillon said. "I mean, what's special about you? Tell me about yourself."

"Well, my father was General Comte Jean de Brissac, and a war hero. He's been dead for some years. My mother died a year ago and I still haven't got over that. It means I am now Comtesse de Brissac. The title goes that way. From my mother or my father."

"But nobody would snatch you for that reason," Dillon told her.

"I am also wealthy. Perhaps they want a ransom."

"That could have made sense, except that it doesn't explain why they've snatched me." He poured some more tea. "Look, from what this character Judas said to me, they're some sort of Jewish extremist group."

"Which makes it even more absurd. I have no Jewish connections." She frowned. "Our family lawyer in Paris, Michael Rocard, is Jewish, but what's that got to do with anything? He's been a lawyer to the de Brissacs for at least thirty years. The cottage I rented in Corfu is his."

"Is there anything else?" Dillon demanded. "Anything in your life? Come on, girl."

"Not that I can think of." But there was a great reluctance there and he seized on it at once.

"Come on, the truth."

So she sighed and sat back. And she told him.

Dillon was stunned. He walked to the table by the window and helped himself to one of her cigarettes. "Jake Cazalet. That's got to be the reason."

"But why?"

He sat on the edge of the table as he talked to her. "Just listen and you'll see the connection." And he told her all about Sicily and the people who were killed there, then about Judas and the Maccabees, and finally about the Nemesis plan.

When he was finished, she could only shake her head, her turn to be stunned. "I can't believe it," she said. "It's so *awful.* All that death, and on such a grand scale."

"Personally, I believe Judas is barking mad, but then many extremists are."

"But they're Jewish. You don't—"

"You don't expect Jews to be terrorists? And who was it assassinated Prime Minister Rabin? All it takes is one small, hard, dedicated group. Take Ireland. More than twenty-five years of the bomb and the bullet, thousands killed, hundreds of thousands wounded, sometimes crippled for life, yet at no time has there been more than three hundred and fifty active members of the IRA. The majority of the Irish people hate the violence and condemn it."

She frowned. "You're well informed."

There was a question there, and he replied to it. "I'm from Belfast originally. When I was nineteen, I was a young actor in London. My father went home on a visit, got caught in an exchange of fire on a Belfast street, and died from British Army bullets."

She said, "And you joined the IRA?"

"The kind of thing you'd do at nineteen. Yes, Countess, I became a gunman for the glorious cause, and once you put your foot on that road there's no turning back."

"But you changed. I mean, you work for British intelligence and this Brigadier Ferguson."

"I didn't have much choice. I had the prospect of a Serb firing squad in Bosnia in front of me or accepting Ferguson's offer to go and work for him."

"Doing the same sort of things you'd been doing," she said shrewdly.

"Exactly, though usually on the side of the right."

"I see."

She was very calm, very still, and Dillon said, "I never believed in the bombs, Countess, and for what it's worth—in Sicily? I'd have shot Hakim and his men, but not the old couple and the girl."

"Yes, I think I believe you."

He smiled then, that special Dillon smile, warm and immensely charming, changing his personality completely.

"You better had, Countess, because I'm the only friend you've got here."

"I believe you, so give me one of those cigarettes and tell me what you think we should do."

"I wish I knew." He gave her a light from his old Zippo. "Interestingly enough, Judas didn't say a word about you being Cazalet's daughter, but he obviously knows."

"Then why didn't he tell you?"

"Oh, I think he enjoys playing games, like the cellar and the well last night. I think he wanted me to find out for myself."

She nodded. "So he intends to use me as a bargaining counter to persuade my father to sign this order? This total destruction of three countries?"

"That's about it."

She shook her head. "Jake Cazalet is a good man, Mr. Dillon. I can't believe he would sign such an agreement, no matter what the threat."

"Normally I'd agree." Dillon got up and walked to the window. "But with you, he obviously feels he has something out of the ordinary. A piece of leverage like no other." He turned. "Tell me about it. Tell me about him and your mother. Anything and everything. It could help. There might be something there."

"I don't know if I can." She frowned. "My mother told me how it happened, pieced it together over the years, and it was no sordid affair—anything but." She laughed bravely, but her voice shook. "Rather tragic, really."

"Nothing better to do, girl dear. Just tell me while we have the time. They could come for me at any minute."

"Well, it started in Vietnam a long time ago," she said. "My age actually, so that means it was twenty-eight years . . ."

EASTERN MEDITERRANEAN

SICILY • LONDON

WASHINGTON

---

1 9 9 7

NOW THAT'S ONE HELL OF A STORY," DILLON SAID.

She nodded. "Remember how he swept in to power?"

"Have you seen him since?"

"Once, the Paris visit last year, just after he was elected. I was a guest at the Presidential Ball. Very unsatisfactory. A few moments only, all very formal, but Teddy spent time with me. Dear Teddy. My father has created a special post for him. Principal Secretary. He has more power in the White House than the rest of the staff combined. He'd kill for my father."

"But all this leaves us with an unanswered question," Dillon told her.

"And what's that?"

"If Judas knows who you are, how did he find out? You, your father, and Teddy Grant are the only people who knew."

"I know. That bothers me, too."

"You mentioned your family lawyer, this Michael Rocard. Could he have known?"

"Definitely not. When my mother was dying and we were discussing the whole business, she made it plain that he knew nothing."

Dillon helped himself to one of her cigarettes and gave her one. "Now listen to me. I'm on your side in all this, whatever happens. He'll send for us soon, I'm sure of it, and then we'll know the game plan. I'm telling you now that I'll go along with anything he wants. No choice really, but whatever happens, my only concern will be to get you out of here eventually. Do you believe me?"

"Yes, Mr. Dillon, I do."

"Good. Now there's one thing you can do for me, you being an artist. Judas has an old silver lighter with a crest on the side, some sort of black bird, a hawk maybe, with lightning in its claws. Do you have any charcoal pencils?"

She went to the easel, opened her paint box, and returned to the table with a piece of cartridge paper. "Show me." Dillon did his clumsy best. "So, wholly black with wings spread," she said and took the charcoal pencil and sketched. "Was the head and the beak like that, because that's a hawk?"

"No, the beak was a sort of yellow."

She rubbed out the head and started again. "That's it," Dillon said.

She laughed. "A raven, Mr. Dillon," and she went to the box again and got two crayons, one black, the other yellow, and finished the bird off.

"Red lightning in its claws," Dillon told her.

When it was finished, she sat back. "Not bad."

"Bloody marvelous." Dillon folded it and put it in his pocket.

"Is it important?"

"I think it's some sort of military crest. It might be a lead."

At that moment, the door opened and David Braun and Aaron came in. "This way, if you please," Aaron said. "Both of you."

Braun led the way, Aaron following, and they found themselves standing before Judas again in his study.

"So there you are," he said. "Had a nice chat?"

"All right," Dillon said. "Let's get on with it."

"Okay, old buddy, this is how it goes. Nemesis comes up before the Future Projects Committee next week, and this time the President signs it."

"Why should he?"

"Because if he doesn't, I'll execute his daughter here."

There was a long pause before Dillon said, "What are you talking about?"

"Don't fuck with me, Dillon, I know who she is."

"And how could you?"

"I told you, I have Maccabees everywhere. MI5 in London, the CIA. Make a computer inquiry about me, for example, and one of my people will know. Anybody in intelligence will tell you it isn't the big people you have to worry about, it's the invisible people. The computer operators, filing clerks, secretaries." He laughed. "So I know who she is and don't ask me how."

Marie de Brissac said, "My father will never sign this insanity."

"Oh, I think he might be tempted. Cazalet has a lot of emotions wrapped up in you, Marie—love, guilt, a profound sense of loss, and missed opportunities. You are no ordinary hostage. And he can always invent a provocation by the Arabs. The CIA is good at that kind of thing, and we'll be glad to help, of course. No, I think we can expect him to cooperate, after he thinks about it."

Dillon said, "Now what?"

"You'll be returned to Salinas. London and Ferguson next stop." He opened a drawer and took out a mobile phone. "Latest model, old buddy, satellite-linked and untraceable. You can't phone me, but I'll phone you."

"And why would you do that?"

"To prove my power. Let me explain. It would be understandable, once you've spoken to Ferguson, if he decided to check through British Secret Intelligence Service computer files for any reference to a terrorist group known as the Maccabees. If he does, I'll know quicker than you can imagine, and I'll phone to tell you. If Cazalet does the same through CIA records, I'll know, and again I'll phone you. This is just to demonstrate the power of the Maccabee organization. They're everywhere, my invisible people. By the way, both inquiries will be a waste of time. There is no information about me or my organization anywhere."

"So what's the point of the exercise?"

"It demonstrates my total power in this matter, but let me get down to brass tacks. You're going back in one piece. We'll drop you in at Salinas. You'll return to Ferguson and tell him that if Jake Cazalet does not sign Nemesis at the coming meeting of the Future Projects Committee, I shall execute his daughter."

"You're mad," Marie de Brissac said.

"Tell Ferguson I don't think it would be helpful for the Prime Minister to know this. You and he will proceed to the White House in Washington, where Ferguson should have no difficulty in obtaining an audience with the President."

"I see," Dillon said. "And we convey the message to the President?"

"Exactly, with this in addition. If any approach is made to involve the CIA or FBI or any military special forces, I will know, and—again—the countess will be executed at once. I've people everywhere, Dillon, as your inquiries and my phone calls to you will demonstrate."

Dillon took a deep breath. "So what it comes down to is simple. Either Cazalet signs to put Nemesis into operation or she dies."

"Exactly, old buddy, couldn't have put it better myself."

"But he won't do it."

"That's too bad—too bad for the countess here."

"You bastard!" Marie de Brissac told him.

Judas nodded to David Braun. "Get her out of here and back to her room."

"Good-bye, Mr. Dillon, and God bless you. We won't be seeing each other again. My father will never sign such a document," Marie de Brissac said.

"Keep the faith, girl dear," Dillon told her, and David Braun eased her out.

Dillon walked to the desk, helped himself to a cigarette, picked up Judas's ornate lighter and flicked it on. He blew out smoke. "You might as well kill her now. Cazalet won't sign. It's too big."

"Then you'd better persuade him." Judas turned to Aaron. "Get Mr. Dillon on his way. Salinas next stop."

Aaron spoke quickly in Hebrew. "He's trouble, this one. You've seen his record."

"Not for long. I'll have him shot after he's seen the President in Washington. It's all arranged. A nice professional job. A street crime. You know Washington? People get mugged and shot all the time. I know the hotel where Ferguson always stays. The Charlton. Very unsafe, underground parking lots these days."

"And Ferguson?"

"No, not him. Too important, and he could be useful."

"And what's that all about?" Dillon asked, having fully understood. "Have you changed your mind? Do I go over the side of the boat with twenty pounds of chain around my ankles?"

"I just love your imagination, old buddy. Now on your way."

He put a cigar in his mouth and Aaron took the special mobile phone from the desk and ushered Dillon out.

On returning to his room, he found his jacket on the bed. "Cleaned and pressed," Aaron told him. "You'll find your wallet, cards, and passport and your own mobile phone so you can call Ferguson the moment you hit Salinas." He held up the special mobile. "Your present from Judas. Don't lose it."

Dillon pulled on the jacket and put the mobile phone in a pocket. "Fuck Judas," he said.

"A great man, Mr. Dillon. You will see just how great." Aaron took a black hood from his pocket and said, "Now pull this over your head." Dillon did as he was told and Aaron opened the door and took his arm. "We'll go to the boat now," and he led him out.

. . .

WHEN THE BOAT tied up at the jetty at Salinas, it was dark. Dillon checked his watch. It had taken around twelve hours and he had been drugged as before, but only for the first eight hours. When they took him up the companionway, it was dark and raining, silver rods driving down through the sickly yellow light of a lamp.

"Eight o'clock on a fine Sicilian evening, Mr. Dillon," Aaron said, "and good old Salinas awaits you."

"What a pleasure."

"Good luck, Mr. Dillon," Aaron said, and added rather surprisingly, "You're going to need it."

Dillon went over the rail and walked along the jetty through the rain. At the far end, he moved into a shelter, lit a cigarette, and watched the boat move out to sea, the red and green lights fading into the night. He took out his personal mobile phone and punched in Ferguson's number at the Cavendish Square flat.

It was surprising how quickly he got a response. "Ferguson."

"It's me," Dillon told him.

"Thank God."

"They've dumped me back on the jetty at Salinas with a message for the President via you and me."

"Is this as bad as it sounds?"

"Your worst nightmare."

"Right. I'll have Lacey and Parry leave Farley Field within the hour for Palermo. I'll phone Gagini and get him to arrange transportation for you as soon as possible. Where will you be?"

"The English Café."

"Just wait there." There was a pause. "I'm glad you're in one piece, Sean."

Dillon switched off his phone. Surprise, surprise, he thought, sentiment from Ferguson.

. . .

FERGUSON PHONED HANNAH Bernstein first at her flat. When she answered, he said, "He's safe, Chief Inspector, back at Salinas. I'm arranging to have him back as soon as possible."

"What was it all about, sir?"

"I don't know. I'd like you to come round now. You can use one of the spare bedrooms. Kim will fix it up."

"Of course, sir."

"I'll see you then."

Next, he phoned Transportation at the Ministry of Defense and arranged the flight to Palermo. Finally, he spoke to Gagini.

"Look, I can't tell you what this is about, Paolo, but it's big, and I want Dillon out of Salinas and safe in Palermo as soon as possible."

"No problem," Gagini told him. "Let's say you'll owe me a favor."

"My pleasure."

"Ciao, Charles," Gagini said and put down the phone.

Ferguson sat by the fire and Kim served him tea and crumpets, and although he enjoyed them, he felt extremely uneasy.

"Damn you, Dillon!" he said softly. "What have you come up with now?"

A little while later, Kim answered the door and Hannah entered with an overnight bag, which she gave him. Her raincoat was dripping and Kim took it from her.

"God, you're soaking," Ferguson said. "Come and sit by the fire."

"I'm fine, Brigadier, but what about Dillon?"

"They dumped him back at Salinas, as I told you. All I know is that he said it's big and something to do with the President."

"My God!" she said.

"I don't think we need to involve the Almighty just yet. I'll get Kim to provide fresh tea and we'll just have to possess ourselves in patience."

. . .

At Salinas, Dillon was sitting on the terrace, rain dripping from the roof. He'd just finished a bowl of spaghetti Napoli and half a bottle of some local red wine when a police car drew up. The driver stayed behind the wheel, but a young sergeant got out and came up the steps.

"Excuse me, signor." He paused, his English obviously poor.

Dillon helped him out in fluent Italian. "My name is Dillon, Sergeant. How can I help?"

The sergeant smiled. "I've had orders from Colonel Gagini in Palermo. He has ordered us to deliver you there as soon as possible."

Another police car pulled up behind with two officers in it, the one in the passenger seat holding a machine pistol.

"A long drive," Dillon said.

"Duty is duty, signor, and Colonel Gagini insists you are delivered in one piece." He smiled. "Shall we go?"

"A pleasure," Sean Dillon said, swallowed his wine, and went down the steps.

It was raining at Farley Field at nine o'clock the following morning when the Lear jet landed. Dillon disembarked and grinned at Lacey. "I wouldn't bank on a holiday, Flight Lieutenant. You're going to be very active."

"Really, sir?" Lacey grinned and turned to Parry. "Ah, well, we find it breaks the monotony."

Dillon walked toward the Daimler and found only Hannah Bernstein inside. He got in. "The great man too busy, is he?"

"He's waiting at the office." She pulled his head down and kissed him on the cheek. "You had me worried, you bastard."

"Now, then, that's bad language for a nice Jewish girl." He lit a cigarette and opened the window. "Let's blow the passive smoke away."

She ignored him. "What happened? What was it all about?"

So he told her.

When he was finished, she said, "This is monstrous."

"Yes, you could say that."

"And this Judas. He must be mad."

"Yes," he said. "You could say that."

THE BRIGADIER, AT his desk in his office at the Ministry of Defense, listened to everything. When Dillon was finished, Ferguson sat there thinking about it, and finally spoke.

"It's the most fantastic thing I've ever heard of. I mean, is this man for real?"

"I questioned Gagini about Hakim," Dillon said, "and I believe you've had his report."

"Yes, a right old blood bath."

"Judas and his Maccabees mean business, Brigadier. As I said, your worst nightmare, but real enough."

"So what do we do?"

"All right," Dillon said. "Let's try him out." He turned to Hannah. "Access the main Secret Intelligence Service computer. Tell it to select Judas Maccabeus and the Maccabees."

She turned to Ferguson, who nodded. "Do it, Chief Inspector."

She went out and Ferguson said, "That poor woman with you out there, she must be terrified."

"She's quite a lady. She'll cope," Dillon said.

"Cope?" Ferguson said savagely. "He's going to kill her."

"No, he won't, because I'll kill him first," Sean Dillon said, his face like stone, and Hannah returned.

"Nothing, sir, a total blank. The computer has never heard of Judas Maccabeus and the Maccabees."

"Good," Dillon said. "So now we wait and see if he phones me on the special mobile," and he took it from his pocket and placed it on the desk.

Ferguson said, "Chief Inspector, you've heard what Dillon has to say about the worries the Maccabees have about the future of Israel, their fears and so on. As a Jew, what do you think?"

"My grandfather is a rabbi, as you know, sir, my father very orthodox, and yet they give me loving support, even when I must break the laws imposed by my religion because of the demands of my profession. I am very proud to be Jewish, and I support Israel."

"But?" Ferguson said. "You appear to hesitate."

"Let me put it this way, sir. During the Second World War, the Nazis did terrible things, the British did not. They behaved as we would expect. There are Arab terrorist groups who butcher women and children. I do not expect such actions from Israelis. However, there are minority fundamentalist groups, the kind who applauded Rabin's murder, who are as bad as any of them."

"And you don't approve?"

"If my grandfather, the rabbi, were here now, he would tell you that it is a fundamental tenet of Jewish law that one cannot secure one's own survival by deliberately depriving another of life."

"So what does that tell you about Judas?" Dillon asked.

"That this man is no religious fanatic. A practical nationalist is my guess."

"Just like the original Judas Maccabeus?"

"Exactly."

"And you are sure you have no sympathy for him?"

She bridled. "Why? Simply because I'm a Jew?"

Ferguson held up a placating hand. "I had to ask, Hannah, you know that."

The mobile phone tinkled. Dillon picked it up. "Dillon here."

"Ah, there you are, old buddy. Request to Number Three Delta computer, source, Chief Inspector Hannah Bernstein, for any information regarding the Maccabees. Response nil."

"Yes, we are aware of that. Do you want to speak to Brigadier Ferguson?"

"What for? Just tell him to get his arse over to Washington. Time is running out, and tell Hannah Bernstein *shalom* and that I'm a big admirer."

The line went dead. Dillon said, "He knew all about the inquiry."

"That's incredible," Ferguson said.

"No, it's the invisible people."

"One of his network of Maccabees," Hannah said.

"Exactly. By the way, he said he was a big admirer of yours."

"The cheek of it. I've never even met him."

"How do you know? How do I know? Interesting point. The fellas who kidnapped me, the others at the castle, all showed their faces, and why?"

"Because they're just foot soldiers," Hannah said.

"Exactly, but Judas wore a hood. Now put your fine police mind to that, Chief Inspector."

"It's obvious," she said. "He has a face that could be recognized."

"What you're saying is he's a somebody."

Ferguson cut in. "Never mind any of this. What we've established is that he's telling the truth. We've just put a question to our most powerful intelligence information computer and he has instant access. In other words, he's cut our legs off."

"So what do we do?" Dillon asked.

"Go to Washington and see the President, but first, I'm going to phone Blake Johnson. As for you, Chief Inspector, make sure the Lear is standing by at Farley Field."

BLAKE JOHNSON WAS forty-eight, a tall and handsome man with jet-black hair who looked years younger than he was. A Marine at nineteen, he'd come out of Vietnam with a Silver Star, two Purple Hearts, and a Vietnamese Cross of Valor. His law degree at Georgia State had taken him into the FBI.

One day in June three years earlier, he had been shadowing Senator Jake Cazalet because of death threats received from certain right-wing fascist groups. The police escort had lost the Senator's limousine, but Blake Johnson, carving his way through heavy evening traffic, had arrived just as an attack was taking place. He had shot both men involved, had taken a bullet in his left thigh.

It was the start of an enduring relationship with Jake Cazalet and had brought him to his present appointment as Director of the General Affairs Department at the White House.

This was supposed to be an outfit responsible for various administration matters and was known, because it was downstairs, as the Basement. In fact, to those in the know, it was the President's private investigative squad and one of the most closely guarded secrets of the administration. It was totally separate from the CIA, the FBI, the Secret Service. In fact, the whispers about it were so faint that few people believed it existed. Cazalet had inherited it, and had taken advantage of the retirement of the previous incumbent to offer the job to Blake Johnson.

FERGUSON USED HIS direct Codex Four line to the Basement office, and Johnson, at his desk, answered at once.

"Say who you are."

"Charles Ferguson, you bugger."

"Charles, how goes it?"

"Bad, I'm afraid. I've got very serious trouble for you and the President, and I mean serious. I know it's strange, but no communication with the Prime Minister, please."

"That bad?"

"I'm afraid so. I'll leave in an hour with Dillon and Chief Inspector Bernstein. Dillon's been up to his neck in this thing. We must see the President at the White House the moment we get in."

"Not possible. He's gone down to his own house for a couple of days on the beach at Nantucket. Time to reflect."

"This is life and death, Blake."

There was a pause. "I see."

Ferguson took a deep breath. "You're his friend, Blake. Tell him it refers to the safety of . . . one who was lost but now is found."

"Jesus, Charles, what is this, a parlor game?"

"I can't say more, not now. Just tell him. He'll know what I mean.

So will Teddy Grant. You've got to trust me on this, Blake—this is as important as it comes."

And Johnson was all efficiency now. "Okay. Don't come into Washington International. Make it Andrews Air Force Base. I'll tell them to expect you. They'll arrange a helicopter to drop you on the beach at Nantucket as they do for the President."

Ferguson said, "No CIA, Blake, no security services of any description. Just come yourself."

"I'll take your word for it, Charles. Okay, I'll go ahead and prepare the President. I'll see you there," and he put down the phone.

Ferguson said, "Right, let's get moving. No time to waste on this one," and he led the way out.

ON THE BEACH at the old house near Nantucket, the President walked, tracked by two Secret Service men and his dog, Murchison, a black flatcoat retriever. The wind was blowing, the surf tumbling in, and it was good to be alive and away from Washington. He called the nearest Secret Service man over, an enormous black ex-Marine called Clancey Smith, who had served in the Gulf.

"Light me a cigarette, Clancey," the President said. "Can't manage in this wind."

Clancey took two Marlboros from his pack, lit them inside his storm coat, and passed one to the President.

Cazalet laughed. "Didn't Paul Henreid do that for Bette Davis in *Now Voyager?*"

"Must have been before my time, Mr. President."

At that moment, there was a cry and they turned and saw Teddy Grant running toward them. Murchison bounded forward to meet him and they arrived together, Teddy breathless.

"For God's sake, Teddy, what is it?" Cazalet demanded.

Teddy gestured to Clancey, who withdrew, and only then did he deliver the bad news.

. . .

THERE WAS THE usual press of people outside the White House on Pennsylvania Avenue, tourists mostly, taking pictures and hoping for a sign of the good and the great, maybe even the President, but there were no TV cameras.

Mark Gold turned up the collar of his coat against the light rain and smiled at the nearest policeman. "No TV today. They can't have lost interest in Cazalet that quickly."

The policeman shrugged. "He ain't here. Went down to Nantucket for a day or two. If you'd been here earlier, you'd have seen the helicopter."

"Heh, I'm sorry I missed that."

Mark Gold turned away through the crowd and walked some distance along Pennsylvania Avenue to where he had left his car. He was a senior computer operator in the Defense Department, a graduate of Columbia University in computer science. He couldn't remember when he'd last visited a synagogue. His older brother, Simon, had been different, a deeply religious man who'd given up a lucrative job as a broker on the New York Stock Exchange to emigrate to Israel to farm on a kibbutz in the north near the Golan. He had been killed, along with twelve other people, when Hamas terrorists had blanketed the kibbutz with seven rockets.

Gold had gone to Israel, too late for any funeral, but to pay his respects, had stood at the grave of a much-loved brother, filled with a deep rage, so that when Aaron Eitan had accosted him, ostensibly for sympathy, but sounding him out, it was good to have someone to pour out his anger to.

It had ended with him being picked up by car, blindfolded, and delivered to a back street house in Jerusalem. When his blindfold had been removed, there was Judas in his black hood seated at a table.

So, Mark Gold was a Maccabee and proud to serve. It gave his life a sense of purpose, and his ability to access Defense Department computers was more than useful to the organization. He could even hack in to CIA records at Langley.

Before starting the car, he took out the special satellite-linked mobile phone and punched the coded series. Judas answered very quickly.

"It's Gold. The President's gone to his house at Nantucket for the weekend. I presume that's where our friends will go."

"Did you check the hotel?"

"Yes, reservations confirmed."

"They're certain to go there after Nantucket. Dillon, of course, will have performed his task. You can take care of him at the Charlton as we agreed."

"Consider it done."

Gold put the phone in his pocket, switched on the engine, and drove away.

WHEN THE LEAR jet landed at Andrews Air Force Base, the news wasn't good. The young major who was waiting to greet them saluted formally.

"My respects, General."

"Brigadier," Ferguson told him.

"We could have a problem. Nantucket, the whole area, is subject to fog a lot. We usually drop the President on the beach right outside his home by helicopter. That may not be possible today."

"So where would we go?"

"There's an air force base nearby. You'll proceed onwards by limousine. It's all been taken care of."

"Then let's get on with it," Ferguson said.

Ten minutes later, the three of them were strapping into a helicopter that took off almost instantly.

. . .

When Mark Gold went into Sammy's Bar, it was early evening and the place was almost empty. The black man with dreadlocks at the corner table was Nelson Harker and just now he was reading the *Washington Post*.

Gold sat down. "Would you like a drink?"

"Not when I'm working."

Harker looked up. He had an interesting face, a quick, intelligent look to him that Gold found surprising in a professional hit man, and Harker had killed often, sometimes for as little as one thousand dollars. This time, he was getting ten, but with Dillon's reputation, it seemed merited. He took a photo from his pocket and passed it over.

"Another photo of Dillon, just to make sure."

"Heh, I've already seen one. So he's been a big name with the IRA, the kind of shitheads who bomb women and kids. That ain't no way to be. I spit on them."

"Well, spit on Dillon at the Charlton Hotel later tonight. I want you there no later than ten."

"And then?"

"If we don't see him around, you can take him in his suite. There's a night elevator in the basement garage to all floors."

"Sounds good to me. Where's my money?"

Gold took out an envelope and slipped it across. "Half now, half after." He stood up. "See you later," and walked out.

ON THE BEACH, THE SURF ROARED IN AS THE PRESIDENT walked with Blake Johnson and Teddy Grant. They all wore storm coats against the wind, and Murchison, barking madly, made occasional forays into the water. Clancey Smith trailed them over to the left.

"For God's sake, Blake, what can it mean?" the President demanded.

"I don't know, Mr. President. What I do know for certain is that if Charles Ferguson says that this is serious, then you'd better believe it. The very fact that he had Dillon with him speaks for itself."

"Yes, of course." The President turned to Teddy. "You were in the hospital last year when I made the London trip and those Protestant activists tried to kill me. Dillon proved his worth that day. A remarkable man."

"That's one way of putting it, Mr. President, I've looked him up.

I mean, whose side is he on? He tried to mortar the British War Cabinet in ninety-one during the Gulf War and damn near succeeded."

"Yes, well, he's on our side now."

It was at that moment that Clancey Smith called, "I'm getting the word, Mr. President. The chopper's landed and they're on their way."

"Thank God," Jake Cazalet said, and a moment later a black limousine appeared on the beach, speeding toward the President's house. "This way, gentlemen." He ran along the beach through clinging strands of mist, Murchison snapping at his heels, and arrived at the house as the helicopter settled.

THERE WAS A fire in the main room and they sat round it while Dillon delivered the bad news. When he was finished, the President seemed shocked but also incredulous.

"Let me get this straight. This Judas creature insists that he has access to our main computer systems. CIA at Langley, FBI, Department of Defense?"

"That's correct, Mr. President."

"So that if we make any inquiry, attempt to discover who he and his people are, he will kill my daughter."

"Yes, that's about the size of it," Dillon said. "He takes a hard line. They not only killed Hakim and his men in Sicily, they killed the old couple and the girl."

"And probably the prison guard, Jackson, in London," Ferguson put in.

"And if I don't sign Nemesis, he'll kill her anyway?"

"I'm afraid so." Dillon took the mobile phone Judas had given him and put it on the coffee table. "That's what he gave me. Two chances to prove him right or wrong."

"As we told you, Mr. President," Ferguson said, "my check for any information on the Maccabees through British intelligence computer sources in London drew an almost instant response."

"So now you want to try the Defense Department's system."

Ferguson nodded. "If we get the same response, we'll know exactly where we are."

It was Hannah Bernstein who interrupted. "I wonder if you mind my asking you something, Mr. President. It's the policeman's mind, I'm afraid. In my job you develop a nose for things, just a hunch with nothing to back it up."

"And you have one now, Chief Inspector?" Cazalet asked her. "Okay, fire ahead."

"The Basement, who knows about it? Is it as secret as they say?"

The President turned to Blake Johnson. "You have my permission."

Blake said, "Officially, I'm the General Affairs Department, and that's all people know. I have a secretary named Alice Quarmby, a widow and entirely trustworthy, and that's it: no other staff. People imagine I've something to do with White House administration."

"Then how do you manage?"

"Rather like Judas. I have a circle of people in other employment, former FBI, for example, scientists, university professors, whom I call on for a specific job. Always totally reliable people."

"Are you saying the Secretary of Defense or the National Security Advisor, people like that, don't realize the true nature of the Basement?" Ferguson asked.

"Teddy knows, but then Teddy knows everything." The President managed a grin. "Let me explain. Several Presidents ago, and I won't say which one, there were a series of scandals to do with Communist infiltration of the CIA and the Defense Department. You may recall the legend of the Russian mole in the Pentagon."

"I do indeed, Mr. President."

"The President of the day, on his own initiative, charged an old personal friend, an ex–CIA man, to set up the General Affairs Department, which meant that he had someone totally trustworthy to rely on. It worked very well, and when his successor took office, the President spoke to him privately on the matter and the Basement carried on."

"And still does," Blake Johnson said. "Of course, there have been a few whispers over the years, but nothing concrete enough to invade our secrecy. Our only connection abroad has been with you, Charles, and that's a special relationship."

"Indeed it is," Ferguson said and turned to Hannah. "What are you driving at, Chief Inspector?"

"Listening to what Dillon had to say, it would seem that Judas mentioned his connections with the main security services, but he never mentioned the Basement."

"My God, girl, you're right," Dillon said. "There's a grand copper's mind for you."

"I would have thought he would, particularly in a matter so personal to the President."

"What you're saying is that he doesn't know about the existence of the Basement," Ferguson said.

She nodded. "And we can prove it one way or the other." She turned to Blake. "I presume that because of the extreme secrecy of your activities you have your own computer bank?"

"I sure do. I can access Langley, FBI, the Defense Department, but mine is locked up tight with our own security codes."

"Good. He told Dillon he could make another security computer inquiry after London to prove his power. Let's not access the other security services, let's put our question to the Basement's computer bank."

There was a short pause, and it was Teddy who said, "I always did say we should have more women policemen. It's the devious minds women have."

"We'll give it a try," Blake said. "I'll use the control room, Mr. President."

He got up and went out and Jake Cazalet stood up. Murchison, lying on the floor, got up also and the President said, "No, lie down."

Instead, Murchison went to Hannah and she stroked his ears. Dillon said, "If it works, it changes a lot of things."

"We'll see," Ferguson said.

Johnson came back. "I asked for any terrorist group known as the Maccabees and an individual known as Judas Maccabeus. The response was negative. Nothing known."

"So now we wait," the President said. "But for how long?"

"He was on to us on the instant in London," Ferguson said.

"Well, I tell you what," Jake Cazalet told them. "This is one of the worst scenarios in my life, but a man must eat and I believe a light meal's been organized in the kitchen. Let's go in for an hour and see what happens."

"I told Mrs. Boulder to go early," Teddy said, when they went into the kitchen. "It's all ready. I'll serve. She left the potatoes in the oven on a low heat and everything else is cold."

Hannah helped him and the President opened two bottles of ice-cold Sancerre. They had cold salmon, new potatoes, salad, and crusty bread, but the conversation was episodic. Everyone had eyes only for the mobile phone that Judas had given to Dillon and which lay on the table.

Teddy said, "I'll make some coffee."

Dillon glanced at his watch. "It's been an hour. What the hell. I say we access the Defense Department's computer and ask the same question. Let's get on with it."

Blake Johnson glanced at the President, and Jake Cazalet said, "Go for broke, Blake."

Blake got up and went out. Dillon said, "Right, let's clear the table and you do the coffee, Teddy, though I'd rather have a teabag myself."

He and Hannah cleared and had barely finished when Blake returned. "I accessed on the joint plan Langley, FBI, and the Defense Department. Totally negative response on Judas and the Maccabees."

"So now we wait," Ferguson said.

Teddy produced the coffee and Dillon's tea, and they all sat down again at the kitchen table. It was quiet, very quiet and Jake Cazalet said, "It's no good, nothing's happening."

The phone rang.

. . .

JUDAS SAID TO Dillon, "Hey, old buddy, you tried me out and didn't find me wanting. Just like London, you access those computer systems looking for me and my people and I'll know."

"Stuff you, you're a bloody sadist." Dillon deliberately made himself sound outraged and frustrated.

"Don't lose your cool, old buddy. Just tell the President that now he knows the score. If he tries to involve security forces in this, his daughter dies instantly. If he refuses to sign Nemesis, she dies."

"You're crazy," Dillon said.

"No, just practical. Give the President my best."

Judas switched off and Dillon turned to Hannah. "You're a bloody genius. He doesn't know the Basement exists. What's just happened is proof."

"Okay," Blake Johnson said. "So the situation is something like this. The Basement computer is clear, although there's no information on him. If we try the other main security services, he knows, and knows very quickly."

"And we've had our two goes," Dillon said. "If we try to involve any of the other security services, he'll kill Marie."

"And you believe that?" the President said.

"I've never been more certain."

"But he can't access our telephone systems, and that includes mobiles if we persist in using Codex Four systems," Hannah said. "So at least we can have closed communication."

"That's true," Ferguson agreed.

"But any whiff on any regular communication circuit and we've had it," Blake Johnson said. "Frankly, Mr. President, the fact that when I accessed such sensitive areas as those security computers, he knew in less than half an hour, really does show the power of the Maccabee organization. I believe that if we do try to involve the CIA and other institutions, the odds are that he will know."

"But what can I do?" the President demanded. "I'm already breaking every damn rule in the book, all protocol, by not informing the Secretary of State and the Joint Chiefs, not to say the heads of the CIA and FBI."

"Exactly," Blake said, "which is why one of your predecessors invented the Basement. We can't trust anyone, that's the point."

"Fine, but there is another point. I'll hit Arab terrorists hard if they merit it and if I have to, but I can't in all conscience sign Nemesis when the Committee meets next week. I mean, what do I do?"

There was stillness and, for some reason, it was Dillon they turned to. He said, "There could be a way forward if we move fast, but the next step is me catching my death, according to Judas. I think that's rather a good idea."

"What on earth do you mean?" Ferguson asked.

"I'll take my chances when we get back to Washington. I'll wear a bullet-proof vest."

"Not much good if the shooter goes for a headshot," Johnson said.

"Well, you take a chance every day of your life."

"Then what, Mr. Dillon?" Cazalet asked.

"I used to be a student at the Royal Academy of Dramatic Art in London, Mr. President. I even acted with the National Theatre. I've always had an ability to change and not just with makeup. Let me show you. Here, give me your glasses, Teddy."

Teddy handed them over and Dillon went out and closed the door. When it opened again, he shuffled in, limping heavily on the right leg, his head slightly down, a look of pain on his face, but it wasn't just that, not only the glasses. His body language had changed. It was as if he had become another person.

"Good God," the President said. "I wouldn't have believed it if I hadn't seen it with my own eyes."

"The Man of a Thousand Faces he was called in international intelligence circles," Ferguson said. "On the run in Ireland twenty years with the IRA and we never touched his collar once."

"Once I'm officially dead in Washington, I'll change," Dillon said, "dye my hair a different color, tinted glasses, perhaps cheek pouches, we'll see. Another passport, of course, but no problem. I always carry two or three with me, and makeup according to the photo on whichever I choose."

"If you need help, I have a friend who lives in my apartment block," Teddy said. "Mildred Atkinson. She does makeup for a lot of the big stars. She was telling me she did DeNiro last week."

"Is she safe?"

"Absolutely."

"Well, I'll see."

Hannah said, "As regards general security, we only have five days anyway before the Future Projects Committee meets."

"So what happens?" the President said.

"The heart of the problem is quite simple," Dillon told him. "Where is she being held? All I know definitely is that it's within twelve hours by boat from Sicily."

"Yes, but you can't account for those twelve hours," Ferguson said. "It could be less than that."

"Yes, but if we accept twelve hours maximum, within the range could be Corsica if we went west, the Tunisian or Egyptian coasts, Italy, Greece, Turkey."

"Have you missed anything?" Johnson said ironically.

"God knows. Marie told me that when David Braun kidnapped her in Corfu, he said she was going for a little plane ride."

There was a pause. The President said, "Okay, you end up dead, you change your identity. Then what?"

"The Brigadier and the Chief Inspector go home in the Lear, grieving. I'll go to Ireland and run down Riley. I'll bring him to London and he can identify the lawyer for us from the Wandsworth Prison surveillance tapes."

Johnson said, "You actually think you can find Riley?"

"I believe so. I think he'll head straight for his cousin's farm in Tullamore. He had the Irish passport the Brigadier got him, he had my operating money. There would be no sense in him not going back to Ireland. He's safe there."

The President nodded. "Yes, it makes sense." He turned to Blake. "It seems to me what Mr. Dillon needs is instant transportation. He doesn't want to have to hang around wasting time wherever it is he goes."

"No problem, Mr. President. I have the new Gulfstream Five private jet on hand, flown in it several times lately. It's a hell of a plane."

The President turned to Dillon. "You could fly to Ireland in not much more than six hours in the Gulfstream." He nodded to Blake Johnson. "I'd like you to go with him. Teddy can hold the fort here."

"At your orders, Mr. President," Blake said.

Cazalet nodded. "That's it, then. All I can say is get to it. Is the helicopter ready, Teddy?"

"Standing by."

"You go with them. I'll see you tomorrow."

Dillon said, "Just one thing. I like your daughter and I don't like Judas and I'll do anything to get her back, even if it means playing public executioner again. Is that all right with you?"

"It sure as hell is," Jake Cazalet said, his face white with passion.

IN HIS CAR along the street from the Charlton Hotel, Mark Gold tapped away at his laptop. He gave a sigh of satisfaction as the screen disclosed what he wanted. He had accessed the traffic information section at Andrews Air Force Base and it was all there. The time the British-registered Lear had landed, names of passengers. The Air Force helicopter used by the President was logged out ten minutes later for Nantucket. Passenger details were always classified on that one, but no prizes for guessing who they were. The helicopter was due to land again at Andrews in half an hour. He got out and looked up the street. There was no sign of Harker and he got back into the car, fuming impatiently as a downpour started.

. . .

MARIE SAT AT the window in front of the easel painting. The door opened and David Braun came in with coffee and cookies on a tray. He placed it on the table.

"Working away, I see."

"What do you expect me to do, make out my last will and testament?"

"Marie, please, I hate all this. I care for you. I'd do anything for you."

"Well, that's good. Go and shoot Judas, then. That really would help."

His shoulders sagged, he went out, and the key turned in the door.

AT ANDREWS, THEY all packed into Blake Johnson's limousine. As they drove down into Washington, he said, "Sean, I've been thinking. Why put yourself at risk? You know, setting yourself up as a target? Why not simply change identity as planned and clear off to Ireland?"

"Because Judas might smell a rat, whereas if I'm officially dead he'll be much happier. Anyway, the first thing you do is find us a cab and the Brigadier and the Chief Inspector and I will transfer. That's so we'll be seen arriving at the hotel on our own."

"And what do I do?"

"Drop Teddy off, no sense in putting him in harm's way."

"And screw you too, Mr. Dillon," Teddy said.

"All right, have it your own way."

"What about a life preserver?" Johnson asked.

"I've got a nylon and titanium vest in my suitcase, I always carry one. Anyway, as you'll be watching my back, this is how it goes."

THE CAB DEPOSITED the Brigadier, Hannah Bernstein, and Dillon at the steps leading up to the Charlton. The concierge came out with an umbrella and porters hurried to get the luggage.

"Shit!" Mark Gold said. "Where are you, Harker?"

At that moment there was a tap on the window. He glanced out and saw Harker peering down at him. Gold got the window down.

"Where in the hell have you been?"

"Stealing a car, you dummy. You didn't imagine we'd drive into the garage in yours so somebody could take your number if we have to move fast? It's down the street."

Gold got out, locked the car, and followed him.

AT THE SAME moment, Blake Johnson and Teddy Grant drove into the hotel's underground garage, which was reasonably full. Blake found a space well surrounded by other vehicles and parked. He switched off, opened the glove compartment, took out a Beretta with a silencer already in place, and checked it.

"Loaded for bear," Teddy said.

"You better believe it," Johnson told him grimly.

A moment later, a limousine drove in and parked near at hand. They eased down as a white-haired, rather portly man got out and walked to the elevator.

"No, I don't think so," Blake said.

Two or three minutes later, a sand-colored sedan moved in. Blake had a quick flash of Gold at the wheel and Harker.

"Down, Teddy," he said urgently, and they went low in their seats. "I think this is it. Hard-looking black man with dreadlocks and a guy in a Brooks Brothers suit at the wheel. It doesn't fit."

The sedan parked between a couple of panel trucks near the elevator and its lights went out. "Keep down, Teddy." Blake raised his head cautiously. "They're just sitting there. Call the Brigadier on your mobile."

IN HIS SUITE, Dillon had stripped to the waist to put on the nylon and titanium vest, Hannah Bernstein watching anxiously. He pulled on a polo sweater in navy blue silk, then his jacket.

"You're sure you want to do this?" Ferguson said.

"He wants me dead, he said so. He also said underground garages like the hotel's were dangerous places."

"I think it's madness," Hannah said.

"But that's only because you love me, girl dear."

"For God's sake, Dillon, can't you take anything seriously?"

"Could never see the point." He smiled. "I've seen the President, and Judas knows that, so now he wants me out of his hair. A fatal error, not for me, but for him."

Ferguson's mobile phone rang and he picked it up, listened, and nodded. "Right."

He turned to Dillon. "Sand-colored sedan by the elevator. Two men, one black, the other white and he has the wheel. Johnson says: When you're ready."

Dillon took out his Walther, checked it, and stuck it in his waistband at the back. He kissed Hannah on the cheek. "We who are about to die and all that good old Roman rubbish. Just stick to the plan. It will work. The great Dillon is never wrong."

"Oh, get out of here, damn you!" she said angrily, and he did just that.

HARKER AND GOLD waited in silence. After a while, Harker said, "How long are we going to give this guy before I go upstairs? We could be here all night. You got the number of his suite?"

"Sure, I tipped a porter."

At that moment, the elevator door opened and Dillon stepped out. He moved into the open between rows of cars and lit a cigarette, taking his time.

"It's him," Gold said excitedly.

"I've got eyes, haven't I? I seen his picture." Harker took out a Colt automatic and screwed on a silencer. "Here goes. It's kiss-of-death time."

He opened the door, stepped out, and immediately took aim,

shooting Dillon in the back twice. Dillon, driven forward, went down on his knees and fell on his face, the back of his jacket smouldering where the bullets had entered.

Blake Johnson jumped from his limousine. "What's going on there?" he shouted.

Harker fired at him twice, but Blake was already ducking, and Harker leapt into the sedan. "Move it!" he snarled, and Gold gunned the engine, swung out into the aisle, and made for the entrance.

THERE WAS TOTAL silence and Teddy was already leaning over Dillon, beating out the tiny flames. "Sean, speak to me, for God's sake."

"I'm trying to get my bloody breath first." Dillon got to his knees.

Johnson was on his mobile. He switched it off. "You okay, Sean?"

"Feels like I've been hit with a sledgehammer twice, but I'll survive."

"Just hang in there. The ambulance is on the way," Blake said. "I'll call the Brigadier and tell him you're okay."

GOLD PARKED THREE streets away and Harker laughed excitedly. "Did I stiff that little bastard or did I stiff him?"

"You certainly did. A pity that idiot happened to turn up."

"Ah, screw him. Where's my money, man?"

Gold took an envelope from his pocket and gave it to him. Harker grinned. "Pleasure doing business with you. I'd get moving if I were you."

He got out of the sedan and walked away through the rain. Gold followed him. No need to wipe anything, since he'd worn gloves. He walked back to the hotel, unlocked his car, and got in. A few moments later, an ambulance appeared and went in the hotel garage.

Gold got his mobile out and called the special number. "Gold here, mission accomplished."

"Are you sure?" Judas said.

"Two in the back. I saw him go down myself. An ambulance has just gone in to pick him up."

"Follow it," Judas said. "Make sure and contact me again."

Gold switched off and as the ambulance emerged, turned his ignition key, and went after it.

IN THE AMBULANCE, Ferguson and Hannah watched as Dillon removed his jacket and shirt. The two rounds were embedded in the bulletproof jacket. Dillon parted the velcro tabs and Johnson helped him off with it.

"You're going to have one hell of a bruise," Blake said. "Only two inches between them. That bastard is good. I've got a friend at the Washington criminal procedures department who owes me a favor to take a look at the garage security video. He's going to see if he can identify the men, then he'll erase our little comedy. All highly illegal."

"The fella at the wheel would be the Maccabee," Dillon said as Hannah handed him a clean, checked country shirt. "Our black friend will be hired muscle. We can't have anyone arrested, that would tip off Judas."

Hannah gave him a leather bomber jacket. "Are you sure you're all right?"

"I could do with a Bushmills whiskey, but that comes later. Did you bring the makeup box from my suitcase?"

She nodded. "Yes."

"Good. I think it's time for the second act, then."

GOLD BRAKED TO a halt and watched the ambulance enter the District Three morgue. There had been no police presence, but then they would be back at the hotel pursuing their inquiries. He waited for quite a while, then took a deep breath, got out of his car, and went in.

The night attendant was a black former Marine sergeant called

Tino Hill. He'd known Blake from the old days, when Hill had been an FBI spotter on a monthly retainer to keep an eye out for bad people with their faces on posters.

Blake, Teddy, Ferguson, and Hannah stood in the back office, the door slightly ajar. Dillon was seated at the table, the makeup box open, looking at himself in a small glass while he coated his face, first with a green-white base, then streaked it with false blood.

He turned. "Will I do?"

"You look horrible," Hannah told him.

"Good. Let's see what happens."

"Are you sure about this?" Johnson asked.

"I think Judas will want confirmation."

The outer bell rang. Johnson peered through the slightly open door. "That's him, the driver. Do as I told you, Tino."

Tino went out. "Can I help you?"

"Well, I don't know," Gold said. "My cousin was supposed to meet me outside the Charlton Hotel and he didn't come and someone told me there was a shooting."

"Just wait a minute."

Tino went back inside, nodded to Dillon, opened a door and led the way into an air-cooled room with several surgical tables containing bodies, three of which were naked, the rest draped with sheets.

"Ready for the pathologists in the morning," he said. "Okay, Mr. Dillon, up you go."

Dillon lay on a vacant table and Tino covered him with a sheet, went out, nodded to the others, and confronted Gold.

"Now let's see." He looked in his register. "You say near the Charlton?"

"That's right."

"What was your cousin's name?"

"Dillon." Gold almost whispered it.

"Hey, that's the victim of the shooting at the Charlton garage. They just brought him in. Will you identify him?"

"If I must."

"Okay. This way, and if you feel like vomiting, run for the green door."

In the receiving room, Gold paused, shocked particularly by the sight of the naked dead bodies. "Don't look good, do they?" Tino said. "Comes to us all. Mind you, look at the size of the dick on the one at the end. I sure as hell believe he had a good time."

Gold breathed deeply. Tino slipped the sheet, revealing Dillon's face only. His eyes were fixed and staring. He looked truly dreadful and Gold did indeed run for the green door, where he found himself in a lavatory, and was thoroughly sick.

When he came out, Tino led him through to the front desk. "Can I have your details, sir? The police will need them."

"I'm too distressed now," Gold said. "I'll be back tomorrow," and he hurried out.

In the back room, Blake switched off his mobile. "I've got an unmarked car to follow him. We'll leave him in place, naturally. If we didn't, Judas would be unhappy, but I'd like to know who he is for future reference."

"And the shooter," Teddy said, "he gets away with it, too? A bastard like that."

"I know, Teddy, but guys like that could get it on the street any night."

Dillon came in, sat down, took cleansing cream from the makeup kit, got rid of the grunge on his face, then washed at a sink in the corner.

He smiled as he toweled it off. "Frightened the bastard to death."

Blake's phone rang. He listened, then said, "Thanks, owe you a favor." He looked at them. "My friend at criminal procedures. He recognized the shooter at once, one Nelson Harker. The driver's face was obscure. Harker is a number-one hit man, who frightens the hell out of people so much, no one will ever testify. He lives on Flower Street."

"Will you visit him?" Hannah asked.

"One of these days. We'll see. Let's get back to the hotel. I'll drop you off, then go home and pack. Ireland next stop."

HIS MOBILE SOUNDED again on the way to the hotel and he answered. When he switched it off, he said, "My man followed our unknown to an apartment block in Georgetown. Mark Gold is his name. My secretary, Alice Quarmby, checked him on our computer, and guess what? He's a Senior Computer Operator at the Defense Department, a very bright young man. His brother, also American, emigrated to Israel. He was killed in some Hamas rocket attack on the kibbutz where he worked."

"So Gold is a Maccabee?" Hannah said.

"Undoubtedly."

He pulled in under the marquee at the front of the hotel. "I'll see you at Andrews as soon as possible."

They got out and went in and Blake Johnson drove away with Teddy.

GOLD HAD LEFT his call to Judas until he reached his apartment. The bodies at the morgue had horrified him, the sickly sweet smell of corruption.

He had a brandy and made the call on the special mobile. "It's Gold," he said, when Judas answered. "I got access to the morgue. He's dead all right."

"Excellent," Judas said. "I'll be in touch."

IN HER ROOM, Marie de Brissac was having a rest, lying on the bed when the door opened. David Braun came in, followed by Judas in his hood. Marie sat up and swung her legs to the floor.

"What do you want?" She was alarmed but refused to show it.

"I just wanted to share some news with you." Judas was laughing, she could tell. "Your friend Dillon was knocked off a little while ago."

"You're lying."

"He's lying in a morgue in Washington right now with two bullets in the back. He won't be returning, Countess."

He laughed out loud and went out and she started to cry. David Braun put a hand on her shoulder, but she shrugged him off.

"Go on, get out! You're as bad as he is!"

IRELAND • LONDON
FRANCE
EASTERN MEDITERRANEAN

DILLON SAT IN FRONT OF THE SINK IN THE BATHROOM AT Teddy's apartment, a towel about his neck and shoulders. Teddy stood in the corner smoking a cigarette, and Mildred Atkinson was behind Dillon, looking at him in the mirror.

"Can you do something, Mildred?"

"Of course I can. Lovely face." She nodded. "The hair, really, but I hate giving people black dye jobs. No matter how good you do it, it looks wrong. I mean, I adore this hair of yours, love," she said to Dillon, "like pale straw. What I'll do is crop it, crew cut really, and I'll bronze it up just like the photo on the passport you've shown me. It'll change the shape of your skull. Then the eyebrows." She frowned. "Glasses are tinted, I see. I'll check on what I have in my bag of tricks."

She picked up her scissors and started. "You're English," Dillon said.

"That's true, love. I'm from Camden in good old London town. Started in this game as a kid at Pinewood Studios."

"What brought you here?"

"Love, my dear, for the biggest American bastard you ever met in your life. By the time I discovered that, I'd made my bones in the business, so I decided to stay. Anyway, stop talking and let's get on with it."

DILLON SAT BACK, a different Dillon staring at him from the mirror. Teddy said in awe, "You're a genius, Mildred. The tinted glasses are just right."

She packed her bag. "Good luck, Mr. Dillon. The dye should be good for two weeks."

"Let me give you something," Teddy said.

"Nonsense, it was a pleasure." She patted his face and smiled at Dillon. "Lovely boy, Teddy," and went out.

AT ANDREWS, THEY parted, Ferguson and Hannah Bernstein first in the Lear. Blake, Dillon, and Teddy watched them go, standing just inside the hangar out of the rain.

Teddy shook hands. "Well, it's up to you guys now."

Dillon started to turn away, then remembered something and produced his wallet. He took out the sketch Marie de Brissac had made for him and unfolded it.

"The President's daughter did this for me. It's the crest on the side of the silver lighter Judas used."

"Looks like an army divisional flash to me," Blake said.

"Yes, and as we know Judas served in the Yom-Kippur War, it must be Israeli. A raven with lightning in its claws. Check it out, Teddy. There must be listings of Israeli Army shoulder flashes somewhere."

"Probably in the public library." Teddy laughed. "Okay, I'll take care of it."

A large black man wearing a standard airline navy blue uniform came across with an umbrella. "Sergeant Paul Kersey, gentlemen. I'm your flight attendant. I think you know the pilots, Mr. Johnson."

"I certainly do."

Dillon held out his hand. "Keogh—Martin Keogh." No sense giving his real name, since he was supposed to be dead.

"A pleasure. This way, gentlemen."

He held the umbrella over them and they crossed to the steps where the pilots waited. Johnson greeted them like old friends and made the introductions.

"Captain Tom Vernon and Lieutenant Sam Gaunt. This is Martin Keogh."

"Nice to meet you," Vernon said. "As you can see, we wear civilian uniform. We find it doesn't pay to advertise. Usually this plane has a crew of four, but we manage with three. The Gulf Five is the finest private commercial airplane in the world. We can manage six hundred miles an hour and a range of six thousand five hundred."

"So Ireland is no problem."

"Good winds tonight. We should make Dublin in six hours."

"So let's get on with it," Johnson said. "After you, gentlemen," and he followed the pilots up the steps.

TEDDY GRANT, AT his apartment, felt restless, unable to sit down. There was so much at stake, so damn much, and it was as if he was unable to do anything and that frustrated him. He looked at his watch. It was just nine o'clock, and then he remembered the sketch Dillon had given him. There were bookstores in Georgetown that stayed open until 10 P.M. It would give him something to do. He got his raincoat and went out.

His sedan was an automatic and had certain adaptations because of his one-armed status, and he drove expertly through the traffic to Georgetown. He parked at the side of the street, opened the glove compartment, and took out a folding umbrella. There was also a short-barrelled Colt revolver in there. He checked it and put it in his raincoat pocket. Muggings were frequent these days and it paid to be careful.

He pressed the automatic button on the umbrella and it jumped up above his head. He still had forty minutes before the stores closed and he found the area around which the bookstores clustered and went into the first one he came to.

He found the military section and browsed through it. Most of the books seemed to concentrate on the Second World War, the Nazis and the SS. Strange the obsession some people had with that. Nothing on the Israeli Army at all. On his way out, he paused at a stand where a new book was displayed on the history of Judaism. He looked at it morosely and walked out.

Although Teddy was a Christian, his grandmother on his father's side had been Jewish and had married out of her faith, as the phrase went. Long since dead, but Teddy remembered her with affection and was proud of the Jewish roots she had given him. He'd never advertised the fact, because religion of any kind meant nothing to him, but the Jews were a great people. The religious precepts, the morality they had given the world, was second to none. It made him angry to think of people like Judas and his Maccabees soiling the very name of their own race by their actions.

He tried three more shops before he struck it lucky. A small corner place was just closing, the owner a very old white-haired man.

"I won't hold you up," Teddy said. "I've been looking for a handbook on Israeli Army units, divisional signs, shoulder flashes."

"Just a minute." The old man went to a shelf, searched it, and returned with a small paperback. "It's a series this company does. Armies of the World. They're quite popular. In fact, I've only got volumes for the Russian and Israeli armies left. I must reorder."

"How much?" Teddy said.

"Fifteen-fifty."

Teddy got the cash out. "No need for a bag, and many thanks for your help."

He walked back to the sedan in the rain, feeling elated, got in, switched on the light, and opened the book. It was mainly text with about twelve pages in color covering the shoulder flashes of various

Israeli units. He closed the book. There was nothing remotely resembling the raven.

He sat there, frustrated, and for some reason angry. He lit a cigarette and started to go over the day's events, culminating in the attempted killing of Dillon. That Mark Gold had to be left untouched made sense, but Harker, an animal who had killed many times for money? That didn't sit well with Teddy at all.

"I mean, what was it all for, Vietnam?" he asked himself softly. "Did it produce a better society? Hell, no. Downhill all the way."

He opened the glove compartment, found his silencer, and clipped it on the end of the Colt and replaced it in his pocket. What was it Blake had said about Harker? *That guys like that could get it on the street any night.* Teddy smiled tightly and drove away.

WHEN NELSON HARKER turned onto Flower Street, he was more than a little drunk and soaked to the skin in the heavy rain. With cash in his pocket, he'd really hung one on and had also paid for the services of two prostitutes right off the street, just the way he liked it. He stumbled on the uneven pavement and paused, swaying.

"Excuse me."

He turned and found a small one-armed man in a raincoat staring intently. Harker peered at him. "What do you want, you little creep?"

Teddy's hand was on the butt of the Colt in his raincoat pocket. With all his being he wanted to pull it out and shoot the bastard—but suddenly he couldn't. Some providential second sight had filtered in through the rage. It was not a question of morality. In Vietnam he had killed for poorer reasons, but if this all went wrong and he ended up in police hands, the ensuing scandal would bring down the President himself, the one human being he valued most. Jesus, what had he been thinking?

He took a deep breath. "Well, excuse me. I was only going to ask the way to Central."

"Go on, fuck off," Harker said and lurched drunkenly away.

Teddy walked off briskly, turning from one street to another until he reached the sedan. A mile further on, he had to cross the river. He paused halfway, got out, and dropped the Colt into dark waters. It was unregistered, untraceable, but that didn't matter. It would sink in the mud and be there for all time, a memorial to what had almost been the stupidest action in his entire life.

"Damn fool," he said softly. "What did you think you were playing at?" and he got in the sedan and drove away.

DILLON WAS ENORMOUSLY impressed with the Gulfstream. It was so quiet as to be unbelievable. There were enormous club chairs that tilted for sleep, a settee at one side, and the tables were maple wood veneer. He'd already noticed the galley and the crew-rest quarters, and there was even a stand-up shower.

"You do yourself well," he said to Johnson.

"It's the best," Blake said. "The best in the world, and that's what I need. It can even use runways half the length of those required for commercial airliners."

"I like the way they've done the five after Gulfstream," Dillon said. "Roman with a V."

"That's style for you," Blake told him. "We also have a state-of-the-art satellite communications system."

"I'll try that right now."

Captain Vernon's voice came over the speaker. "We're cruising at fifty thousand feet and we have a brisk tail wind. By the way, Ireland is five hours ahead of us, so I suggest you adjust your watches."

Kersey brought coffee, and tea for Dillon. "There you go, gentlemen. Sing out if you want anything. I'll serve dinner in an hour if that suits."

"Well, a large Bushmills whiskey would go down fine right now," Dillon told him. "If you have such a thing."

"Mr. Dillon, we've got everything." Kersey was back with the Bushmills in seconds. "Okay, sir?"

"Very okay," Dillon said.

After Kersey had gone, closing the door to the galley, Blake said, "You wanted to make a call?"

"Yes, to my old friend Liam Devlin, the greatest expert on the IRA alive. He helped us out considerably with the Irish Rose affair, remember?"

"I surely do." Blake was adjusting his watch. "But it's two-thirty in the morning over there."

"So I'll wake him," and Dillon picked up the phone.

IN BED AT his cottage in the village of Kilrea outside Dublin, Liam Devlin was aware of the phone's incessant ringing. He cursed, switched on the light, and picked up the phone, checking the time on the bedside clock.

"Jesus, Mary, and Joseph, do you know what time it is, whoever you are?"

"Oh, shut up, you old rogue, and listen, will you? It's Sean—Sean Dillon."

Devlin pushed himself up. "You young devil. Where are you calling from?"

"A Gulfstream making its way across the Atlantic, Liam. I've a friend with me and we need you."

"Is this an IRA thing?" Devlin asked.

"Worse, much worse, but Dermot Riley's involved, only not on IRA business."

"Sure, and he's doing fifteen years in Wandsworth Prison."

"He was until he offered Ferguson a deal, the whereabouts of another Active Service Unit in London and an arms dump."

"And you believed him?" Devlin laughed out loud. "And he did a runner on you?"

"Something like that, but much more complicated, and like I said, not IRA business. I need to get to him, Liam. It's desperately important. Nose around and see what you can find out."

"Well, there's always his cousin, Bridget O'Malley down at Tullamore. Her farm's near the Blackwater River."

"Could be or he might think that too obvious. We'll see you at Kilrea around nine-thirty. He was using the name Thomas O'Malley, by the way."

"Fine. Can I go back to sleep now?" Devlin asked.

"Sure, and when have you ever done anything except what you wanted to do?" Dillon asked and put the phone down.

DEVLIN SAT THERE thinking about it. From what Dillon had said, this was special, very special, and at his age that excited him. He reached for a cigarette and lit it. His doctor had tried to get him to cut down, but what the hell did it matter at his age? He got up, found a robe, went into the kitchen and put the kettle on, then he picked up the phone and dialed a number.

"Is that you, Michael?" he asked. "Liam Devlin here."

"Jesus, Liam, you're up late."

"And you."

"Well, you know I've taken to the novel-writing, and I like to work through the night."

"I heard that and I also heard you have breakfast at the Irish Hussar around seven o'clock most mornings."

"That's true."

"I'll join you. I need to pick your brains."

"And I know what that means, you old sod. I'll see you then and we'll have a crack."

Devlin put the phone down, switched off the kettle, and made a pot of tea, whistling softly.

. . .

On the Gulfstream, they had an excellent meal of fillets of lemon sole with potatoes and a mixed salad followed by Italian ice cream with hazelnuts. They shared a bottle of Chablis.

Afterwards, Dillon said, "I wonder what the poor sods in first-class are getting tonight on the commercial flights. That was great."

"We aim to please." Blake drank some of his coffee. "Devlin seems an extraordinary individual. Are all the stories I've heard true?"

"Probably. He was a university graduate of Trinity College, Dublin. A scholar and a poet and one of the most feared gunmen the IRA ever had. In the Spanish Civil War, he fought against Franco and was taken prisoner by the Italians, who handed him over to the Nazis in Berlin."

"And he worked for them?"

"Well, he was no Fascist, but the IRA were dickering with Hitler at the time. They thought that England losing the war would be Ireland's opportunity. Devlin parachuted into Ireland for the Abwehr and only got back to Berlin by the skin of his teeth."

"Then what? Is there any truth in the old legend about a German attempt to kidnap Churchill with Devlin as a middle man?"

"Norfolk, nineteen forty-three," Dillon said. "Crack force of German paratroopers. Devlin was there all right, but the attempt failed. Once again, he got out by a small miracle."

"But you said he was anti-fascist?"

"They paid him well and the money went to funds for the organization. He once said he'd have tried to snatch Hitler if someone had paid him enough. He knew them all personally. Himmler, General Walter Schellenberg. He was even instrumental in saving Hitler from assassination by the SS late in the war."

"Good God!" Blake said.

"The idea was it was better keeping him alive and cocking things up, whereas with the SS in charge the war might have gone on longer."

"I get the point."

"Hitler gave him the Iron Cross First Class. Devlin falls about laughing when he tells you that."

"And then the Troubles?"

"Yes. He was one of the original architects of the Provisional IRA. On the British Army's most-wanted list."

"Which is when you met him?"

"He taught me everything I know, but Liam was an old-fashioned revolutionary and I was going through a Marxist phase; all purity of violence, being young and foolish. Shots were exchanged, but no great harm done. We made up in recent years."

"A strange man."

"A great man, the best I've ever known."

Blake nodded. "This name on your false passport, Martin Keogh. Any significance?"

Dillon shrugged. "An alias I've used on and off for years."

Blake nodded. "So you think Devlin might be able to help us find Riley?"

"If anyone can. Once we have Riley, we haul him back to London to identify that phoney lawyer from the Wandsworth security cameras. Once we have his face, we'll move on to his identity."

"You sound confident!"

"I am. With luck, he could be a stepping stone to Judas."

Blake nodded slowly. "It's not much."

"It's all we've got, and another thing. If we do find that place where Judas is holding her, it won't do any good to call in the Navy Seals or any kind of special forces. He'll kill her stone dead at the first sound."

"You mean you'd want to go in on your own?"

"I'd need backup," Dillon told him. "But I did see a fair amount of the interior. I know she's on the third floor and things like that."

"But one man." Blake shook his head. "That's crazy."

"He only has five Maccabees with him," Dillon said. "And no indication of staff. But then he wouldn't have staff for obvious reasons. So, five plus Judas is six."

"And you'd do that on your own?"

"Why not? You've heard the old joke about the tailor in the fairytale by the Brothers Grimm? Five at one blow? I'll make it six."

"That was flies on a slice of jam and bread," Blake said.

"Same difference." Dillon called Kersey. "Another Bushmills and I'll turn in."

"Right away, sir."

"You know," Blake said, "there's one thing that really bugs me about the whole business."

"And what's that?" Dillon asked, taking the drink that Kersey brought.

"From what Marie de Brissac told you, the general knew from that anonymous letter only that his wife had spent the night with an American officer. He didn't know it was Jake Cazalet."

"So it would appear."

"So only Marie and her mother and the President knew the secret."

"You're forgetting Teddy Grant."

"Okay, but that means only three left when the countess died. So how in the hell did Judas find out?"

"God knows. All that matters is he did." Dillon switched off the overhead light. "I'm going to sleep while the going's good," and he tilted back his seat.

DEVLIN PARKED HIS car on a quay on the River Liffey and walked through soft rain to the pub called the Irish Hussar. It was a pleasant, old-fashioned place with booths and a mahogany bar with a mirror behind it, rows of bottles on the shelves. Normally much favored by Republicans and Sinn Fein supporters, at that time in the morning the clientele were mainly workers of every kind tucking into a full Irish breakfast. He found his quarry, one Michael Leary, in the end booth just starting his meal.

"Liam, you old dog."

"Same to you," Devlin told him.

A young woman, all smiles, for Devlin was a great favorite, came to the table. "And what can I get you, Mr. Devlin?"

"The same and lots of breakfast tea, and mind I can stand the spoon in it." He turned to Leary. "Is the work going well, Michael?"

"That thriller I did sold nicely in the airports. To be honest, Liam, I've cleared fifty thousand pounds in the past twelve months and it seems to be climbing."

"And still working through the night?"

"It's the leg. I get a lot of pain. Can't sleep," and he banged it with his fist.

Leary, an active member of the Provisional IRA for more than twenty years, had lost the leg when a bomb he was supposed to run across the border in an old truck had exploded prematurely, killing his two companions and taking his leg. At least the incident had kept him out of a British prison, but it had brought an end to his career as an active member of the Movement.

The young woman brought Devlin his breakfast and a pot of tea and withdrew and he started to eat.

"What is it, Liam? What do you want?" Leary asked.

"Fifteen years ago when I was sixty and should have known better, I saved your life in County Down. When the RUC peelers shot you in the shoulder, I got you over the border."

"True," Leary said, "but false as my left leg in one respect. You weren't sixty, you were seventy."

"A slight digression from the truth, but you owe me one and I've come to collect."

Leary paused, frowning slightly, then resumed eating. "Go on."

"We both know you're still heavily connected with the organization. You were still running the intelligence section in Dublin for the Chief of Staff until the peace process started."

Leary pushed his plate away and the young woman came and took it. "Is this IRA business, Liam?"

"Only indirectly. A favor for a friend."

"Go on." Leary filled his pipe from a pouch.

"You've still got your ear to the ground. Would you know if Dermot Riley got back in one piece? You see, last I heard, he was in Wandsworth Prison doing fifteen years, then it seems he got out. I understand that when last seen, he was using an Irish passport in the name of Thomas O'Malley."

"Who saw him?"

"My friend, but it's confidential."

"Well, there's more than one would like to see Dermot, including the Chief of Staff. All right, he's back. He passed through security at Dublin airport three days ago in the identity of Thomas O'Malley. A security man recognized him. As he's one of our own, he simply checked him through, then reported the matter to the Chief of Staff."

"And what did he do?"

"Put in a call to London, then sent two enforcers, Bell and Barry, to pay a visit to Bridget O'Malley on her farm by the Blackwater River. That was yesterday. She swore he hadn't been there. Thought he was still in prison, so they came back."

"Knowing those two, I'm surprised they didn't try burning her with cigarettes."

"You think he's there, Liam?"

"Or thereabouts. Where else would he go?"

There was a pause as Devlin drank his tea, and finally Leary said, "The thing is, it stinks. We have friends everywhere, you know that, even at Wandsworth Prison. It seems Riley was booked out on a warrant signed by Brigadier Charles Ferguson a few days ago."

"Do you tell me?" Devlin lit a cigarette.

"And we all know who his strong right hand is these days—Sean Dillon. Would he be this friend of yours, Liam?"

Devlin smiled. "Now how would I be knowing a desperate fella like that?"

"Come off it, Liam. You taught him everything you know. You used to say he was your dark side."

Devlin got up. "A grand breakfast, and you the successful author now, Michael, I'll let you treat me. If you run into Dermot Riley, I'd like a word."

"Don't be stupid, Liam. Even the living legend of the IRA can come to a bad end."

"Jesus, son, at my age who cares? Oh, and you can tell the Chief of Staff when you phone him that this isn't an IRA matter. He has my word on it."

He walked away and Leary sat there thinking about it and then it came to him. Why would Ferguson take Riley out of Wandsworth? Obviously for some sort of deal, and Riley had done a runner or if he hadn't, was he in Ireland on a false passport to do some job or other for Ferguson?

In any case, only one course of action was open and he got up and left, walking quickly to his car.

HE SAT IN the parlor of the small suburban house that was the Chief of Staff's home. His wife served tea and the Chief sat there stroking the cat on his lap, listening.

When Leary was finished, the other man said, "Get hold of Bell and Barry and send them to me."

"And Liam?"

"Nobody likes him more than I do, but if the old bugger turns up there, especially if Dillon's with him, then Bell and Barry can stiff them both."

DEVLIN'S COTTAGE AT Kilrea was next to the convent. The garden was a riot of color and the cottage itself was Victorian, with Gothic gables and a steeply pitched roof. Blake Johnson and Dillon arrived in a rental car from Dublin Airport at nine-thirty.

"This is nice," Johnson said.

"Yes, he likes his garden," Dillon said and rang the bell.

The door opened and Devlin appeared in black sweater and slacks. "You young bastard," he cried and hugged Dillon tightly, then he smiled at Blake. "And who might this be?"

"A friend from Washington, Blake Johnson."

"A friend, is it? Well, I've been around long enough to recognize a peeler when I see one. That's Belfast for policeman, Mr. Johnson, but come into the kitchen. I've had breakfast, but I'll make you some coffee. Which variety of cop are you?"

"I used to be FBI," Johnson said as Devlin filled the kettle.

"And now?"

Johnson glanced at Dillon, who said, "Let's say he does for the President what Ferguson does for the Prime Minister."

"That must be a tall order." Devlin smiled. "All right, sit down and tell me about it."

Which Dillon did, Blake Johnson making a point or two here and there. When they were finished, Devlin said, "Not good, not good at all, and I can see where you'd need Riley."

"Will you help us, Mr. Devlin?"

"Liam, son, Liam. Actually, I've already tried." He went on to tell them of his breakfast with Leary.

When he finished, Dillon said, "So Bell and Barry are still around?"

"Are they special?" Blake asked.

"The worst. If they get to work on her, she'll know about it." He took out his Walther and checked it. "Are you carrying?" he asked Blake.

"Sure, my Beretta. Will I need it?"

"Could be. Leary will tell the Chief of Staff and he'll send them back to see her."

"I know. I thought it would help to stir the pot, Sean," Devlin said.

"You certainly have. We'll get going now."

"Not without me." Devlin smiled at Blake. "Lovely country where Bridget has the farm. Tullamore, between the Blackwater River and the Knockmealdown Mountains. A grand day out in the country. What could be better?"

AT THE SAME time, in Ferguson's office at the Ministry of Defense, Hannah was phoning through to security of Wandsworth. She spoke to a chief officer and outlined her request, then she knocked on Ferguson's door.

"I've spoken to someone responsible for surveillance tapes, Brigadier. He's digging out what they have now, and I've told him I'll be there directly."

"Take my car and driver," Ferguson said.

"I've been thinking. I don't think Judas can have violated the integrity of the Department as such. If he'd had a plant here, surely his people wouldn't have needed to eavesdrop on Dillon's cottage with directional microphones."

"A point which had occurred to me, Chief Inspector."

"That still leaves us with the fact that there would seem to be a Maccabee at work in the computer section of both MI5 and the SIS."

"We'll have to leave hunting that person down until this unhappy affair is resolved one way or the other."

"Good, sir."

"As it happens, the first thing I did on getting to the office was to check the CV of every member of the Department on my computer."

"For religious orientation, Brigadier?"

"God forgive me, but yes."

"And I was the only Jew." She smiled. "When is a Maccabee not a Maccabee?" She smiled again. "I'll see you later, sir," and went out.

AND HOW FAR did you say?" Blake Johnson asked Devlin.

"Well, we've come thirty miles or so. Maybe another hundred or a hundred and twenty. It's the country roads that twist and turn. No superhighways or turnpikes here."

Dillon said, "I'll give Ferguson a call and see what he's up to."

He pressed the Codex button on his mobile, then called Ferguson. "It's me," he said, and in spite of the coded nature of the call added, "Martin Keogh."

"No need for that," Ferguson said. "The machine indicator is on green. Where are you?"

"Driving down from Dublin to Carlow, and Waterford after that."

"You're going to see the O'Malley woman?"

"Yes. Devlin found out from an IRA source that Riley passed through Dublin airport three days ago using the O'Malley passport. The thing is, the Provos would like to have words with him, too. The Chief of Staff sent a couple of heavies to Tullamore to try and find him, but they got nowhere."

"I see."

"Devlin stirred the pot nicely with his contact. We think it will make the Chief of Staff send his goons down there again. They may even be ahead of us."

"Watch yourself," Ferguson told him, "and do keep Johnson in one piece. You're expendable, Dillon, but his demise would make for an international incident."

"Thanks very much." Dillon switched off his mobile, sat back, and started to laugh helplessly.

AT THE FARM OUTSIDE TULLAMORE, DERMOT RILEY FINISHED milking the last cow. He carried the churns of milk over to the tractor, lifted them into the trailer, then drove out of the barn and down the track a quarter of a mile to leave the milk churns on the platform by the gate to be picked up by the truck from the dairy in the village.

He drove back up to the barn, parked inside and lit a cigarette, and stood in the entrance, the slopes of the Knockmealdown Mountains looming above him. He wore a cap and an old donkey jacket and Wellington boots, and he had never been happier. Karl, the German Alsatian, lay on a bale of hay watching him, tongue hanging out.

"This is the life, dog, isn't it?" Riley said, "the only bloody life."

The dog whined and Bridget called across the yard, "Come away in, Dermot."

She was in her early sixties and looked older, a stout, motherly looking woman with the red cheeks that came from country living, and white hair. When Dermot had arrived on her doorstep by night she had been overjoyed. The shock of seeing him in the flesh when she had thought him in prison was almost too much to bear. Of course, he'd told her his presence had to be kept a secret for the time being until he got himself sorted out with the IRA. She'd found blankets and pillows and driven him half a mile up the track in her old jeep to the barn at High Meadow, where they dealt with the sheep in lambing season. There was a room with a secret door above the loft and Riley had used it often in the old days when on the run.

"You manage here until I see old Colin and Peter and tell them to take a week off," she said, referring to the two pensioners who worked at the farm part-time.

But in the morning, Bell and Barry had arrived from Dublin in a silver BMW, truly frightening men who had asked about Dermot. She'd lied through her teeth, which was a thing she didn't like to do as a good Catholic, had insisted Dermot was in prison. Two things had helped. When they interrogated Colin and Peter, the two old men were genuinely bewildered, had also insisted that Dermot was away in prison in England, and were patently telling the truth. Secondly, Bridget had been able to produce a letter written by Dermot in Wandsworth only ten days before.

The two men had insisted on searching the house and farm buildings. Barry, who was six feet three and built like a wall, told her in a low, dangerous voice as they were leaving, "You know who to phone in Dublin if he turns up, you've done it over the years. He has nothing to worry about. The Chief wants words, that's all."

Not that she'd believed him, not for a moment.

In the kitchen, she passed him an egg sandwich and a mug of tea. "You're spoiling me," Dermot said.

"Ah, you're worth spoiling." She sat at the table and drank tea herself. "What happens now, Dermot? Bad enough to be on the run from the police, but the IRA is something else."

"I'll make my peace. All I need is a chance to tell my side of the story. It's going to be fine, you'll see."

"And you'll stay?"

"I'm never going to leave again." He grinned. "Find me a nice girl in the village and I'll settle down."

AT THAT MOMENT, Bell and Barry were approaching Tullamore in the BMW. Their meeting with the Chief of Staff had been brief.

"I'm concerned Riley's been up to no good. He was last heard of leaving Wandsworth in the company of Brigadier Charles Ferguson, and we all know what that means. I want the bastard, so go back and get him for me."

As they entered the village, it was Bell who noticed Colin and Peter emerging from the post office. "That's interesting," he said. "The two old men from the farm. Why aren't they working?"

"Maybe they're part-timers," Barry said.

"But they'd still work mornings, that's when all the hard work's done," Bell said. "Driving in the cows, milking, and so on. I know about these things, I was raised on a farm. I'm going to have words."

Colin and Peter had vanished into Murphy's Select Bar, and Bell followed them. At that time in the morning, there was only Murphy, the two old men with a pint of stout in front of each of them already, and a hard-looking young man in cloth cap, jacket, and jeans at the bar.

The old men stopped talking, frozen with fear, and Murphy, who knew very well who Bell was, turned pale. The young man drank some of his ale and frowned.

"Now then, you old bastards," Bell said, "I don't think you were telling the truth when we spoke yesterday."

"Jesus, mister, I swear we were."

"Then tell me one thing. Why aren't you working?"

"It was the missus wanted to give us the day off," Peter said.

"Hey, you," the young man at the bar called. "Let them alone."

Murphy put a hand on his arm. "Leave it, Patrick, this is IRA business."

Bell ignored him. "So you haven't seen Riley?"

"I swear to God I haven't."

Patrick moved in and tapped Bell on the shoulder. "I said leave them alone."

Bell swung his right elbow backwards, catching him full in the mouth, and as Patrick staggered back, Barry, who had appeared in the doorway, gave him a vicious punch to the kidneys, which sent him on his knees. He stayed there until Bell pushed him over.

"Silly boy," he called to Murphy. "Tell him to mind his manners in future," and they left.

Barry took the wheel and drove out to the farm. He paused at the entrance where the truck from the dairy was parked, two men manhandling Bridget's milk churns on board.

"Interesting," Bell said. "She's given her laborers a holiday, so how in the hell did that old woman manage those milk churns?"

"Well, we'll see, won't we?" Barry told him and drove along the track.

BRIDGET HAPPENED TO be in the storeroom at the back when they arrived, so she didn't hear them, and the Alsatian was up at the barn at High Meadow where Dermot was checking on some ewes. She came into the kitchen carrying a bag of flour and stopped dead in her tracks. Barry and Bell were standing just inside the kitchen door.

"You're back," she whispered and placed the bag of flour on the table.

"Yes, we are, you lying old bitch," Barry said. He took a pace forward and slapped her across the face. "Now where is he?"

She was terrified out of her mind. "I don't know, truly I don't, Mr. Barry."

"You're a bad liar." He slapped her again. Blood ran from her nose and he grabbed her hair and nodded to Bell, who lit a cigarette.

She started to struggle. He pushed her down across the table and Bell blew on his cigarette until it was red hot and touched her right cheek.

She screamed, writhing in agony. "No—please! I'll tell you."

Barry let her get up. "You see, everything comes to he who waits," he said to Bell and turned to Bridget, who was sobbing bitterly. "Where is he?"

"Half a mile up the track, the barn at High Meadow. There's a room with a secret door above the loft. He sleeps there."

Barry smiled. "That wasn't too hard, was it?" and he and Bell walked out.

"Oh, Dermot, what have I done?" Bridget said and started to cry bitterly.

AT HIGH MEADOW with the ewes, Dermot saw the flash of silver on the track below and knew he was in trouble. He hurried into the barn, Karl following. He couldn't take the dog with him to the secret room, for any kind of a whine would give him away, never mind barking.

"Off you go, boy, home to Bridget." Karl hovered uncertainly. "Go on, get moving!" Dermot told him.

This time, the Alsatian did as he was told. Dermot climbed the ladder to the loft, then clambered over bales of hay and got the secret door in the wood paneling open. He climbed inside. It was dark, just the odd chink of light, and he waited.

When Barry and Bell got out of the BMW, the Alsatian sat looking at them. "Get rid of that for starters," Barry said, and Bell took out a Smith & Wesson revolver.

The moment he pointed it, Karl took off, scattering the sheep, making for the valley below. Bell laughed and put the revolver back in his pocket.

"A smart bugger, that dog."

"Well, let's see if Dermot is," Barry said and led the way inside.

They stood looking up at the loft crammed with the bales of hay and Barry called, "We know you're there, Dermot, so you might as well come out. Bridget was very forthcoming after a little persuasion."

Dermot, in the darkness, almost choked with rage, but he didn't have a gun, that was the thing, couldn't take them on.

It was Bell who spoke now. "There's a lot of straw in here, Dermot, not to say hay. If I drop a match, you'll be in serious trouble. Of course, if you want to end up like a well-done side of beef, that's your affair."

A moment later, the secret door opened and Dermot scrambled out. He made his way to the edge of the loft and stood looking at them.

"You bloody bastards," he said, "if you've hurt Bridget, I'll do for you." Then he climbed down the ladder.

Barry grabbed his arms from the rear. "You shouldn't talk like that, you really shouldn't." He nodded to Bell. "Just his body. I want his face to look normal when he's sitting in the back of the car on the way back to Dublin."

"My pleasure," Bell said and punched Riley very hard beneath the ribs.

WHEN THE RENTAL car pulled up in the farm yard, Blake Johnson was at the wheel. The kitchen door was open and Karl erupted, jumping up at the car, growling fiercely. Dillon opened a window and whistled, a low and eerie sound that put the teeth on edge. Karl subsided, his ears flattening.

"Jesus, but I taught you how to do that well," Devlin said.

As they got out of the car, Bridget appeared in the doorway. She looked terrible as she tried to staunch the blood from her nose with a tea towel.

"Liam Devlin, is that you?"

"As ever was," Devlin said and put an arm around her shoulders. "Who did this to you?"

"Barry and Bell. They were here yesterday seeking Dermot. I told them he wasn't here."

"But he was," Dillon said and put a hand on her shoulder. "I'm Sean Dillon. I fought with Dermot in Derry in the old days."

She nodded vacantly. "They turned up a little while ago, beat me and burned me with a cigarette."

"The bastards," Devlin said.

"The thing is, I told them where Dermot's hiding. Half a mile up the track. The barn at High Meadow." She was crying now. "I couldn't help it, the pain was terrible."

"Go in, make yourself a cup of tea. We'll be back with Dermot, I promise you."

She did as she was told, and Devlin said grimly, "I think a lesson is in order here."

The three men got in the car, Blake taking the wheel again. Dillon took out his Walther, checked it, and screwed on the silencer.

"Take it nice and easy and let's see the lay of the land. It could be a hot one. They'll be carrying, and they're good. What about you, Liam?"

Devlin grinned. "And what would I be needing with a shooter, with a couple of desperate individuals like you two to look after me?"

They climbed up toward the crest of a hill, Blake choosing a low gear. There were trees along the edge of the track and a row of trees bordering the meadow, the barn beyond them.

"They'll see us coming," Blake said.

"Which is why I'm going to bail out on the bend and take to the trees," Dillon told him, "so slow down for me. You take care of the confrontation, Liam, and don't worry. A hard man, this one with all that FBI training. He'll manage, especially with me coming in the back door."

"Well, that's a comforting thought," Blake said and slowed on the bend.

Dillon opened the door and made for the ditch as Devlin closed the door behind him. The car picked up speed and Dillon hurried through the trees.

. . .

AWARE OF THE sound of the engine as the car approached, Bell left Barry clutching Riley and went to the door, drawing his revolver.

"What is it?" Barry demanded.

"Don't know. Black saloon car, driver and one passenger."

"Get in the loft." Bell did as he was told, climbing the ladder, and Barry dropped Riley to the ground and kicked him. "Stay still." He moved behind the open door.

He heard the car stop outside and steps approaching. Devlin appeared in the doorway, Blake Johnson at his back. He paused, then came forward.

"Well, now, Dermot, you don't look too good."

"Watch yourself, Mr. Devlin, the bastard's behind the door," Riley told him.

Barry stepped out, holding his revolver. "Easy, the both of you, or I'll blow your spines out." He rammed the barrel into Blake's back, patted his pockets and found the Beretta. "Would you look at that now? And what about you, Devlin?"

"Don't be daft. Would a seventy-five-year-old man like myself be carrying a pistol?"

"Add ten years to that, you lying old bugger."

Devlin sighed and said to Blake, "Neanderthal man come back to haunt us. He only learned to walk erect this morning."

"I'll do for you, you old sod." Barry was furiously angry. "You've had your day. You've been due for the knacker's yard for years."

"Well, it comes to us all." Devlin gave Riley a hand. "Up you get, Dermot. Don't let bastards like this grind you down."

Barry exploded in rage. "I warned you. I'll put you on sticks."

"And why would you want to do that, I wonder?" Sean Dillon called.

He stood just inside the other door to the barn, rain increasing in a great rush at that moment. His left hand was behind him holding the Walther against his back. With his right, he shook a cigarette from his pack, put one in his mouth, and lit it with his old Zippo.

Barry was totally thrown by the change in Dillon's appearance. "Sean Dillon, is that you?"

"Your worst nightmare," Dillon said.

"The loft, watch the loft, Sean," Riley croaked.

Barry kicked him. "Take him!" he cried.

Bell stood up on the edge of the loft, gun ready, and Dillon's hand came round in one smooth motion. He fired twice, catching Bell in the heart, the sound of the silenced weapon flat on the damp air. Bell fell headfirst.

In the same moment, as Barry raised his revolver, Liam Devlin shot him in the back with the Walther he was holding in his raincoat pocket, sending him into the ground. There was silence, only the sound of the rain on the roof.

Blake Johnson said, "My God, that was something."

Dillon pocketed the Walther, went and stirred Bell's body, then checked Barry. "Well, we've done the world a favor." He looked at Devlin and shook his head. "You told me you weren't carrying."

"I know," Devlin said. "I'm a terrible liar." He turned to Dermot. "Are you all right?"

"My ribs don't feel too good."

"You'll live. This is Mr. Johnson, an American and former FBI, so mind your manners. He and Dillon are working on the case you were involved in. You'll go back to London with them."

"And why would I do that?"

"Because it's the safest place for you at the moment," Dillon told him. "Ferguson will keep his word. All you have to do is look at the security video for the day that phoney lawyer, George Brown, visited you in Wandsworth and put a face to him. Stay here and the Provisional IRA will have your balls."

"Maybe not," Devlin said. "I'll speak to the right people, Dermot, explain the truth. You haven't done anything against the organization. I still have influence."

"With two enforcers lying here dead?"

"Scum, Dermot, and the Chief of Staff knows it. Sometimes you have to dirty your hands. Now let's get out of here."

DEVLIN PHONED MICHAEL Leary on his mobile. "Is it yourself, Michael? You'd better get a disposal squad down here to Tullamore. You'll find Bell and Barry in the barn at High Meadow, very dead. I had to stiff Barry myself. Sean took care of Bell."

"Liam, what have you done?"

"Nothing that hadn't been coming to those two animals for years. A disgrace to the organization. Dillon is taking Riley back to London this afternoon. Nothing affecting the IRA. Afterwards, I want you to allow him back."

Leary sounded shocked. "You must be crazy."

"I'll see you in the Irish Hussar late afternoon and I'll explain and you can tell the Chief of Staff. I won't take no for an answer."

Dillon said, "Still the hard man, Liam."

"Hard enough." Devlin led the way back into the kitchen. Blake stood by the open door and Bridget was at the table. "You'll get the doctor, Bridget, promise me."

She nodded. "All right."

"Later, some men will turn up in a hearse or a truck, something like that. They'll take the bodies away. Bell and Barry never existed. Just forget about them."

"And Dermot?"

"He's going to London for a day or so with Sean, then he'll be back. I'll fix it with the IRA."

"God bless you, Liam."

Riley came in wearing corduroy trousers and a jacket and tie. He looked very respectable. "Will I do?"

"Definitely," Dillon said. "Let's get going."

Riley hugged Bridget. "I'll see you soon."

"I'll pray for you, Dermot," and then she flooded with tears and rushed out of the kitchen.

. . .

IN HIS OFFICE at the Ministry of Defense, Ferguson switched off the Codex, frowning, then pressed the old-fashioned buzzer on his desk. Hannah Bernstein came in.

"Brigadier?"

"Just had Dillon on the phone. They've got Riley. They're on the way back to Dublin now."

"Was it messy, sir?"

"Always seems to be where Dillon's concerned. Two IRA enforcers went down, one to Dillon, and would you believe Devlin got the other?"

"I wouldn't exactly be surprised."

"Apparently, they'd tortured Bridget O'Malley into saying where Riley was hiding. No great loss."

"Then we should be able to show the video to Riley this evening?"

"I would imagine so."

"Excellent." Hannah nodded. "Then if you've no objection, I'll take a few hours off, go home and freshen up. I'll be back at five."

"Off you go then," Ferguson said.

IN THE OVAL Office at the White House, the President took a call from Blake Johnson on his Codex line. He pressed the special buzzer that brought Teddy in. Teddy stood by the desk, waiting, as the President listened and then said, "Excellent, Blake, I'll await a further report."

He switched off and Teddy said, "Good news?"

The President nodded and gave him a quick run-down on what had happened at Tullamore as related to him by Blake.

"So they're on their way back to London with Riley so he can look at the video to try and identify Brown?" Teddy asked.

"That's it."

"Okay, but even if they put a face to him, they still have to identify him."

"He told Riley that he really was a lawyer, but that Brown wasn't his real name," Cazalet said.

"A lot of lawyers in London, Mr. President."

"Teddy, I don't need this," the President said. "These men are all I've got."

There was agony on his face and Teddy was immediately contrite. "That was stupid of me. Forgive me." He turned and went out, closing the door behind him and stood there in the corridor cursing. "You fool," he said softly. "You stupid damn fool!"

DEVLIN SAW THEM off at Dublin airport, watching the Gulfstream climb away, then went and got a taxi into town. He told the driver to stop on the way at a phone box and called Leary.

"It's me, Liam," he said. "I'll be at the Irish Hussar in twenty minutes," and he put the phone down.

ON BOARD THE Gulfstream, Blake was enjoying a coffee while Dillon and Riley drank tea. "One thing," Dillon said, "I owe you, Dermot, for warning me that Bell was in the loft."

"And tipping Devlin and me off about Barry being behind the door," Blake said.

"Not that it did any good," Riley told him.

"Yes, it did," Dillon said. "We stiffed both the bastards in the end."

Riley seemed troubled. "Tell me, Sean, will Ferguson play square with me? Will he let me go once this thing is over?"

"My hand on it."

"But go where? I still can't see me being safe in Ireland."

"Leave it to Liam. He'll fix it."

Blake said, "Do you really think he can pull it off?"

"Look at it this way. As I've said, nothing Dermot did in this affair was against the interests of the IRA. Once Liam's explained that, it'll be okay. He can be very persuasive."

"But what about Bell and Barry?"

"Plenty more rubbish where they came from, whereas Liam Devlin is the living legend of the IRA. It will work because he'll make it work."

"God, I hope so," Riley said fervently.

AT THAT MOMENT, Devlin was paying off the taxi outside the Irish Hussar. When he went in, it was half full and many of the drinkers nodded in recognition and he heard his name mentioned. Michael Leary and the Chief of Staff were in the end booth.

"God save all here." Devlin sat down and neither of them said a word. "God save you kindly was the answer to that."

"Liam, what in the hell have you done?" Leary demanded.

"Cut his own throat is what he's done," the Chief of Staff said.

Devlin waved to a waitress. "Three large Bushmills over here." He took out a cigarette, lit it, and eyed the Chief of Staff. "I haven't always approved of the tactics, but haven't I always supported the organization?"

"You've served us well," the Chief of Staff said reluctantly.

"None better," Leary agreed.

"Then why would I lie now, and me an old man with one foot in the grave?"

"Ah, fug you, Liam," the Chief of Staff said. "Get on with it."

So Devlin gave them a truncated version of the story, embellished a little.

"A phoney lawyer called Brown sees Dermot in Wandsworth and offers him a way out. Contact Ferguson and say he would offer knowledge of where a very nasty terrorist called Hakim was hanging out. Sicily, as it happens."

"So?"

"Well, the whole thing was a scam by another Arab fundamentalist group who Dillon had done a bad turn to. They knew it was Dillon that Ferguson would send after Hakim, and Riley, as ordered, offered to go with him to show good faith."

"And what happened?"

"Oh, they grabbed Dillon at some Sicilian fishing port, Riley with them, only by this time he was beginning to suspect he'd get shafted himself, so he jumped overboard while they were leaving harbor and swam back. The rest you know."

"No, we don't," Leary said, but the strange thing is it was the Chief of Staff who was laughing.

"Go on," he said, "and how did Dillon get away? I mean, it must have been good."

"He had one gun in his pocket, another in his waistband at the rear under his coat. They found those and missed the Walther he had under his left trouser leg in an ankle holster. He shot three and took to the water himself. Of course, when he reached the shore, Dermot was long gone."

"And that's the way of it?" the Chief of Staff said.

"Absolutely. Dermot's wanted in London for one purpose only. To see if he can put a face to this phoney lawyer, Brown, on the security video. Once he's done that, he's free."

"I see."

"Nothing to do with the IRA in any of this," Devlin said. "My word on it. The person who's really scored is Dermot. He could have been sitting in a cell for the whole fifteen years, even twelve if he got remission, the Brits are the losers on that one. I'd have thought you'd have liked that."

The Chief of Staff glanced at Leary, then grinned reluctantly. "All right, Liam, you win. Riley can come home and we'll drink to it."

When Ferguson picked up his phone, Devlin said, "So there you are, you old sod. Are they in yet?"

"Too early," Ferguson said. "Long car trip once they've landed. You did sterling work."

"Keep the soft soap for those who need it. Tell Dillon I've good news for Riley. I've seen Leary and the Chief of Staff and he's to be allowed home."

"How did you manage that?"

"I told them a half-truth, if you like." He carried on and told Ferguson the story he had sold to Leary and the Chief of Staff.

Ferguson said, "My God, you're the most incredible man I've ever known."

"I agree with you." Devlin laughed. "Tell Sean to watch his back," and he put the phone down.

HANNAH DROVE OUT of the Ministry of Defense garage in her red Mini car, the one she found best in London traffic. She parked on the forecourt of her ground floor flat in Ebury Place, unlocked the door, and went in.

The man who called himself George Brown straightened behind the wheel of the black Ford Escort parked along the street and reached for his mobile.

"She's here. Get over as quickly as you can. If she leaves before you get here, I'll follow and contact you."

Hannah at that moment was having a quick shower. She stepped out, toweled dry, then put on fresh underwear and a blouse. She found a fawn trouser suit, dressed, and went downstairs.

She phoned her father's office in Harley Street, only to discover from his secretary that he was doing a heart and lung transplant at the Princess Grace Hospital that would probably take eight hours.

Not that it mattered, for she knew who she really wanted to see. She grabbed her handbag, went out, and drove away in the Mini car just as an ambulance turned the corner. Brown cursed and went after her, but five minutes later and proceeding along the Embankment beside the Thames, was comforted to find the ambulance on his tail.

The driver was Aaron Eitan, Moshe in the seat beside him. "Keep close," Moshe said. "This traffic is terrible."

Aaron laughed. "It's years since I last drove in London. What fun."

RABBI THOMAS BERNSTEIN was seated at his study desk, a small but distinguished-looking man with a snow-white beard and hair topped by a plain *yarmulke* in black velvet. There was a knock, the door opened, and his granddaughter came in.

He put down his pen and held out his arms. "So there you are, light of my life."

She embraced him warmly. "Your sermon for *Shabbes?*"

"Queen of the week. It's like show business. I have to catch their attention. How are you?"

"Busy."

He laughed. "I've learned enough about you and your work to know that means you're on a big case."

"The biggest."

He stopped smiling. "Can you tell me about it?"

"No, highly secret and all that."

"You're troubled. Why?"

"All I can say is there's a Jewish element and it disturbs me."

"In what way?"

"Let me ask you a question. The man who shot Prime Minister Rabin—"

He interrupted her. "Murdered is a more accurate word."

"The man who did that, and those who support him, claimed some sort of biblical authority for what he did."

His voice was stern. "No such authority exists in either the Bible or the Torah. That despicable act of violence was a great sin in the eyes of God."

"So, if I had to hunt down such people, it would not disturb you?"

"Because they are Jews? Why should it? We are the same as other people. Good, bad, average, sometimes evil."

"Tell me," she said, "why does God allow these things to happen, the evil that men do?"

"Because he gave us free will, the possibility of choice. In that lies the only true meaning of salvation." He held her hands. "Trust in what you believe is right, child, do what you have to do. You have my blessing as always."

She kissed his forehead. "I must go. I'll see you soon."

She went out. He sat staring at the door, then started to pray for her.

CHAPTER 10

THE AMBULANCE WAS PARKED IN THE STREET, BROWN'S BLACK Escort behind it, and he stood beside it. As she came out of the gate of the small garden in front of her grandfather's house, she had to pass the Escort and the ambulance to get to her Mini car. Brown knocked on the rear doors of the ambulance and spoke to her at the same time.

"Detective Inspector Bernstein?"

She paused instinctively, turning toward him. "Yes, who are you?"

The doors of the ambulance opened and Moshe jumped down, grabbed her arm, and pulled her between the doors. Aaron reached down and lifted her inside. Moshe followed and produced a pistol with a silencer.

"Now be good, Chief Inspector. If he had to shoot you, no one would hear a thing." Aaron took her handbag, opened it, and removed her Walther. "I'll look after this."

"Who are you?"

"Jews like you, Chief Inspector, and proud of it."

"Maccabees?"

"You are well informed. Wrists, please." He cuffed them in front of her with plastic handcuffs. "Now behave yourself."

He got out and closed the doors. Brown said, "I'll be right behind. I'll join you in Dorking."

"Let's get moving, then," Aaron told him, and he got behind the wheel and drove away.

MOSHE SAID, "YOU want a cigarette?"

"I don't smoke," she said in Hebrew.

He smiled delightedly and replied in kind. "But of course, I should have known."

"Where are you taking me?"

"You'll find out soon enough."

"You'll never get away with it."

"I'm ashamed of you, Chief Inspector, that's just a line from a bad movie. We are Maccabees, as Dillon must have told you. We can do anything. We kidnapped the President's daughter. We kidnapped Dillon and where is he now? On a slab in a Washington morgue."

"So you animals did that, too? I wasn't sure, now I know. How do you justify that?"

"He served his purpose, but Dillon was the kind of man who could have become a serious liability."

"You had him murdered?"

"Sometimes the end does justify the means and our cause *is* just. More important than the life of a man like Dillon."

"That sounds familiar." Hannah nodded. "Ah, yes, Hermann Göring, nineteen thirty-eight. Don't let's get upset over the deaths of a few Jews, that's what he said."

Moshe was pale and the pistol trembled in his hand. "Shut your mouth!"

"Gladly. Actually, I'd rather not talk to you at all," Hannah Bernstein told him.

IN HIS OFFICE, Ferguson checked his watch. It was just after five and no sign of Hannah yet. At that moment, his phone rang and he switched on the Codex. "Ferguson."

"It's me," Dillon said. "Just hit Farley Field. Thanks for the RAF Range Rover."

"Straight down to the Ministry," Ferguson told him. "So much traffic in and out of our garage, you'll be swallowed up."

"No one would recognize me, anyway."

"One good thing. No directional microphones in here. I've had a fresh detection outfit brought in so we're secure."

"All except for our computer system," Dillon said. "See you soon."

AARON REACHED DORKING within half an hour and pulled into the parking lot of a huge supermarket crammed with vehicles. Brown parked his car and came round and Aaron leaned out.

"Okay, you get in the back. Afterwards, drive back here in the ambulance, dump it, and clear off in your own car."

"Fine."

Brown went round, opened the rear door and climbed in, closing it behind him. Hannah looked him over as the ambulance drove away, and a kind of realization dawned. "Well, now, you wouldn't be George Brown by any chance?"

Brown was put out. "What do you mean?"

"Oh, an informed guess. Put it down to twelve years as a copper. One develops a nose for these things."

"Damn you!" he said.

"No, damn you!" Hannah Bernstein told him.

. . .

ONWARDS FROM DORKING, Aaron made for Horsham. On the other side, he moved further into Sussex toward the River Arun, finally turning into a maze of country lanes following signs to Flaxby. He reached it, the kind of village which was a single pub and a scattering of houses. A mile on, he turned into a narrow lane that emerged into a huge overgrown airfield, a tower and several hangars decaying with age. He braked to a halt outside the hangars.

He went round and opened the rear doors. "All out."

He put a hand up and helped Hannah. She said in Hebrew, "Where are we, or am I being naive?"

"Not really. We're in the depths of rural Sussex. This used to be a Lancaster bomber base during the Second World War. Notice the lengthy runway, still usable in spite of the grass and weeds. We need a long runway."

Engines started up, and a moment later a Citation jet moved out of one of the hangars. It stopped close by and the door opened, steps dropping down.

"Do I get to know our destination?" Hannah asked.

"Magical mystery tour. Take her on board, Moshe."

Moshe urged her up the ladder, and one of the pilots pulled her in and seated her. Outside, Aaron said to Brown, "On your way. We'll be in touch."

"I suppose if I was an Arab fundamentalist I'd say, 'God is good,' " Brown told him.

"But he is," Aaron said. "Our God, anyway."

He went up the steps, pulling them up behind him, and closed and locked the door. The Citation taxied to the end of the field and turned. It paused, thundered down the runway, and lifted. Brown watched it go, then got into the ambulance and drove away.

. . .

IN ONE OF the control rooms of the Ministry of Defense, Ferguson, Dillon, Riley, and Blake Johnson sat back and watched as the operator ran the relevant section of the video through.

"All right, enhance the image and work through the crowd."

The operator did as she was told, bringing up a larger image, concentrating on faces, and Riley cried out, "That's him there in the raincoat with the briefcase."

"Freeze where possible," Ferguson urged.

There were a number of views of Brown from the front and from the side, all different perspectives.

"That should do," Dillon said. "Now print."

In a matter of seconds the machine had disgorged several colored prints of various views of the man calling himself George Brown. Dillon passed them to Blake one by one.

"There's our man." He turned to the operator. "You can go now."

"But how do we find him, Dillon?" Ferguson glanced at his watch. "And where the hell is the Chief Inspector? It's six-thirty."

The mobile Judas had given Dillon sounded in his pocket. Dillon pulled it out and switched on. He held it up, face expressionless, and handed it over to Ferguson.

The Brigadier said, "Ferguson here."

"This is Judas, old buddy. I figured you might have hung on to that special mobile I gave the late, lamented Sean Dillon."

"What do you want?"

"I thought you might be short one Detective Chief Inspector."

Ferguson had to breathe deeply to stay in control. "What are you saying?"

"She's winging her way toward me at this very moment at thirty thousand feet in her very own private Citation jet."

"But why?"

"Just to make sure you don't step out of line, Brigadier. It's not one, but two of them now. One wrong move and they both die. Have a good night."

The line went dead and Ferguson switched off the mobile, his face pale. "That was Judas. He says he's got Hannah."

There was a heavy silence and Blake Johnson said, "I suppose I'll have to inform the President."

"Yes, by all means. Use the phone in my office." Blake went out and Ferguson said, "What in the hell are we going to do?"

"It alters nothing," Dillon said and took a deep breath to combat his rage. "Our task's still to find Judas."

"And how do we set about that?"

"With these." Dillon held up the photos. "We find Brown."

"Well, we can't put him on bloody television," the Brigadier said.

"Then we'll have to find another way."

THE PRESIDENT SWITCHED off the Codex in his sitting room, sat there for a while, and then buzzed for Teddy, then he went and poured a whiskey. He was drinking it when Teddy came in.

"Anything I can do, Mr. President?"

"I'm beginning to think there's nothing anyone can do. I've just spoken to Blake. The good news is that Riley has put a face to the phoney lawyer on the video."

"That's great," Teddy said.

"The bad news is that Judas has kidnapped Chief Inspector Bernstein. Not one, Teddy, but two to worry about now. He told Ferguson it was to keep him in line."

"The sadistic swine," Teddy said.

"Which is true, but doesn't help at all," the President told him.

ONE THING WE do know," Dillon said. "He's a lawyer, because he told Riley that he was, isn't that true, Dermot?"

"Definitely." Dermot frowned. "He knew his way round, knew the system. I had a sod of a prison officer in charge of me and Brown sorted him with no trouble at all. Anyway, what about me? Anything more I can do?"

"Not really," Ferguson said. "Go and wait in the outer office. I'll have someone arrange a bed for the night. We have rooms here for special circumstances. I'll see you're on your way back to Ireland in the morning."

"Thanks." Dermot turned to Dillon. "Sorry, Sean."

"Not your fault. Good luck, Dermot."

Riley went out. Ferguson said, "What in the hell do we do?"

Dillon smiled suddenly. "I've just had a thought. We could go to the man who has the widest knowledge of criminal lawyers of any man I know, because he's used them so much."

"And who in the hell do you mean?"

"Harry Salter."

"Good God, Dillon, the man's a gangster."

"Which is exactly my point." Dillon turned to Blake. "Are you game?"

"I sure as hell am."

"Good, we'll get a car from the pool and I'll show you something of the murkier side of the London underworld."

HARRY SALTER," DILLON said to Blake as they drove along Horse Guards Avenue, "is in his late sixties, a dinosaur. He did seven years for bank robbery when he was in his mid-twenties. Never been in prison since. He has warehouse developments, pleasure boats that show you the delights of the Thames, and he still hangs on to his first buy, a pub on the Thames at Wapping called the Dark Man."

"And he still works the rackets?"

"Smuggling mainly. Illegal duty-free cigarettes and booze from Europe. Big business since the Common Market has exploded. Diamonds from Amsterdam are a possibility, too."

"You haven't mentioned drugs or prostitution," Blake said. "Could we possibly be into an old-fashioned gangster here?"

"Exactly. Mind you, he'll blow your kneecap off if you cross him, but that's business. He's your kind of people, Blake."

"Well, I look forward to meeting him."

As they moved down Wapping High Street, Blake said, "I wonder why Judas didn't snatch Hannah at the same time he took you in Sicily?"

"He needed her to go back to Ferguson as a witness to what happened is my guess. Sure, he could have taken her, too, and got in touch with Ferguson personally, but leaving it to her made it stronger. It meant that Ferguson knew beyond any doubt that what had happened was true."

"Yes, that makes sense." Blake nodded. "But I think we have an unstable guy here. He likes to play games."

"He certainly does."

"You've used Salter before?"

"Oh, yes, he helped me out on a little gig I had a while back where I had to prove I could breach security at the House of Commons and make it to the terrace by the river front. He doesn't run much of a gang these days, just his nephew, Billy, a real tearaway that one, and two minders, Baxter and Hall. The rest is accountants and an office, all legitimate."

They turned along Cable Wharf and pulled up outside the Dark Man. It was an old-fashioned London pub, a painted sign of a sinister-looking individual in a black cloak swinging in the wind.

"This is it," Dillon said. "Let's go."

He pushed open the door and entered the saloon. There were no customers, the place totally deserted. At that moment, the door at the rear of the bar opened and the barmaid came through, a trim blonde in her forties, her hair swept up from a face that was heavily made up. She was called Dora, and Dillon knew her well. She looked upset.

"It's you, Mr. Dillon. I thought the bastards might have come back."

"Take a deep breath, Dora. Where is everybody?"

"The customers all made themselves scarce and who can blame them? Harry and the boys were in the corner booth having shepherd's pie half an hour ago when Sam Hooker and four of his men came in with sawed-off shotguns."

"Why would he do that?"

"He's working the river these days like Harry, pleasure boats as a front. Wanted a partnership, but Harry told him to stuff it."

"So what happened?"

"They took Harry, Baxter, and Hall. Billy put up a fight, but they knocked him unconscious. I've just been seeing to him in the kitchen. Come through."

She lifted the bar flap and led the way into the kitchen. Billy Salter sat at the table drinking Scotch, a pump action shotgun in front of him. He was twenty-six, a hard young man who'd done prison time for assault and affray. Just now, the left side of his face was bruised and swollen. He glanced up.

"Dillon, what in the hell are you doing here?"

"I was hoping to see your uncle. I need his help on something, only it looks more like he could do with mine."

"Fucking Sam Hooker, I'll do for him myself."

"All on your own with that shotgun? Don't be a silly boy, Billy. According to Dora, Hooker has four goons with him. Who do you think you are, Dirty Harry? It only works in the movies because the script makes it work."

Billy poured a little more whiskey into his glass and looked at Blake. "Who's your friend?"

"If I said he was former FBI you wouldn't believe me. Blake Johnson."

"Your face doesn't look too good," Blake said. "Maybe a cracked cheekbone. I'd say you need the casualty department of your nearest hospital."

"Stuff that. What I need is Sam Hooker's head on a platter."

"Well, you won't get that standing here," Dillon told him. "Where did they take him?"

"Hooker usually operates from a pleasure boat called the *Lynda Jones.* He ties up at the old dock at Pole End. That's half a mile downriver from here."

Dillon turned to Blake. "Look, this is personal, you don't need to get involved."

"For Christ's sake, don't let's stand around talking," Blake said. "Let's do it," and he led the way out.

POLE END WAS a desolate place, a symbol of the decay of what had once been the greatest port in the world, rusting cranes etched against the night sky. Dillon braked to a halt some distance away and they got out, Billy carrying the shotgun, and approached the dock.

"Damn it to hell," Billy said. "Will you look at that. They've moved her. That's the *Lynda Jones* out there."

There were two arms to the docks stretching out into the river, the area between about three hundred yards across, and the *Lynda Jones* was anchored in the center.

"You're sure that's where your uncle will be?" Blake asked.

"Where else? Another thing, why move out there to the middle of the dock?" Billy said. "I'll tell you. Because it's impossible for anyone to get out there without them knowing."

"Not quite," Dillon said. "I introduced you to scuba diving the other year, Billy, remember? And didn't Harry see the possibilities? I happen to know you went to Barbados on holiday and got your diving certificate."

"So what?"

"Come on, Billy, you've been working a new racket. Diamonds from Amsterdam dropped overboard with a floating marker from ships passing upriver. You go out later underwater and retrieve them. That means you have the diving gear at the Dark Man, right?"

"Okay, so you've got me, but what are you getting at?"

"You hurry back to the pub, pick up an inflatable, a tank, fins, and a mask and get back here fast. Don't bother with a diving suit."

"You mean you're going to swim out there?"

"Can you think of anything else to do?"

"But there's five of them."

"Well, that means with the way I'm loading my Walther, I'll have two rounds for each of them. On your way, Billy, and don't forget a dive bag. Here are the keys."

Billy hurried away and Blake went to the edge of the dock and peered down through the shadows. He straightened. "Not even a rowboat down there. Are you sure about this, Sean?"

"Why not? All I need to do is hold them up, free Salter and the other two, and bring the boat in."

"You sure as hell make it sound easy."

They looked out toward the lights of the boat. There was a burst of laughter. "People on deck," Dillon said.

"I make it three, and one of them's going down the ladder," Blake said. "It's kind of dark down there, but I think there must be a boat."

Which there was, for an engine roared into life and a speedboat moved across the water toward the dock. Dillon and Blake stayed in the shadows by a crane.

"You're bigger than me, so get him from the rear, hand over his mouth and not a sound, while I have words," Dillon said.

"You're on."

Strange, but standing there in the shadows, Blake Johnson felt more alive than he'd done in years, and he flexed his hands, waiting, as the speedboat coasted in to the stone steps. The man behind the wheel got out and came up. As he reached the dock, Blake moved fast and grabbed him.

Dillon put the barrel of the Walther under the man's chin. "Not a sound or I'll kill you. This is a silenced weapon. They won't hear a thing. Do you understand?" The man nodded, Blake removed his hand. Dillon said, "Salter and his boys are out there with Hooker—right?"

The man was terrified. "Yes."

"Where?"

"In the main saloon."

"Nicely tied up?" The man nodded and Dillon said, "Hooker and three others, so what are you doing here?"

"There's a Chinese restaurant on the main road. Hooker phoned an order through to them. He sent me to get it."

"Considerate of him. That's a nice tie you're wearing." Dillon pulled it off and passed it to Blake, who tied the man's wrists.

"Are you thinking what I am?" Blake asked.

"I presume so. The minute you see me board at the stern, you and Billy come out in the speedboat. Hooker will think it's his man with the Chinese." He grinned. "Shows you where greed gets you." He shook the man fiercely. "Where's your transport?"

"Over there in that old warehouse."

Dillon marched him over and found a Ford van parked in the darkness. Blake opened the rear doors and Dillon shoved the man in. "Not a sound or I'll come back, and you know what that will mean."

They closed the doors and returned to the edge of the dock.

Billy arrived a few minutes later, engine off, coasting down a slight incline over the cobbles. He switched off, got out, and went and opened the trunk of the car.

"Everything okay?"

"Tell him, Blake," Dillon said, opened the rear door of the car, sat on the seat and undressed down to his underpants, slipping his glasses into a jacket pocket.

He pulled on the inflatable jacket, then clamped the tank to it. "Give me five minutes. The light under the awning at the stern is bright enough for you to see me go over the rail, then you two come out in the speedboat like I said."

"Bloody cold out there," Billy told him.

"Not for long." Dillon put his Walther in the dive bag and hung it around his neck, then he went down the steps, sat on the last one and pulled on his fins. He adjusted his mask, reached for his mouthpiece, and slipped into the dark waters.

. . .

BILLY WAS RIGHT, it was bitterly cold, but he kept on going, surfacing once to check his position, then going back under. He surfaced again by the anchor line, dumped the inflatable, the tank, his mask, and the fins, then pulled himself up to the anchor chain port. He peered through cautiously. The stern deck under the awning was empty, the sound of laughter coming from the saloon and then a cry of pain. Dillon hauled himself through, took the dive bag from around his neck and produced the Walther. He waved to the dock, and as he moved toward the saloon, the speedboat started up.

There was another cry of pain and he peered in through the porthole in the door. Salter and his two minders, Baxter and Hall, were seated on three chairs, arms bound behind them. A large man in a dark suit, presumably Hooker, was holding a butane cylinder, the kind of thing used for stripping paint. His brutal face had an expression of joy on it as he touched the flame to Baxter's left cheek.

Baxter yelled in pain, and Harry Salter said, "I'll do for you, I swear it."

"Really?" Hooker said. "I don't think so, because by the time I've finished you'll be a well-done hamburger. How's this for starters?"

The trouble was there were only two of his men there, laughing, glasses in their hands, so where was the third? But Dillon couldn't afford to wait, and as Hooker advanced on Salter, he flung open the door and stepped in.

"I don't think so."

Hooker stared stupidly at him. "What in the hell have we got here? Take him, boys."

One of them slipped a hand inside his pocket and Dillon shot him in the thigh.

Salter leaned back and laughed out loud. "Dear God, Dillon, you little Irish bastard. I don't know what you've done to yourself, but I recognize the voice."

Dillon said to Hooker, "Just switch the burner off and put it on the table."

"Fuck you!" Hooker told him.

"What a pity," Dillon said and shot off part of Hooker's left ear.

Hooker screamed and dropped the burner, which for some reason went out. Hooker had a hand at his ear, blood pouring between his fingers, and Dillon nodded to the one man left undamaged.

"Cut them loose."

He wasn't aware of any movement behind him because the door stood open, only the barrel of a shotgun against his neck. He turned his head slightly and saw, in the mirrored wall, a small, gypsy-looking man with dark, curling hair, holding a sawed-off.

The man reached for the Walther in Dillon's hand and Hooker snarled, "Kill him! Blow his bleeding head off!"

In that moment, Dillon saw the door at the other end of the saloon open, and Blake Johnson, Billy behind him, stepped in. Dillon dropped to one knee, Blake's hand swept up holding the Beretta, a perfect shot that caught the gypsy in the right shoulder, spinning him round as he dropped the sawed-off.

"What kept you?" Dillon asked.

Billy raised the pump gun. "I'll kill the lot of you!"

"No, you won't, Billy, leave off," Harry Salter told him. "Just cut us free." He glanced at Baxter's burnt face. "Don't worry, George, I'll get you patched up at the London Clinic. Only the best for my boys." Released, he stood, flexing his hands. "Dillon, you look ridiculous, but I'll remember you in my will."

The one Dillon had shot in the thigh and the gypsy were sprawled on the bench seat beneath the mirror. Hooker leaned against the table, moaning, blood everywhere.

Salter laughed. "Out of your league, but you never realized it."

"Let's go," Dillon said. "Your speedboat awaits."

"All right." Salter turned to Hooker. "Very good Indian surgeon near Wapping High Street. Name of Aziz. Tell him I sent you." He went out on deck, and they all followed. He paused at the top of the steps down to the speedboat. "I was forgetting. Let me have that Walther, Dillon."

Dillon handed it over without hesitation and Salter went back into the saloon. There was a shot followed by another, a cry of pain. He reappeared and handed the Walther back to Dillon.

"What did you do?" Dillon asked as they went down the ladder.

"What your lot do, the bleeding IRA. I gave him one in each kneecap, put him on sticks," Salter said. "I could have killed him, but he'd be a better advert that way. Now let's get the hell out of here, and introduce me to your friend. He seems to know what he's doing."

BACK AT THE Dark Man, Hall took Baxter away for medical assistance and Salter, Blake, and Billy sat in a booth on the empty bar.

"Champagne, Dora," Salter called. "You know this bugger likes Krug, so Krug it is."

Billy said, "Here, I'll help you, Dora," and he got up and went behind the bar.

Salter said, "Bloody lucky for me you came along. What was it you wanted to see me about?"

"Something special," Dillon said. "Very hush-hush, but mixed in is a lawyer who called on a prisoner at Wandsworth using a phoney name. One George Brown."

"How can you be sure he was a lawyer, or not, for that matter?"

"Let's put it this way. The way he handled himself would seem to indicate that he knows his way round the criminal system. I thought you might recognize him."

He took four photos of the mysterious Brown from his inside pocket and spread them out. Salter looked them over. "Sorry, old son, never seen him before."

Dora came over wrestling with the cork of a bottle of Krug and Billy followed with an ice bucket. He put it down on the table and looked down at the photos. "Blimey, what's he doing there?"

There was a slight, stunned silence and Dillon said, "Who, Billy, who is he?"

"Berger—Paul Berger." He turned to Salter. "You remember how Freddy Blue was up for that fraud case nine months ago, taking down payments for television sets that never arrived?"

"Sure I do."

"This guy, Berger, was his lawyer. He came up with some law nobody had ever heard of and got him off. Very smart. He's a partner in a firm called Berger and Berger. I remember because I thought it sounded funny."

Dillon said to Dora, "Get me the telephone book, will you?"

Billy poured champagne. "Was that what you wanted?"

"Billy, you just struck gold for us." Dillon raised his glass. "Here's to you." He took the champagne straight down and got up. "I'll phone Ferguson."

He moved down the bar and made his call. After a while, he came back. "Okay?" Blake asked.

"Yes, Ferguson's having a check via BT."

"Let's hope they don't have a Maccabee on their information service staff," Blake said.

"Hardly likely. They can't be everywhere, so no sense in getting paranoid."

"And what's a Maccabee?" Salter asked. "Sounds like a bar of chocolate to me."

"Anything but, Harry," and Dillon held out his glass for a refill.

His mobile rang and he switched on, taking out a pen and writing what Ferguson told him on the back of a bar mat.

"Fine, we'll be in touch." He switched off and nodded to Johnson. "I've got his home address. Camden Town. Let's move."

He got up and Salter took his hand. "Hope you find what you need."

"Glad to have been of service, Harry."

"Not as bloody glad as I am," Salter said.

THE ADDRESS WAS IN A LANE CALLED HAWK'S COURT OFF Camden High Street. "Fifteen—that's it," Blake said, and Dillon slowed.

The street was lined with villas built on the high tide of Victorian prosperity and varied greatly. It was obviously what real estate agents call an up-and-coming area, with young professionals moving in and improving the properties they had bought. The result was that some of the houses looked seedy and rundown and others had new windows and shutters and brightly painted doors with brasswork.

Number fifteen filled neither category. It wasn't exactly rundown, but it didn't look particularly up-market. Dillon turned at the end of Hawk's Court. There was an old church there, very Victorian in appearance, with a cemetery. There was a gate through railings, one or two benches, a couple of old-fashioned street lamps. Dillon turned, drove back, and parked on Camden High Street at the side of the road.

They walked back. Blake said, "How do you intend to handle this?"

"I haven't the slightest idea," Dillon told him.

"Well, we can't just leave him around like a loose cannon after speaking to him."

"We have a suitable safehouse where he could be kept," Dillon said.

"And what if Judas misses him? Smells a rat?"

"What have we got left, Blake, four days? Maybe the time has come to take chances. Let's find this Berger and put the fear of God in him. To hell with him anyway. Marie and Hannah are more important."

They opened the gate, went up a few steps, and rang the doorbell. The house stayed quiet and dark. Dillon tried again. "No good," he said finally. As he turned to Blake, the door of the next house, one of the rundown variety, opened and a young woman appeared.

She had blond hair topped by a black beret and wore a black plastic mac and plastic boots in the same color. "Sure you're not looking for me?" she asked.

"No. Mr. Berger," Dillon told her.

She locked her door. "Sorry, I thought it might be business. He's out most of the time. Lives on his own since his wife left him. Does he owe you money?"

"Jesus, no," Dillon said. "We're just clients. He's our lawyer."

"Well, he usually goes to Gio's Restaurant in the evenings. Turn right at the end and it's a hundred yards."

"Thanks very much," Dillon told her, and she walked away very quickly, high heels tapping.

"Come to think of it, I haven't eaten," Blake said.

"Then Gio's it is. There's only one problem. We know my cottage in Stable Mews was bugged with directional microphones. Maybe Berger was personally involved, maybe not, but there's a chance he knows me, so you'll have to eat alone."

"Poor old Sean, you'll starve," Blake said. "But I see your point."

. . .

GIO'S WAS A small Italian family sort of place with checked table cloths, lighted candles, and one or two booths. Dillon stayed back and Blake stood and consulted the bill of fare in the window. He turned his head and said quietly, "He's alone, second booth from the window, reading a book and eating pasta. He's heavily into the book. You can look."

Dillon did as he was told, recognized Berger for himself, and dropped back. "In you go. I'll just hang around. When he leaves, we'll take him in Hawk's Court."

"You mean follow him into his house?"

"No, he probably has good security, with the kind of clients he's got. It could be messy. We'll take him up to that churchyard and have words there."

"See you later, then."

Blake went inside, to be greeted by a waiter who showed him to a table on the other side of the room from Berger. The American ordered a glass of red wine from the bar and spaghetti with meat balls. Someone had left a newspaper on the chair next to him and he started to read it, one eye constantly on Berger.

DILLON WENT INTO the general store two doors down where they had a selection of sandwiches. He chose ham and tomato on French bread, obtained tea in a plastic cup from a machine, and went back outside. It was raining slightly and he stood in the doorway of a shop that had closed for the night and ate the sandwich and drank the tea. Then he had a cigarette and strolled past the window of Gio's.

Berger still had his nose in the book, but seemed to have reached the coffee stage, while Blake was halfway through his spaghetti. The rain increased in volume and Dillon walked back to the car, opened the door, and checked inside. There was a folding umbrella on the shelf by the rear window. He opened it and went back along the pavement, passing Gio's in time to see Berger settling his bill. As the waiter turned away, Blake waved him over.

Berger stood up, went and got his coat from a wall peg while Blake was still settling, then he picked up his book and made for the door. Dillon stood back. Berger paused, turned up his collar, and stepped into the rain and Dillon followed, keeping him a few yards ahead. As they turned the corner into Hawk's Court, Blake caught up and they walked on, side-by-side, until Berger reached his gate.

As he opened it, Dillon called, "Mr. Brown?"

Berger paused and turned. "I beg your pardon?"

"George Brown?" Dillon said cheerfully.

"Sorry, you've made a mistake. My name is Berger—Paul Berger."

"Sure, we know that, but you called yourself Brown when you visited Dermot Riley in Wandsworth Prison," Blake Johnson said.

"Don't deny it," Dillon advised him. "We've got you on the security video, so we know who you are, just as we know you're a Maccabee, one of dear old Judas's merry band of brothers."

"You're mad," Berger said.

"I don't think so." Dillon had a hand in the right pocket of his raincoat and he pushed back the flap to disclose the Walther. "As you can see, this is silenced, so if I shoot you now, no one will hear a thing."

"You wouldn't dare."

"After what you lot have done, I'd dare anything, so start walking, straight up to the cemetery. We're going to have words." He pushed the Walther hard into Berger's belly. "Go on, move!"

THERE WAS A porch just inside the railings of the cemetery, a bench inside it. One of the lamps was close by, so there was a certain amount of light. Dillon pushed Berger down.

"Right, Judas Maccabeus is a right-wing Jewish terrorist. His followers are called Maccabees and you are one of them. He's kidnapped the daughter of the President of the United States. He's now also kidnapped Chief Inspector Hannah Bernstein."

"This is nonsense."

Blake said, "Come now, let's be reasonable. We know you're the George Brown who visited Dermot Riley in Wandsworth. We've got you on the video surveillance tape from the prison and we've also got Riley."

"Rubbish, you can't have," Berger said, giving himself away.

"Absolutely. Picked him up in Ireland this morning and brought him back to London. He's at the Ministry of Defense now. He'll swear to the fact that you promoted a plan to get him out of prison to set up one Sean Dillon in Sicily, and Dillon will also confirm that."

"But that's impossible," Berger said, falling into the trap.

"Why, because he's dead, murdered in Washington?" Dillon's smile was terrible as he removed his glasses for a moment. "No, he isn't, because I'm right here."

Paul Berger cried out in terror.

"EVERYTHING SO SLICK," Dillon said, "right down to the very convenient death of that prison officer, Jackson. Was that you, Berger? I mean, he might have identified you. Who knows?" Dillon lit a cigarette. "But even the great Judas gets it wrong. He's going down, Berger, and you'll go down with him, so talk."

"I can't. He'll have me killed."

Dillon went into the act beloved of policemen the world over, good guy and bad guy. He turned to Blake, shaking with rage. "Did you hear that? Well, I'll tell you what. I'm going to kill this bastard myself. I mean, we're in the right place to do it." He gestured at the monuments and headstones looming out of the night. "Plenty of room to bury him in there." He turned on Berger and rammed the Walther under his chin. "I'll do it now—right now."

Blake pulled him away. "You didn't say there would be killing." He sat beside Berger. "For God's sake, tell him."

Berger was shaking. "What do you want to know?"

"How does Judas communicate?"

"I have a special mobile, that's how he gave me the job of getting Riley out of Wandsworth. He talks personally."

"Have you ever met him?"

"No, I was recruited by another Maccabee."

Blake took over now. "So where does Judas operate from?"

"I don't know."

"Come off it, son, I can't believe that," Dillon said.

Berger was close to breaking and it was obvious he was telling the truth. "I honestly don't know. I don't."

There was a pause. Blake put a hand on his shoulder. "What about Chief Inspector Bernstein?"

"She was picked up outside her grandfather's house in an ambulance by two Maccabees from Judas's personal staff."

"Names?" Dillon demanded.

"Aaron and Moshe."

Dillon turned to Blake. "They're the lads who knocked me off in Salinas."

"Were you there?" Blake asked.

Berger nodded. "We took her down to a place on the other side of Flaxby in Sussex. There was one of those old overgrown bomber bases from the Second World War. They had a Citation jet waiting and flew off with her. My job was to dump the ambulance in Dorking."

"And you don't know where they're flying to?" Blake asked.

"No idea, I swear it."

It was obvious to both of them that he was telling the truth, and it was a sudden thought of Dillon's that gave them what they needed.

"You said you were recruited by a Maccabee. Why was that?"

"I was at a conference on the future of the State of Israel. It was held at the University of Paris. I took part in a seminar, spoke out. I've always held strong views."

"And?"

"I was approached by a lawyer. He said he'd admired my speech and asked me out to dinner."

"A Maccabee?" Blake said.

"That's right. We sat on one of those restaurant boats on the river and talked. I was there four days and saw him every day."

"And he recruited you?"

"Haven't you any idea how it sounded? God, I wanted to join, to be a part of it all."

"Then Judas spoke to you, the Almighty himself," Dillon said.

"He's a great man. He loves his country." Berger seemed to have recovered some of his courage.

Dillon said, "What was the name of the lawyer in Paris who recruited you, and don't tell me you can't remember."

"Rocard—Michael Rocard."

"Jesus, Mary, and Joseph!" Dillon turned to Blake Johnson. "The de Brissac family lawyer. He's got to have been the leak to her identity in some way. Dammit, he even owned the cottage she was using in Corfu when she was kidnapped."

"Paris next stop, it would seem," Blake said. "What about him?"

Dillon turned to Berger. "Come on." He pulled him up. "We'll deliver him to the safehouse. They can hang on to him there until everything's resolved, then we'll see Ferguson."

They started down Hawk's Court, Berger in between, and passed his house. He said, "You're going to kill me, aren't you? There's no safehouse."

Blake said, "Yes, there is, don't be a fool."

"You're lying!" Berger said in a low voice, and suddenly ran away very fast.

They went after him. He reached the corner and made to cross Camden High Street on the run, head down, at the same moment as a double-decker bus approached. Collision was unavoidable and he was bounced into the air.

There was pandemonium as a crowd gathered and the driver of the bus dismounted in considerable distress. A police car pulled in and two officers got out and pushed through the crowd. One dropped to one knee beside Berger and examined him.

He looked up and said to his partner, "No good, he's dead."

There were expressions of shock from the crowd, and the wretched driver said, "It wasn't my fault."

Several people called, "He's right, the man just ran into the road."

At the back of the crowd, Dillon nodded to Blake. They walked back to the car and drove away.

THE TRIP IN the Citation had been uneventful. Hannah had kept herself-to-herself and as far away from Aaron and Moshe as possible. She accepted the coffee and sandwiches passed to her and leafed through a few magazines, a banal thing to do, but what else was there, except looking out of the window occasionally. Flying at thirty thousand feet with plenty of cloud below meant that she hadn't the slightest idea where she was.

After three hours, there were glimpses of sea far below which could only be the Mediterranean. There was the coast of an island that could have been anywhere and then cloud again.

Moshe busied himself preparing more coffee and took some through to the pilots. Aaron ignored her, apparently deep in the book he'd been reading for the past three hours. Moshe returned and busied himself with refreshments again. He passed Aaron some sandwiches and coffee.

"The same for you, Chief Inspector?"

"No, just coffee."

She peered out of the window again, catching a glimpse of another piece of land far below, and then the clouds blanketed everything. She turned to a tap on the shoulder and Moshe gave her the coffee.

As she drank it, she became aware of Aaron watching her as he sipped coffee himself, and there was a slight smile on his face, which of course irritated her.

"You find me amusing?"

"On the contrary, I think you are a very remarkable woman. Your grandfather a rabbi, father a great surgeon, a wealthy woman who goes to Cambridge, then joins the police and becomes a top Scotland Yard detective who is not afraid to kill when she has to. How many times? Is it two or three?"

God, how she hated him, and yet when she searched for the harsh reply, it wouldn't come. He put down his cup in slow motion and reached for hers.

"I'll take it, Chief Inspector," he said. "You just lie back and go to sleep. We're almost there, you see. Better for everyone if you don't know where you are."

The coffee. Too late, of course, far too late, and in the moment of realization she slipped into darkness.

IN HIS FLAT at Cavendish Square, Ferguson sat by the fire and listened as Dillon and Blake Johnson filled him in between them. When they were finished, he sat there thinking about it, frowning.

"Strange, it all coming down at this stage to the de Brissac lawyer, this Michael Rocard."

"Yes, but he's managed the family affairs for years," Dillon said. "If anyone would appear to be above suspicion, it would be he, and yet I suspect he must be the source of Marie's true identity. He must have found out. Perhaps by accident."

"Like we used to say in the FBI," Blake told him, "if it's murder, always check the family first. There is an interesting question here. Why would a man like Rocard, famous, part of the establishment, ever get involved with the Maccabees in the first place?"

Ferguson came to a decision. "I'm going to check him out."

"Is that wise?" Dillon asked.

"Oh, yes. Conditions of the tightest security, man-to-man. I'm talking about Max Hernu."

THE FRENCH SECRET Service had probably been more notorious than the KGB for years, and as the SDECE it had enjoyed a reputation for ruthless efficiency second to none. Under the Mitterand government it had been reorganized as the DGSE, which stood for Direction Générale de la Securité Extérieure.

It was still divided into five sections and numerous departments, and Section 5 was still Action Service, the department which had smashed the OAS in the old days and most illegal organizations since.

Colonel Max Hernu, who headed Section 5, had served as a paratrooper in Indochina, been taken prisoner at Dien Bien Phu, then afterwards fought a bitter and bloody war in Algiers, though not for the OAS that was supported by so many of his comrades, but for General Charles de Gaulle.

He was an elegant, distinguished-looking man with white hair, who at sixty-seven should have been retired, the only problem being that the French Prime Minister wouldn't hear of it. He was sitting at his desk in DGSE's headquarters in Boulevard Mortier, studying a report of ETA supporters living in France, when he took Ferguson's call on the Codex line.

"My dear Charles." There was genuine pleasure on his face. "It's been too long. How are you?"

"Hanging in there, just like you," Ferguson told him. "The Prime Minister won't let me go."

"A habit they have. Is this business or pleasure?"

"Let's just say you owe me a favor and leave it at that."

"Anything I can do, you know that, Charles."

"You know the de Brissac family?"

"But of course. I knew the general well and his wife. Both, alas, dead now. There is a charming daughter, Marie, the present comtesse."

"So I understand," Ferguson said carefully. "The family lawyer, Michael Rocard. Anything you can tell me about him?"

Hernu was immediately alert. "Is there a problem here, Charles?"

"Not as such. His name has cropped up, let's say, on the edge of an affair I'm involved in. I would be grateful for any information you have on the man."

"Very well. Absolutely beyond reproach. Legion of Honour, a distinguished lawyer who has served some of the greatest French families. Accepted at every level in society."

"Married?"

"He was, but his wife died some years ago. No children. She suffered poor health for years. She had a bad war."

"What do you mean by that?"

"Rocard is Jewish and so was the woman he would later marry. As children, they were handed over to the Nazis during the time the Vichy government was in power, together with their families and thousands of others. In their case, they ended up in Auschwitz concentration camp. I suppose they must have been fifteen or sixteen when the war finished. I believe Rocard was the only member of his family to survive. I'm not sure about his wife's family."

"Thank you," Ferguson said. "Very interesting. Where's he living these days?"

"I believe he still has an apartment on Avenue Victor Hugo. Look, Charles, I've known you long enough to tell when something's going on."

"Max, you couldn't be more wrong," Ferguson lied smoothly. "His name came up because he'd had legal dealings with an arms firm we've been worried about. Trade with Iran, that sort of thing. Nothing for you to worry your head about. I'd tell you if there was, you know that."

"Charles, you're lying through your teeth."

"Leave it, Max," Ferguson said. "If there is something you should know, I'll tell you."

"That bad?"

"I'm afraid so. I'd appreciate it if you faxed me his picture."

"All right, but keep me informed."

"The moment I can, I will, you have my word."

"The word of an English gentleman," Hernu laughed. "Now you really do have me worried," and he switched off.

. . .

In the Oval Office, Jake Cazalet was trying to review a speech for a luncheon the following day to welcome a delegation of visiting Japanese politicians. It was difficult to concentrate in any way at all. It just went round and round in his head, the whole rotten business. He put down his pen and sat there brooding about it when the phone rang, the special Codex line, and he reached for it.

"Mr. President, Charles Ferguson."

"Any progress?" Cazalet was suddenly alert.

"I think you could say that. We managed to trace the lawyer who called himself George Brown."

And now Cazalet was excited. "The one who saw Riley at Wandsworth?"

"The same."

"And he told you where she is?"

"He didn't know."

"How in the hell can you be sure?" and there was anger there now.

"Let me put you on to Blake Johnson, Mr. President."

There was a pause, he could hear them talking, and then Johnson's voice sounded. "Mr. President? Dillon and I questioned the man involved thoroughly and he didn't know where she is."

"You're using the past tense."

"Yes, well, he's dead. Let me explain, please."

When Blake was finished, the President said, "So Judas was just a voice on the phone."

"That's obviously the way he runs things. It's a little like the old Communist cell system. Each individual only knows one or two other people."

"Like Berger knew this lawyer in Paris, Rocard?"

"That's right."

"So, it's Paris next stop?" Cazalet said.

"Absolutely. Too late tonight, but Dillon and I will be on our way in the morning."

"Fine, put me back to the Brigadier."

A moment later, Ferguson said, "Mr. President."

"What do you think?" Cazalet asked.

"I've spoken to a contact in the French Secret Service, very much on the old pals basis. As a boy, Michael Rocard was in Auschwitz, and so was his wife. He was the only survivor of his family."

"Good God," the President said. "So that's why he's a Maccabee?"

"It would appear so."

"Right, I can only pray that Blake and Dillon can get the right information out of him."

CAZALET SAT THERE thinking about it. There was a knock on the door and Teddy entered, a couple of folders under his good arm.

"A few things for you to sign, Mr. President."

He put one of the folders on the desk and opened it. Cazalet said, "I've just had Ferguson and Blake on the phone."

"Any progress?"

"You could say that," and the President filled him in.

Teddy was immediately excited. "This guy, Rocard, he must hold the key. Dammit, he must have found out about your daughter and told Judas."

"That would make sense. Anyway, where do I sign?"

Teddy led him through a number of papers, and when Cazalet was finished, he folded the file and picked it up. As he did so, the other file slipped from beneath his arm, and a few papers scattered. One of them was the charcoal sketch Marie de Brissac had done of the black raven with the lightning in its claws.

It was the President who picked it up. "What in the hell are you doing with this, Teddy?"

"It's a sketch your daughter did for Dillon, Mr. President. Apparently, Judas has a silver lighter with that crest on it. Dillon thought that as we know Judas served in the Yom-Kippur War, it must be a regimental crest. I got hold of a book of Israeli divisional signs, shoulder flashes, crests, everything. Dillon thought that if we knew the outfit, it might be a lead, but I got nowhere."

"That's because you've been looking in the wrong book," the President said. "Black raven with lightning in its claws. That's the 801st Airborne. One of those outfits thrown up from nowhere by the Vietnam War. I took part in a big clean-up operation in the Delta in January of sixty-nine. They were on the left flank."

"My God!" Teddy said.

"I know," the President nodded. "Remember what Dillon said? Judas sounded American but denied it. He was lying for obvious reasons. If he served with the 801st, he must be American."

"You're damn right he must be an American and you can sure as hell bet, the kind of guy he is, that he was an officer."

"That makes sense." The President sat back. "As I recall, they operated out of Fort Lansing. That's in Pennsylvania. A few of those new airborne units were based there."

"I'm going to go and check," Teddy said and made for the door.

The President said, "Just a minute, Teddy. If they've got an archives section, which they probably have, you could have a problem if you ask for details of officers who served with the regiment."

"Somehow I don't think Judas has his own special Maccabee sitting down there just waiting to see if anyone's going to make that sort of check, but I'll be more subtle. Leave it to me."

Teddy was back within ten minutes. "Yes, they do have an archives setup. I spoke to the curator, a nice lady named Mary Kelly who was just closing up. Twelve airborne units operated out of there. I told her I'm taking time off from the history department at Columbia to do a book on airborne warfare in Vietnam."

"That's pretty clever, Teddy, but what in the hell are you looking for?"

"We know he told Dillon his war was the Yom-Kippur War. Now that was nineteen seventy-three. He wasn't in the Six-Day War, which was nineteen sixty-seven. Why not?"

"I take your point." Cazalet nodded. "Because he was serving in Vietnam."

"So I'll check the list of officers serving with the regiment, and I'll be looking for Jewish officers, naturally."

"But Teddy, there were a lot of Jewish officers."

"Sure, my old company commander for one." Teddy was suddenly impatient and forgot himself. "For Christ's sake, Jake, it's better than doing nothing. I can take one of the jets from Andrews in the morning if you'll authorize it. I'll be there in no time."

Jake Cazalet raised a hand defensively. "Okay, Teddy, go with my blessing." He reached for the Codex phone. "I'll let Ferguson know."

HANNAH BERNSTEIN DRIFTED up from darkness. The light was very bright from a small chandelier in the vaulted ceiling. The room was paneled in dark wood and seemed very old. The bed enormous. There was dark oak furniture, a large Persian carpet spread across a polished oak floor.

She got to her feet and stood up, swaying a little, then walked to the barred window and looked out. What she saw, although she didn't realize the fact, was the same view that Marie de Brissac had from her room—the bay, the jetty with the speedboat beside it, the launch on the other side, a night sky bright with stars, moonlight dancing on the water.

The door opened and Aaron entered, followed by David Braun with a tray. "Ah, up and about, Chief Inspector. Coffee for you, nice and black. You'll feel much better afterwards."

"Like the last time?"

"I had no option, you know that."

"Where am I?"

"Don't be silly. Drink your coffee, then have a shower and you'll feel much better. The bathroom is through there. This is David, by the way."

Braun said in Hebrew to Aaron, "Chief Inspector? It's astonishing."

Hannah said in the same language, "Go on, get out of here, the both of you."

He was right about one thing. The coffee helped. She drank two cups, then undressed, went into the bathroom and stood under a cold shower for a good five minutes. She toweled her short hair briskly, then finished it off with the wall-mounted hair dryer.

"All the comforts of home," she said softly and went back into the bedroom and dressed.

She was standing by the window ten minutes later when the key sounded in the lock. She turned and Aaron opened the door and stood to one side. Judas followed him, a menacing figure in the black jump suit and hood.

He was smoking a cigar and his teeth gleamed in a smile. "So, the great Detective Chief Inspector Hannah Bernstein. What's a nice Jewish girl doing in a job like yours, when she should be married with three kids?"

"Making chicken soup with noodles for her lord and master?" she asked.

"I like it!" he said in Hebrew. "Sorry about your pal Dillon, but when you've got to go, you've got to go. Mind you, from what I hear, the bastard has been on borrowed time for years."

"He was worth ten of you," she said.

He laughed. "Not anymore, he isn't." He turned to Aaron. "Bring her along. Time she met our special guest."

Marie de Brissac was painting, seated in front of the easel, when the door opened and Aaron came in, followed by Hannah and Judas. Marie frowned and put her brush down.

"What's going on?"

"I've brought you a friend, a companion, if you like." He turned to Hannah. "Go on, tell her who you are."

"My name is Hannah Bernstein."

Judas cut in. "Hey, let's get it right. Detective Chief Inspector Hannah Bernstein." Marie looked bewildered. "She was with Dillon in Sicily when we picked him up. I let her go then, because I wanted her to be able to talk to her boss. Then I got to thinking about you up here all alone and upset because we knocked off Dillon, so Aaron and Moshe flew to London and brought her back just for you." He turned to Hannah. "You didn't mind a bit, did you?"

She said calmly, "Why the hell don't you clear off and leave us alone?"

He laughed again. "Hey, I'm being really good to you. You can have dinner together." He turned to Aaron. "See to it," and he went out.

HOW DO I know you're who you say you are?" Marie de Brissac asked.

"You mean who that bastard says I am?" Hannah said, then laughed ruefully. "You'll just have to trust me, I suppose. I didn't realize you painted. That's rather good."

She walked to the easel, paused at the table, picked up a piece of charcoal, and wrote on the first piece of cartridge paper. *Dillon is alive.* Marie read the message and looked at her in astonishment, and Hannah carried on: *The room may be bugged. Go to the bathroom.*

Marie did as she was told and Hannah followed, closing the door and flushing the toilet. "We saw your father—Dillon and I. Dillon knew they were going to kill him afterwards and managed to fool them into thinking he was dead. It doesn't matter how."

"Oh, my God!"

"Maybe your room isn't bugged, but in any case, from now on when we mention Dillon, he's dead."

"Yes, I see that."

"So, he's on your case."

"And yours?"

Hannah smiled. "He's the best, Countess. Judas doesn't know what he's up against. Now back we go." She flushed the toilet again and they returned to the bedroom. "So, you've no idea where we are?"

"I'm afraid not, and you, Chief Inspector?"

"I was kidnapped in London and flown here, wherever it is, in a private jet. We flew over the Mediterranean, I know that, but then they drugged my coffee."

"They drugged me when they grabbed me in Corfu," Marie said.

"I know, Dillon told me." Hannah shook her head. "Poor Sean. To end up like that, shot in the back by some wretched hit man."

The door opened and David Braun came in pushing a trolley. "Dinner, ladies."

He started to lay the dining table and Marie said, "This is David, Chief Inspector, David Braun. He likes me, really, but on the other hand, he believes Judas to be a truly great man."

"Then all I can say is he must be mentally deranged." Hannah pushed David to the door. "Go on, get out of it. We can manage very well alone."

FERGUSON COULDN'T SLEEP. He'd told Dillon and Blake about Teddy Grant's intention of visiting Fort Lansing. He was sitting up in bed, reading, when the special mobile which Judas had given Dillon sounded. Ferguson let it ring for a while, then picked it up.

"Ferguson."

"Hi, old buddy, just thought I'd let you know she arrived in one piece. She's having dinner with the countess now. It's countdown time, Brigadier. How long have we got? Three days. Dear me, Jake Cazalet must be going through hell."

He started to laugh and Ferguson switched off the phone.

CHAPTER 12

As the Gulfstream lifted off from Farley Field the following morning, Captain Vernon came on over the speaker.

"We'll be able to land at Charles de Gaulle, but the weather isn't good. Heavy rain and mist in Paris itself."

He switched off and Blake made a cup of coffee, and tea for Dillon. "Imagine that bastard phoning Ferguson like that."

"He likes sticking pins in people."

"Well, I'd sure as hell like to stick pins in him. How are we going to play this, Sean?"

"I haven't the slightest idea. What do you think?"

"Frankly, I don't see how we can avoid a face-to-face confrontation."

"The same tactic we employed with Berger."

"Something like that."

"And how far would you be prepared to go to save the President's daughter, Blake? Can I shoot an ear off, put a bullet through his kneecap?"

Blake frowned. "For God's sake, Sean."

"The point of the exercise is to save Marie de Brissac's life. Now, how far do I go? I mean, what if Rocard is made of sterner stuff than Berger? What if he tells us to get stuffed? All I'm trying to say is if you don't like what I do, just step out of the room."

Blake raised a hand defensively. "Give me a break. Let's see how it goes, okay? And there's Teddy checking out the 801st Airborne at Fort Lansing. Maybe he'll come up with something."

JUDAS WAS IN his study at that moment, having risen early, seated behind the desk, going through papers and running the fingers of one hand through his cropped hair, when his special phone rang.

"Yes," he said and listened. After a while, he nodded. "Thanks for the information."

"Damn!" he said softly and flicked the intercom. "Aaron, get in here."

Aaron entered a moment later. "Was there something?"

"Hell, no, I just wanted to let you know Berger's dead. I had a call from one of my London people. He was knocked down by a bus in Camden High Street. It was reported on the local television news."

"Unfortunate," Aaron said.

"Yes, he was useful to us."

"Are you ready for breakfast?"

"Yes, I'll have it with you. I'll be along in a moment."

Aaron went out and Judas sat there for a moment, then picked up his special mobile and punched in Rocard's number in Paris. A metallic voice replied in French. "Michael Rocard here. I've gone to Morlaix for three days. I'll be back Wednesday."

Judas cursed softly in Hebrew, then said, "Berger's been killed in an accident in London. Contact me as soon as you can." He switched off, got up, and went out.

. . .

When Blake and Dillon crossed the tarmac at Charles de Gaulle and went into the arrival hall, a young woman in a Burberry trenchcoat came forward to greet them, a large envelope in one hand.

"Mr. Dillon, I'm Angela Dawson from the Embassy. Brigadier Ferguson asked for these." She held up the envelope and passed it over. "Also I've got a car for you outside. This way, please."

She was efficiency itself as she led them to the main entrance and out to the parking lot. She stopped beside a blue Peugeot and handed the keys to Dillon. "Good luck, gentlemen."

She walked away briskly and Blake said, "Where in the hell did Ferguson find her?"

"Oxford, I suspect," Dillon said and got behind the wheel. "Let's get moving."

The weather report had been accurate for once, pouring rain and clinging gray mist. Blake said, "What a greeting."

"I like Paris," Dillon told him. "Rain, snow, mist, I don't give a damn. It always excites me. I've a place here."

"An apartment?"

"No, a boat on the Seine. I lived in it, on and off, for years during what Devlin would have called my dark period." He turned along Avenue Victor Hugo and pulled in at the curb. "This looks like it."

They got out of the Peugeot and went up the steps to the main entrance. As they stood examining the name cards, each beside its bell push, the door opened and a stout, middle-aged woman in raincoat and headscarf, a basket over one arm, emerged.

She paused. "Can I help, gentlemen?"

"We are seeking Monsieur Rocard," Dillon told her.

"But he is not here. He went to Morlaix for a few days. He's due back tomorrow." She went down the steps, put up her umbrella, and turned. "He did say he might be back this afternoon late, but he wasn't sure."

"Did he leave an address? We have legal business with him."

"No, I believe he was staying with one of his boyfriends." She smiled. "He has many, monsieur."

She walked away, and Dillon grinned. "Let's take a look." He pressed a button at random, and when a woman's voice answered said, "It's me, cherie," in French.

The buzzer sounded. The door opened at a push, and they were in.

They found Rocard's apartment on the third floor. The corridor was deserted and Dillon took out his wallet, produced a picklock, and went to work.

"A long time since I had to use one of those," Blake said.

"You never lose the knack," Dillon said. "I've always felt it would be useful if I ever have to take to crime."

The lock yielded, he eased the door open and went in, Blake following.

It was a pleasant, old-fashioned apartment, with lots of antiques and Empire-style gold-painted furniture. The rugs were all collector's items, there was what looked like a genuine Degas on one wall, a Matisse on the other. There were two bedrooms, an ornate marble bathroom, and a study.

Dillon pressed the recall button on the answering machine. The voice said: "Michael Rocard here. I've gone to Morlaix."

"Go through his messages," Blake said.

Dillon pressed the button and the messages, all in French, came through and then Judas cut in.

"Hebrew," Dillon said. "We've just won the jackpot. I'll play it again." He listened intently, then nodded. "Berger's been killed in an accident in London. Contact me as soon as you can."

"Judas?" Blake said.

"Or I'm a monkey's uncle." Dillon looked around the study. "Not worth turning the place upside down. He wouldn't leave incriminating evidence around, a smart man like that."

Blake picked up a photo in a silver frame from the desk. It was very old-fashioned and in black and white. The woman was in a chiffon dress, the man in dark suit and stiff collar. There was a boy of perhaps ten or twelve, a girl of five or six. It was strange, remote, something from another age.

"Family group?" Blake said.

"He's probably the kid in the short pants," Dillon told him.

Blake replaced the photo carefully. "Now what?"

"Better leave quietly. We can try again in case he does come back late afternoon. Otherwise we'll just have to fill in the time." He smiled. "In Paris, that usually means having a really great lunch."

They left the apartment, paused while Dillon relocked the door, then went downstairs. Outside it was still raining and they paused, looking across at the Bois de Boulogne.

"A good address," Dillon commented.

"For a successful man," Blake nodded.

"The man who had everything and in the end found he had nothing."

"Until Judas came along?"

"Something like that."

"So what do we do now?"

Dillon smiled. "We'll go and see if my barge is still in one piece."

IT WAS MOORED in a small basin on the Quai St Bernard. There were pleasure boats tied up to the stone wall, motor cruisers with canvas awnings up against the rain and mist drifting across the Seine. Notre Dame was not too far away. There were a number of flower pots on the stern deck with no flowers in them. Dillon lifted one and found a key.

"How long since you were here last?" Blake asked.

"A year or eighteen months, something like that." Dillon went down the small companionway and unlocked the door.

He stood just inside. "Jesus, smell the damp. It could do with a good airing."

It wasn't what Blake had expected, a stateroom lined with mahogany, comfortable sofas, a television, and a desk. There was another cabin with a divan bed and a shower room and a kitchen galley.

"I'll find us a drink." Dillon went into the galley and searched the cupboards. When he came back with a bottle of red wine and two glasses, he found the American looking at a faded newspaper clipping.

"I found this on the floor. The Prime Minister. It's from the *London Times,* but I can't make out the date."

"Good old John Major. Must have slipped down the back of the desk when I cleared the rest of the material. February nineteen ninety-one, the mortar attack on Downing Street."

"So it really is true and you were responsible for that. You nearly brought it off, you bastard."

"That's true. It was a rush job, no time to weld guidance fins to the mortars, so they weren't quite accurate enough. Come up this way."

He had been very calm, very matter-of-fact as he had spoken. He opened another door that gave access to the aft deck. There was an awning, rain dripping from the edges, a small table and two chairs in wicker. Dillon poured claret into the glasses.

"There you go."

Blake sat down and savored it. "Excellent. I'm supposed to have stopped, but I could use a cigarette."

"Sure." Dillon gave him one and a light and took another himself. He stood by the rail, sipping the wine and looking toward Notre Dame.

"Why, Sean?" Blake said. "Hell, I know your record backwards, but I still don't understand. All those hits, all those jobs for people like the PLO, the KGB. Okay, so your father was caught in the crossfire in some Belfast street battle and you blamed the British Army and joined the IRA. You were what, nineteen? I understand that, but afterwards."

Dillon turned, leaning on the rail. "Remember your American Civil War history. People like Jesse and Frank James? Raiding, fighting, and killing for the glorious cause and that was all they knew, so what came afterwards, when the war was over? They robbed banks and trains."

"And when you left the IRA, you offered yourself as a gun for hire."

"Something like that."

"But when the Serbs shot you down in Bosnia, you were flying in medical supplies for children."

"A good deed in a naughty world, isn't that what Shakespeare said?"

"And Ferguson saved you from yourself, pulled you in on the side of right."

"What a load of cobblers." Dillon laughed out loud. "I do exactly what I was doing before, only now I do it for Ferguson."

Blake nodded, serious. "I take your point, but isn't anything serious business to you?"

"Certainly. Saving Marie de Brissac and Hannah from Judas, for instance."

"But nothing else?"

"Like I've said before, sometimes situations need a public executioner and it happens to be something I'm good at."

"And otherwise?"

"Just passing through, Blake, just passing through," and Dillon turned and looked along the Seine.

AT THE SAME moment and six hours back in time, Teddy boarded an Air Force Lear jet at Andrews. They took off, climbed to thirty thousand feet, and the senior pilot came over the speaker.

"Just over an hour, Mr. Grant, and it should be pretty smooth. We'll put down at Mitchell Field. That's about forty minutes by road to Fort Lansing."

He switched off and Teddy tried to read the *Washington Post* but couldn't take it in. He was on too big a high. He had the strangest feeling about this. There was something waiting for him at Fort

Lansing. There had to be, but what? He reached to the bar, made a cup of instant coffee, and sat there, thinking about things as he drank it.

MARIE DE BRISSAC WAS doing a charcoal sketch of Hannah. "You've got good bone structure," she said. "That always helps. Were you and Dillon lovers?"

"That's a leading question."

"I'm half French. We're very direct. Were you?"

Hannah Bernstein was careful to stay in the past tense where Dillon was concerned, just in case. "Good God, no. He was the most infuriating man I ever knew."

"But you liked him in spite of that?"

"There was plenty to like. He had a ready wit, bags of charm, enormous intelligence. There was only one flaw. He killed too easily."

"I suppose the IRA got to him early."

It was a statement, not a question, and Hannah said, "I used to believe that, but only at first. It was his nature. He was too good at it, you see."

The door rattled and David Braun came in with a tray. "Coffee and cookies, ladies. It's a beautiful day."

"Just put it on the table, David, and go," Marie told him. "Don't let us pretend that things aren't as they are."

It was as if she had slapped him, and his shoulders slumped as he went out.

"He really does like you," Hannah told her.

"I've no time for false sentiment, not at this stage."

She started to fill in the sketch and Hannah poured a couple of cups of coffee and placed one at Marie's hand. She took her own and went to the open window and looked out through the bars.

"Come on, Dillon," she said softly. "Sort the bastards."

. . .

TEDDY'S PRESIDENTIAL AUTHORIZATION had the same magical effect at Mitchell Field that it had had at Andrews. The duty officer, a Major Harding, had an Air Force limousine with a sergeant driver over from the vehicle pool in fifteen minutes.

"You look after Mr. Grant real good now, Hilton," he said.

"Consider it done, sir."

They moved out of the base and took a road that led through rolling green countryside. "Very pretty," Teddy said.

"I've seen worse," Hilton told him. "My last posting was Kuwait. I've only been back two months."

"I thought you had a tan," Teddy said.

Hilton appeared to hesitate. "Were you in the military, Mr. Grant?"

"My arm, you mean?" Teddy laughed. "Don't be embarrassed. I was an infantry sergeant in 'Nam. Left the arm there."

"Life's a bitch," Hilton told him.

"It's been said before. Now tell me about Fort Lansing."

"During the Vietnam War, there was one regiment after another through there, but when the conflict was over it was rundown. There was some kind of resurrection at the time of the Gulf, but it's just a primary infantry training base these days."

"I just want the museum."

"Hell, no problem. It's open to the public." They pulled onto a freeway. As he picked up speed, he said, "There's a diner five miles along the way, and after that nothing for thirty miles. Do you want a coffee or a pit stop or something?"

"Good idea," Teddy said. "But only for ten minutes. I want to get going," and he sat back and tried to concentrate on the *Post* again.

IN PARIS, MICHAEL Rocard parked as close as he could get to his apartment and walked to the front door. He hurried upstairs, only a satchel in one hand, and unlocked the door of his apartment.

Considering his age, his hair had a considerable amount of color in it and he looked ten years younger than he was, although the excellent suit he wore helped in that respect.

He checked the messages on his answering machine, listening to them one by one, then froze almost in panic as he came to Judas's message in Hebrew. *Berger dead.* He went to the sideboard and poured cognac. What even Judas didn't know was that Rocard and Berger had been occasional lovers. In fact, Rocard had developed a genuine and considerable affection for him. He unlocked a drawer in his desk, took out the special mobile, and punched out the numbers. Judas answered almost immediately.

"It's Rocard."

"You fool," Judas told him. "Running off to Morlaix like a dog in heat and at a time like this."

"What can I say?"

"So, Berger is dead, knocked down by a London bus. What's the saying? Everyone is entitled to fifteen minutes of fame? Well, Berger got his, only it was a fifteen-second announcement of how he met his death on London local television."

The cruelty was devastating, but what came next was worse. "You'll need a new boyfriend for your London trips."

Was there anything the bastard didn't know?

Rocard mumbled, "What can I do?"

"Nothing. If I need you, I'll phone. Three days, Rocard, only three days to go."

He switched off and Rocard stood there, clutching the mobile, thinking of Paul Berger, and there were tears in his eyes.

WHEN TEDDY WENT into the museum complex at Fort Lansing, he was impressed. It was modern and air-conditioned, with tiled floors and great murals of combat scenes on the walls. He avoided reception and walked along the main corridor until he came to an office with a sign saying Curator on it. He knocked and opened the door and found a highly attractive black woman seated behind a desk at the window.

She glanced up. "Can I help you?"

"I was looking for the curator, Mary Kelly."

"That's me." She smiled. "Are you Mr. Grant from Columbia?"

"Well, yes . . . and no. I am Mr. Grant, but I'm not from the history department at Columbia." Teddy opened his wallet and took out his card and dropped it in front of her.

Mary Kelly examined the card and the shock was physical, that much was obvious. "Mr. Grant, what is this?"

"I've got a Presidential authorization here if you'd like to see it."

He took it from an envelope, unfolded it, and passed it across. Mary Kelly read it aloud. "My secretary, Mr. Edward Grant, is on a mission on behalf of the White House that is of the utmost importance. Any help offered would be deeply appreciated by the President of the United States."

She looked up. "Oh, my God!"

He removed the authorization from her fingers, refolded it, and put it back in the envelope. "I shouldn't have told you, but I'm taking a chance because I don't have time to fool around. Even now I can't tell you the full story. Maybe one day."

She smiled slowly. "How can I help?"

"You have the records of a number of airborne regiments that passed through here during the Vietnam War."

"That's right."

"One of them was the 801st. I'd like to check the list of officers serving with that regiment from, say, nineteen sixty-seven until seventy."

"What name are you looking for?"

"I don't have a name."

"Then what do you have?"

"Only that he's Jewish."

"Well, that covers quite a bit of territory. There were a *lot* of Jewish people in the army during the war. The draft affected everybody, Mr. Grant."

"I know. It's an incredible long shot. Will you help me?"

She took a deep breath. "Of course I will. This way," and she led the way out.

The archives were in the basement and they had it to themselves. There was only the gentle hum of air-conditioning as Mary Kelly examined the microfilm record, listing names on a pad with her right hand. She sat back.

"There you are. For the four years, nineteen sixty-seven up to and including seventy, there are twenty-three officers listed as being of the Jewish faith."

Teddy examined the list name by name, but it was meaningless. He shook his head. "No damn good. I should have known."

She was distressed for him and it showed. "And you've no other information?"

"Well, he served in the Israeli Army in the Yom-Kippur War in nineteen seventy-three."

"Well, why didn't you say so? We'll have that on his back-up record. The Pentagon requires that a record be kept when American military personnel serve with another country's army."

Teddy said, "And you can check on that?"

"Quite simply. I have a small internal computer here. It's not mainline. It's to facilitate our own records. Over here." She went and sat in front of a screen and tapped the keys. "Yes, here we are. Only one officer serving with the 801st went on to serve with the Israeli Army. Captain Daniel Levy, born nineteen forty-five in New York, left the army in nineteen-seventy."

"Bingo!" Teddy said, a kind of awe in his voice. "That's got to be him."

"A hero," she said. "Two Silver Stars. Father Samuel, mother Rachel, are listed as next of kin, but that was a long time ago. The father was a New York attorney. The address was Park Avenue, so they must be pretty wealthy with an address like that."

"Is that it?" Teddy said. "No more?"

"Nothing that we can help you with." She frowned slightly. "It really is important, isn't it?"

"It could actually save someone's life." He grabbed her hand and shook it. "When I can, I'll come back, I promise, and maybe then you'll be able to hear the full story, but for now, I must return to Washington. If you'd show me the way out, I'd appreciate it."

HE STOOD SOME distance from the limousine, called the President on his mobile, and told him what he'd discovered.

"It certainly sounds promising, Teddy, but where does it lead us?"

"We could check on the family background. I mean, father an attorney, living on Park Avenue. He must have been important. I use the past tense because he's either dead or very old."

"I've just had a thought," Cazalet said. "Archie Hood. He's been the doyen of New York attorneys for years."

"I didn't think he was still alive," Teddy said.

"Oh, yes, he's eighty-one. I saw him at a fund-raiser in New York three months ago when you were in L.A. Leave it to me, Teddy, and you get back here as quick as you can."

Teddy made his way to the limousine, where Hilton held the door open for him. "Okay, sergeant, Mitchell at your fastest. I've got to get back to Washington as soon as possible."

IT WAS ABOUT four o'clock when Rocard put on his raincoat and went downstairs. The concierge was polishing the mirror in the hall and paused.

"Ah, Monsieur Rocard, you are back."

"So it would appear."

"Two gentlemen were trying to reach you this morning. They said it was legal business."

"Then if it's important, they'll come back. I'm going to have an early dinner at one of the *bâteaux mouches.*"

He went out and walked to his car, and at that moment Dillon pulled the Peugeot in at the curb on the other side of the road.

Blake pulled out the photo fax that Max Hernu had sent Ferguson. "It's him, Sean."

Rocard was already getting into his car and drove away. "Let's see where he's going," Dillon said and went after him.

Rocard parked on the Quai de Montebello opposite the Ile de la Cité, not too far from where Dillon's boat was tied up. There were a number of pleasure boats moored there, awnings over the aft and fore decks against the weather. Rocard ran through the rain and went up the gangplank of one of them.

"What's this?" Blake asked as Dillon parked at the side of the cobbled quai.

"Bâteaux mouches," Dillon told him. "Floating restaurants. Sail up the river and see the sights and have a meal at the same time, or just a bottle of wine if that's your pleasure. They follow a timetable."

"Looks as if they're getting ready to cast off now," Blake said. "We'd better move it."

The two deck hands who were starting to pull in the gangway allowed them to board and they moved into the main saloon, where there was a bar and an array of dining tables.

"Not many people," Blake said.

"There wouldn't be with weather like this."

Rocard was at the bar getting a glass of wine from the look of it. He took it and crossed to a stairway and mounted to the upper deck.

"What's up there?" Blake asked.

"Another dining deck, but pretty exposed. The kind of thing that's fun in fine weather. We'd better get a drink and see what he's up to."

They moved to the bar and Dillon asked for two glasses of champagne. "You intend to dine, gentlemen?" the barman asked.

"We'll see," Dillon replied in his excellent French. "I'll let you know."

They crossed to the stairs and went up. As he had indicated, this was another dining deck, but the sides were open and rain was blowing in. The crew had stacked the chairs in the center and the rain increased in force and mist drifted across the river.

There were other boats, of course, barges tied together in lines of three, and another restaurant boat passing in the opposite direction.

"It's quite something," Blake said.

Dillon nodded. "A great, great city."

"So where is he?"

"Let's try the stern promenade."

It was reached by a door with a glass panel in it. Outside were three or four tables under an awning. Rocard was sitting at one of them, the glass of wine in front of him.

"Best get on with it," Blake said.

Dillon nodded and opened the door and led the way through. "A wet evening, Monsieur Rocard," he said.

Rocard looked up. "You have the advantage of me, Monsieur . . . ?"

"Dillon—Sean Dillon, he who was supposed to be dead in Washington, but it's the third day, and you know what that means."

"My God!" Rocard said.

"This, by the way, is a gentleman named Blake Johnson, here on behalf of the President of the United States, who is rather understandably desperate for news of his daughter."

"I don't know what you're talking about." Rocard tried to stand and Dillon shoved him down and took out his Walther. "Silenced, so if I want to, I can kill you without a sound and put you over the rail."

"What do you want?" Rocard looked sick.

"Oh, conversation, cabbages, and kings, Judas Maccabeus, poor old Paul Berger, but most of all Marie de Brissac. Now where is she?"

"Before God, I don't know," Michael Rocard said.

THE BOAT MOVED FORWARD INTO THE MIST. BLAKE SAID, "I find that difficult to believe."

"It's true."

"Look, the game's up," Dillon told him. "We know about Judas and his Maccabees. You wouldn't deny you're one of them?"

"That's true, but I've never met Judas personally."

"Then how were you recruited?"

Rocard thought for a long moment, then shrugged, resigned. "All right, I'll tell you. I'm sick of the whole thing, anyway. It's gone too far. I was at a reunion of survivors of the Auschwitz concentration camp. I was at Auschwitz as a boy with my family. Those Vichy swine handed us over to the Nazis. It's where I met my wife."

"So?" Blake said.

"We all stood up and made testament about what had happened to us. I had a mother, a father, and a sister. We were sent to Auschwitz

Two, the extermination center at Birkenau. A million Jews died there. Can you gentlemen conceive of that? One million? I was the only member of my family to survive because a homosexual SS guard took a fancy to me and had me transferred to Auschwitz Three to work in the I. G. Farben plant."

"I know about that place," Blake Johnson said.

"The girl who became my wife, and her mother, were transferred by the same man as a favor." His face was full of pain. "We survived, returned to France, and picked up the threads of our lives. I became a lawyer, her mother died, we married." He shrugged. "She was never well, always ailing, she died years ago."

"So where did Judas come into it?"

"I was approached by a man at the Auschwitz reunion and offered the chance to help to secure the future of Israel. I couldn't resist. It seemed"—he spread his hands in a very French gesture—"so worthwhile."

"And you served the de Brissac family?" Dillon said.

"I was their lawyer for years."

"And betrayed the fact that Marie's father was really the American President to Judas?" Blake accused.

"I didn't mean it to turn out as it has. Before he died, the general signed a deed acknowledging that he was Marie's titular father under the Code Napoléon to ensure she inherited the title. When I asked for an explanation, he refused."

"So how did you find out?" Dillon asked.

"In such an ordinary way. When the countess was dying of cancer, she was sitting with Marie on the patio one day enjoying the sun. I'd arrived with papers for the countess to sign. They didn't hear my approach, but they were discussing the situation. I heard the countess say: 'But what will your father think?' but of course to me, her father was dead."

"So you listened?" Blake said.

"Yes, and heard all I needed to know. The name of her real father."

"And you told Judas."

"Yes," Rocard said reluctantly. "Look, I deal with many important people, politicians, high-ranking generals. One of my briefs is to keep Judas informed of anything interesting."

"And you told him Marie de Brissac's secret?" Blake said.

"I didn't realize what he would do with the information, I swear it."

"You poor fool," Dillon said. "In over your head, and it all seemed so romantic. Berger was exactly the same."

Rocard stiffened. "You knew Paul?" His eyes widened. "You killed him?"

Blake said, "Don't be stupid, and pull yourself together. I'll get you a cognac."

He went inside. Rocard said, "What happened to Paul? Tell me."

"We traced him and questioned him. He told us how you recruited him. I'd intended holding him in a safehouse until this thing was over, but he panicked, thought we meant him harm. He ran across the road and a bus hit him. That's the truth."

"Poor Paul." Rocard's eyes were moist. "We were . . ." He hesitated. "Friends."

Blake returned with a large cognac. "Try that, it might help."

"Thank you."

"All right," Dillon said. "So tell us how it happened to Marie. Come on, you've nothing to lose now."

"Judas phoned and ordered me to buy a small cottage on the northeast coast of Corfu. I was to persuade Marie to holiday there."

"Why Corfu?"

"I've no idea. It was easy to persuade her to go because, since her mother's death, she's filled her time by taking painting holidays all over the place."

"Didn't it occur to you that he would have a devious motive?" Blake asked.

"I'm used to obeying his orders, that's the way he runs things. I didn't think. The damage had been done." He shook his head. "I just didn't think. I'd no idea that what has happened would happen. I care for Marie, I always have since she was a child."

"But you followed Judas blindly?" Blake said.

"Remember Auschwitz, Mr. Johnson. I'm a good Jew. I love my people, and Israel is our hope. I wanted to help, can't you see that?"

And it was Dillon who put a hand on his shoulder. "I see. I can see perfectly."

"Do you know what he intends to do with her?" Blake asked.

And Rocard didn't, that became immediately plain. "Use her as some sort of bargaining counter, I suppose."

"Actually, he's going to execute her on Tuesday unless her father signs an executive order for an American military strike against Iraq, Iran, and Syria."

Rocard was truly horrified, and seemed to age visibly. "What have I done? Marie, what have I done?" He got up and moved to the rail and looked up at the rain. "I didn't mean any of this, as God is my judge."

Dillon turned to Blake Johnson. "I believe the poor sod."

He turned and Rocard had gone, vanished as if he had never been. He and Blake ran to the rail. Mist swirled across the river, it seemed as if an arm was raised, and then the mist rolled in again. Dillon straightened, hands braced against the rail.

"I'd say there's just about so much pain a person can take."

Blake turned to him and there was anguish in his face. "But we've failed, Sean, we're no further forward. What are we going to do?"

"Well, I don't know about you, but I'm going to go down to the bar to get myself a very large Irish whiskey. After that, it's back to London to break the bad news to Ferguson."

THE PRESIDENT HAD run into roadblocks in his attempts to contact Archie Hood. He wasn't at his apartment, that was certain, but a call to the law firm where he was still a consultant provided a number in the Cayman Islands where he was on holiday.

Finally, Cazalet made contact. "Archie, you old buzzard. It's Jake Cazalet. Where are you?"

"Mr. President, I'm on the terrace of a delightful villa above a palm-fronted beach with a glass of champagne in one hand. I'm also surrounded by beautiful women, three of them, who happen to be my granddaughters."

"Archie, I need your help, ears of the President only. A matter of vital importance. Can't tell you why at the moment, but I hope to eventually."

The old man's voice had changed. "In what way may I be of service, Mr. President?"

"Levy, Samuel Levy, that mean anything to you?"

"Knew him well. He was a multi-millionaire from the family's shipping line, but he chose the law and sold out when he inherited. Brilliant attorney. Did it for the hell of it. Never needed the money. Been dead about five years now."

"And his son, Daniel Levy?"

"Now there was a strange one. Big war hero in Vietnam, then he got all turned on to Israel. Joined the Israeli Army and fought in the Yom-Kippur War. Of course they had a big family tragedy a few years ago."

"What was that?"

"Dan Levy's mother and married sister went out to see him on holiday. They were both killed in the bombing of a Jerusalem bus station. The old man never got over it. It really killed him off."

Jake Cazalet fought to stay calm. "And what's happened to Daniel Levy?"

"Inherited almost a hundred million dollars, a house in Eaton Square in London, a castle in Corfu. Last I heard he was a colonel in Israeli Airborne, but he resigned. There was a scandal. He executed Arab prisoners or something."

"You say a castle in Corfu?"

"Sure, I visited it once years ago when his father owned it. My wife and I were on a cruise and Corfu was one of the stopping-off points.

Strange place on the northwest coast called Castle Koenig. Apparently in the old days it was owned by a German baron. The Krauts have always liked Corfu. If I remember right, Prince Philip was born there." There was a pause. "Does any of this help?"

"Help? Archie, you've done me the greatest service of your career. One day you'll know why, but for the moment, total secrecy."

"Mr. President, you have my word."

WHEN TEDDY CAME into the Oval Office, the President was standing at the window. He turned and the energy in him was visible. "Don't say a word, Teddy, just listen."

When he was finished, Teddy said, "It all fits. Judas told Dillon he'd had relatives killed. I mean, it all damn well fits."

"So, all the indications are that she and Chief Inspector Bernstein are at this Castle Koenig place. When they kidnapped her, telling her she was going for a plane ride before they drugged her, it was just a bluff."

"So what do we do, send in Navy Seals, borrow the SAS from the Brits?"

"No way, Teddy. The first sign of trouble he'd kill them." Cazalet reached for the Codex. "Let's get Ferguson."

IN FACT, FERGUSON had just finished speaking to Dillon in the Gulfstream on the way back to London. He listened to what Cazalet had to say.

"Teddy is right, it fits, Mr. President. I'm afraid Rocard, the de Brissac lawyer, has followed Berger to an early grave, but before he died, he indicated a Corfu connection."

"So what do we do?"

"I have associates in Corfu, because for some years we've operated illegal traffic to Albania just across the water which is, as you know, still Communist-dominated. The people I use are entirely the right kind for this sort of operation. Dillon and Blake Johnson will be arriving at Farley Field in the Gulfstream. I'll join them there, bring them up to date, and we'll leave for Corfu at the soonest possible moment. Trust me, Mr. President. I'll stay in close touch."

Jake Cazalet switched off the Codex, and Teddy said, "Well?"

So the President told him.

FERGUSON SAT THERE thinking about it for a while and then called a number in Corfu. A woman answered the phone and spoke in Greek.

"Yes, who is it?"

"Brigadier Ferguson," he said in English. "Is that you, Anna?"

"It is, Brigadier. Good to hear from you."

"I need that good-for-nothing rogue of a husband of yours, Constantine."

"Not tonight, Brigadier, he's working."

"I know what that means. When will he be back?"

"Maybe four hours."

"Tell him I'll call, and make sure he's there, Anna. A big payday."

He put the phone down, went to the sideboard and poured a Scotch, and stood at the window savoring it. "Right, you bastard, we're coming to get you," he said.

AT THAT MOMENT, Constantine Aleko was at the wheel of his fishing boat, the *Cretan Lover,* halfway between the coast of Corfu and Albania, his head apparently disembodied in the light of the binnacle. It was raining slightly and there was a slight wind from the sea.

Aleko was fifty years of age. Once a lieutenant commander in the Greek Navy, he had ended a reasonably distinguished career by punching a captain in a drunken fight over a woman in a Piraeus bar.

So, he had come home to Corfu to the little port of Vitari, had used his compensation money as a down payment on the *Cretan Lover,* a supposed fishing boat that had the kind of engines that could take her to twenty-five knots.

Backed by his beloved wife, Anna, he had worked the smuggling trade for all it was worth, using the extensive knowledge of the Albanian coast that he had gained in the Greek Navy to his own advantage. The cigarette trade was particularly lucrative. The Albanians would pay almost anything for British and American brands.

Of course they were tricky bastards and needed watching, which was why he had his two nephews, Dimitri and Yanni, on his side, and his wife's cousin, old Stavros. It was Stavros who brought him coffee now, as rain streamed against the wheelhouse window.

"I've got a bad feeling about this. That Albanian bastard, Bolo, I don't trust him an inch. I mean, he tried to do us down last time on that cargo of Scotch whiskey."

"It's taken care of, you old worrier, believe me. I know how to handle scum like Bolo." Constantine drank the coffee. "Excellent. Here, take the wheel for me. I want a word with the boys."

Stavros took over and Aleko crossed the deck, passing the draped nets, the baskets of fish, and went down the companionway. In the main saloon, Dimitri and Yanni were pulling on diving suits. There were two Uzi submachine guns on the table.

"Hey, uncle," Yanni said. "You think these Albanian apes will try and take us?"

"Of course he does, stupid," Dimitri said. "Otherwise why would we be bothering?"

"Bolo owes me five thousand American dollars for this cargo of Marlboro cigarettes," Aleko said. "I've good reason to think he'll try to take them for nothing. So—you know what to do. You don't need tanks. Just go over at the right time and swim to the other side of his boat and don't forget these."

He lifted one of the Uzis, and Dimitri said, "How far do we go?"

"They try to shoot you, you shoot them."

He left them to it and went back on deck. When he went into the wheelhouse, he lit two cigarettes and gave one to Stavros.

"A good night for it."

"It better be," Stavros told him, "because if I'm not much mistaken, there they are now."

The other boat was rather similar, nets draped from the mast to the deckhouse. There were a couple of men working in the stern deck, apparently sorting fish in the sickly yellow light of a lamp that hung from one corner of the wheelhouse. There was a man at the wheel, someone Aleko hadn't seen before, and Bolo was standing beside him, smoking a cigarette. He was forty-five, a large man, shoulders huge in the reefer coat he wore, and the face beneath the peaked cap had the kind of reckless charm possessed only by the truly insincere. He came out on deck.

"Hey, my good friend Constantine. What have you got for me this time?"

"What you asked for, Marlboro cigarettes, for which you will pay me five thousand American dollars with your usual reluctance."

"But, Constantine, I'm your friend." Bolo took a bundle of notes from his pocket bound with a rubber band. "Here, check it for yourself. It's all there." He tossed it across. "Where are my cigarettes?"

"Under the nets here. Show them, Stavros."

As Aleko quickly counted the money, Stavros removed the nets, revealing several cardboard packing cases. Bolo's two deckhands joined him and manhandled them across. When they were finished, they stepped back over the rail.

Aleko looked up. "So, it's all here. Amazing."

"Yes, isn't it, and now I'll have it back."

Bolo reached inside the wheelhouse and produced a Second World War machine pistol, the German variety known as the Schmeisser and much favored by Italian partisans. His two deckhands took out revolvers.

"I might have known," Aleko said. "The leopard doesn't change its spots."

"I'm afraid not. Now give me the money back or I'll kill the lot of you and sink your damn boat."

"Oh, I don't think so."

Dimitri and Yanni, black-cowled figures in their rubber suits, were sliding under the rail on the other side of the Albanian boat. They stood up holding the Uzis ready, menacing figures.

Yanni said, "Good evening, Captain Bolo."

The Albanian turned in alarm and Yanni fired a short burst that caught Bolo in the right arm and tore the Schmeisser from his grasp. Dimitri had already taken careful aim and loosed off a single shot that took one of the deckhands in the back of the leg. He went down and the other dropped his gun and raised his hands.

"I enjoyed that," Aleko said. "Back on board, boys, and cast off."

As the gap widened, Bolo stood clutching his blood-soaked sleeve, his face twisted with pain. "Damn you, Constantine."

"You're only a beginner." Aleko waved. "I don't think we'll be seeing each other for a while."

The boys went below to change, and Stavros made coffee while Aleko took the wheel. When the old man returned, he put the mug of coffee on the chart table and said, "One thing I don't understand. Why didn't we take back the cigarettes?"

"A bargain is a bargain." Aleko grinned. "But I just called up the gunboat working the channel tonight. Lieutenant Kitros in command. He once served under me in the navy. I've given him their position, but it wouldn't be much good without hard evidence."

"The cigarettes?"

"Exactly."

"You wonderful bastard."

"Yes, I know. Now let's get back home to Vitari."

VITARI WAS A small fishing port on the northeast coast of Corfu, and home was a taverna on a hill overlooking the harbor. Anna was in sole charge, a handsome, heavily tanned woman who wore a headscarf and a traditional peasant dress in black. She was devoted to her husband, her only regret the fact that she'd been unable to bear him children.

There were a dozen fishermen in the bar, a young local girl seeing to their wants, and greetings were exchanged when the crew of the *Cretan Lover* entered.

"You three get a drink," Aleko said. "I'll be in the kitchen with Anna."

She was at the stove, stirring lamb stew in a black pot, and turned, smiling. "A successful night?"

He kissed her on the forehead, poured himself a glass of red wine from a jug on the table, and sat down. "Bolo tried to take us."

Her face darkened. "What happened?" He told her, and when he was finished she said, "The swine. I hope Kitros finds him. He should get five years."

"Oh, Kitros will get him all right. I trained that young man myself."

"You had a phone call from London, England. Brigadier Ferguson."

Aleko straightened. "What did he want?"

"He just said it would be a big payday and that he'd call back."

"That sounds interesting. He's always paid well, anyway."

"And so he should. Those drops you made him on the Albanian coast, that's dangerous work, Constantine. If the Communists got their hands on you . . ."

He cut in. "You worry too much, woman." He got up and slipped his hands around her waist. "It's a good job I love you."

Stavros and the boys came in with their drinks. "Still lovebirds at your age?" Stavros said.

"Oh, shut up and sit," Anna said.

They did as she told them and she laid plates. Aleko said, "Anna tells me our old friend Brigadier Ferguson phoned me from London."

They were all immediately interested. "What for?" Yanni demanded. "Albania again?"

"I don't know," Aleko said. "A big payday is what he said and he's phoning back."

"Hell, that sounds good," Dimitri said.

Anna brought the pot and started to spoon out the stew. "Stop it, the lot of you, and just eat."

It was perhaps ten minutes later that the phone rang in the small office and Aleko got up and went in.

"Brigadier," he said in excellent English. "And what can I do for you? Albania again?"

"Not this time. Tell me what you know about a place called Castle Koenig."

"About fifteen miles north of here on the coast. Owned by an American family for many, many years. Name of Levy."

"Is anyone there now to your knowledge?"

"They employ a local couple to caretake. It was inherited by a son named Daniel. Some sort of war hero. Vietnam, I think. He's even fought for the Israelis. He just comes and goes, that's what I hear. Quite popular with the locals. Look, what is this?"

"I've reason to believe he's holding two women there at the moment. One of them is my assistant, a Chief Inspector Bernstein. It doesn't matter who the other is, it's classified."

"This is a political thing?"

"More a terrorist thing," Ferguson said. "I'm going to fly out as soon as possible by private jet, and I'll have two first-class operatives with me. We intend to get those women out, Constantine, and I need your help. There would be very big money in this."

"Forget that for the moment. What are friends for? When will you arrive?"

"Sometime in the morning. I'll have a Range Rover waiting at the airport, and we'll drive across the island and join you at the taverna. The *Cretan Lover* is in good condition, I trust?"

"Perfection. You're thinking of going in by sea?"

"Probably."

"I've got an idea. Give me a contact number."

"No problem. I'll give you my mobile. It's satellite-linked so you can even get me on the plane. What do you have in mind?"

"I'll take a run up there now. If I go by motorbike I'll be there in half an hour. I've got a cousin called Goulos, who has a small farm near the castle. I'll see what I can find out."

"I look forward to hearing from you."

Aleko returned to the kitchen, took his reefer coat from behind the door, and pulled it on. "But you haven't finished your meal," Anna told him.

"Later, this is important." He opened a drawer, took out a Browning and checked it, and put it in his pocket.

"What is this?" Stavros said.

Aleko said, "I'll tell you all about it later. I'm taking your Suzuki, Yanni, so let's have the keys."

Yanni complied. "Where are you going?"

"To see my cousin Goulos. There's something funny going on at Castle Koenig and I'd like to know what it is," and he went out.

THE MESSAGE WAITING for Dillon and Blake when they arrived at Farley Field was explicit. They were to wait to hear from Ferguson. They joined the pilots in the RAF officers' mess for a meal and were halfway through it when Dillon's mobile sounded. He nodded to Blake, got up and went out of the front door of the mess, taking the call standing on the tarmac.

"I know you've been hanging around up there for some time," Ferguson said, "but a lot's happened. I know where she is, Corfu, and I know who Judas is."

"But how?"

So Ferguson brought him up to date.

When the Brigadier was finished, Dillon said, "What now?"

"I'll be joining you at Farley soon. Ask Captain Vernon to prepare a flight plan. I should be hearing from Aleko, of course."

"So we hit from the sea?"

"That would seem logical."

"We'll need tooling up."

"Aleko has a rather extensive range of equipment, but I'll bring a few items from the armorer."

"Fine. We'll see you when we see you, then."

Dillon went back to the mess and sat down. "That was Brigadier Ferguson," he said to Captain Vernon. "He'd like you to file a flight plan to Corfu."

Blake looked up, frowning.

"That might not be possible before the morning." Vernon pushed his plate away and stood up.

"I'll come with you," Lieutenant Gaunt said and followed him.

"What the hell is going on?" Blake asked.

"We've found them, thanks to Teddy and that black raven sketch. It wasn't Israeli, Blake, it was American. Judas is one of your own."

"Then tell me, for Christ's sake," Blake demanded. "Everything."

WHEN THE ARMORER at the Ministry of Defense knocked on the door of Ferguson's office, he found Ferguson at the window looking out at Horse Guards Avenue.

"Ah, Mr. Harley."

"Brigadier." Harley almost clicked his heels. A retired sergeant-major, he had served in the Korean War with Ferguson. "How can I assist, Brigadier?"

"A black operation, Sergeant-Major, very black. Your authorization is on the desk there."

"Thank you, sir." Harley picked it up, folded it and put it in a pocket, then took out pad and pen. "What would you require?"

"Three flak jackets, very latest model, and in black. Black jump suits to go with them. Stun grenades, night-vision goggles, also a pair of good night-vision binoculars."

"Weaponry, sir?"

"Handguns, silenced of course, and silenced machine pistols of some sort. What would you suggest?"

"Silenced Brownings for the pistols, sir, still the preferred handgun of the SAS, and I'd stick to the Uzi for a machine pistol. The latest model the Israelis have come up with is a superb silenced version. Anything else?"

"Semtex is always useful. I'm thinking of blowing doors."

"I'll make up a box for you. Small charges for five-second timer pencils and three- or four-quarter-pound blocks for anything bigger, plus a selection of assorted timers."

"Excellent. At your soonest, Sergeant-Major, and delivered to Farley Field."

"I'll see to it myself, sir." Harley folded the pad. "Sounds like the kind of order Mr. Dillon would have given me." He hesitated. "I heard a whisper, sir. I hope it isn't true."

"Farley Field, Sergeant-Major, at your soonest."

"Of course, sir," and Harley went out.

ALEKO MADE GOOD time on the main road, turning into a narrow track when he was close to his destination, negotiating the way slowly over the uneven surface in the light of the headlamp. When he rode into the yard of the farm, it was midnight, but there was still a light in the kitchen and a dog barked. Aleko switched off the engine and pushed the Suzuki up on its stand. The door opened and Goulos, an aging man with gray hair, appeared, holding a shotgun.

"Who are you?"

"It's your cousin, Constantine, you fool. Put the gun away."

The dog had rushed out, still barking, but now started to whine and lick Aleko's hand.

"What kind of time is this?" Goulos demanded.

"Ask me in and I'll explain."

"Well, come in. My wife's away so you'll have to make do with me."

Aleko took a package from the Suzuki's side bag and followed him. It was a country kitchen with stone floor, open fire, and pinewood furniture. He put the package on the table.

"One thousand Marlboro cigarettes, my gift to you."

Goulos almost went berserk. "These things are like gold, so expensive. Almost too good to smoke, but I will."

"Here, have one of mine for the time being and let's have a drink," Constantine said.

Goulos went to the cistern, opened it, and took out a bottle. "This is a German wine called Hock. Marvellous when cold and the cistern is better than an ice box."

He got a corkscrew and opened the bottle, poured two glasses, and accepted one of Aleko's cigarettes. "Wonderful." He expelled the smoke. "So I die a little earlier. Who cares? I hear you're doing really well with the smuggling these days."

"Fair."

"What nonsense, you make a fortune. So what do you want with your poor old cousin?"

Aleko poured more Hock. "You're family, Goulos, and I love you, but if you let me down in this affair, I'll kill you myself."

"That important?" Goulos said. "Well, what are families for? So tell me."

"Castle Koenig," Aleko said.

Goulos stopped smiling. "You've got a problem there?"

"I could have. A serious problem. Tell me anything you can."

"Well, this American family has owned it for years. The present member is, or was, a colonel in the Israeli Army, name of Levy. The family have always been well liked locally. He used to have holidays as a boy, learned some Greek, but these days"—he shrugged—"it's not the same."

"In what way?"

"Well, he always had caretakers, Zarchas and his wife, because he only came to the castle now and then, but about two months ago he fired them without explanation."

"And then?"

"Five young men turned up, all Israelis. They've been there ever since. One of them, called Braun, does the shopping at the village store. He doesn't have Greek, so uses English." He poured Aleko another glass of Hock. "They're there now, I know that for a fact, also Colonel Levy. What's it about, Constantine?"

"Bad people is what it's about," Aleko told him. "I think they're holding two women captive."

Goulos smiled beautifully. "Now isn't that a coincidence? Little Stefanos, my goat boy, was on the slope close to the castle a few days ago. He was in the olive grove looking for a stray, and he could see into the courtyard. Someone drove in in a vehicle, then two of the Israelis helped a woman out and took her in the main door between them."

"My God," Aleko said. "That's it."

"No, there's more. He was up there again yesterday when the same thing happened, only this time the woman involved had to be carried inside."

Aleko banged on the table. "Like I said, bad people, my cousin."

"So what will you do about them?"

Aleko smiled. "Oh, something appropriate." He stood up and shook hands. "Enjoy your cigarettes," and he opened the door and went back to the Suzuki.

When he returned to the taverna, his nephews and Stavros were sitting at the bar, the only customers, Anna standing behind.

"What happened?" she demanded.

"First I phone Brigadier Ferguson, then I'll explain." He went through to the office and was back in five minutes. "Right," he said. "What do you want to know?"

FERGUSON HAD TAKEN the call while seated in the back of his Daimler on the way to Farley Field. He had never felt such elation. He sat there thinking about it, then phoned the President on his mobile. Cazalet was in the sitting room at the White House having coffee and sandwiches with Teddy, when he took the call.

"Total confirmation, Mr. President. My local contact has established they are there."

"Thank God!" the President said. "What happens now?"

"We'll do whatever we have to tomorrow. I'll be there with Dillon and Blake Johnson and my local people. I'll keep in constant touch."

"Thank you," Cazalet said, then turned to Teddy. "They're there," he said simply. "They are there at Castle Koenig. Ferguson has had it confirmed."

THE ONE FLY in the ointment was the weather. At Farley Field the rain fell monotonously as Ferguson was sitting in the small office the station commander had loaned him, talking to Blake and Dillon. Captain Vernon and Lieutenant Gaunt came in. Gaunt unfolded a chart across the desk.

"There we are, Brigadier, direct flight over France, Switzerland, northern Italy, and down the Adriatic Sea to Corfu."

"How far?"

"Almost fourteen hundred miles."

"How long will it take?"

"I'd normally say three hours to allow for any eventualities, but weather in mainland Britain is so bad at the moment that they won't give me a departure time until eight A.M."

"Damn!" Ferguson said.

"Sorry, Brigadier, nothing I can do."

"Yes, not your fault. Proceed on that time scale, then."

Vernon went out and Dillon opened the French window and looked out at the rain. "A hell of a night."

"I know, don't rub it in," Ferguson said.

It was Blake who stated the obvious. "Even if we don't get to Corfu by noon and still have to cross the island by Range Rover, it won't make much difference. Whatever the plan, when it comes to attacking Castle Koenig, it must be under cover of darkness."

Ferguson nodded. "You're right, of course." He pushed back his chair and stood up. "A few hours sleep, gentlemen. Let's grab them while we can," and he led the way out.

IT WAS STILL RAINING THE FOLLOWING MORNING WHEN THEY took off, rising through the bad weather steadily until they leveled off at fifty thousand. Sergeant Kersey brought coffee, and tea for Dillon, and retired.

"Can we go over again what Sergeant-Major Harley delivered?"

Ferguson told him, and Dillon nodded. "That seems adequate. I'm glad you remembered the door charges."

Ferguson said mildly, "I would remind you, Dillon, that I have been doing this sort of thing for even longer than you."

"Is that a fact?" Dillon said innocently. "I didn't think you were that old."

"A nineteen-year-old subaltern on the Hook in the Korean War, as you very well know."

"I always heard that was a bad place," Blake said.

"You could say that. Trench warfare, just like the First World War.

You'd sit there in a regiment of seven hundred and fifty men and the Chinese would attack in divisional strength, usually around twelve thousand." He shrugged. "Old men's stories. Who cares?"

"Well, you got a Military Cross out of it, and that's not bad for nineteen, you old bugger," Dillon said. "Let's look at that map again."

Ferguson took it from his briefcase and unfolded it. It was quite simply a large-scale map of Corfu. "Here we are, Vitari, that's Aleko's village, and he said Castle Koenig was about fifteen miles north."

"But not marked," Blake said.

"Well, it wouldn't be, it's not that kind of a map." Ferguson looked at Dillon. "You think it can be done?"

"Under cover of darkness, yes."

"There is one problem. Aleko and his chaps are good men and as fine a band of cutthroats as I've ever used, but against Judas, or Levy, as I suppose we must call him now. . . ." Ferguson shook his head. "A first-class soldier, and I would deduce that every one of his men has served in the Israeli Army."

"It doesn't matter," Dillon said. "This is a one-man operation anyway. Aleko and his boys simply land me and stand out to sea and wait for a signal to come back when needed."

"The worst idea I ever heard of," Blake Johnson told him. "I think you've forgotten how to count, Dillon. Levy has five men that we know of—that's six including him—and we got that information from you. Now what the hell are you going to do? Sneak in there and kill them one by one like a bad action movie?"

"I know the interior of the castle, I know where to go."

"You don't damn well know. You were on the third floor, and so was Marie de Brissac, and you only know that because they took you down to the cellar. Oh, I was forgetting. They took you to the great man's study, so you know where that is. Other than that, you know squat."

"So what are you saying?"

"That you need backup, my fine Irish friend, and here I am."

"It's not your kind of game."

"Two tours in Vietnam, Dillon, and I've killed a few times in the FBI. It's beyond argument." Blake turned to Ferguson. "Tell him, Brigadier."

Ferguson smiled. "Frankly, I rather took it for granted. I even brought a jump suit and flak jacket for myself."

"Now I know the world's gone mad," Dillon said.

"Yes, on reflection, I'll stay with the boat. Useful, that flak jacket, though, if we come under fire, but I'm hungry. Sergeant Kersey!"

Kersey came through from the galley. "General?"

"I keep telling you, it's Brigadier in the British Army. I don't know what these two want, but I'd like tea, toast, and marmalade. I'm just in the mood."

"Coming right up, General," Kersey said deliberately and returned to the galley smiling.

IN HIS STUDY, Colonel Dan Levy, also known as Judas, was standing at the window looking out, an unlit cigar in his mouth, when there was a knock at the door and they all came in, led by Aaron, and stood in a semicircle.

Levy turned to face them. "Good morning, gentlemen."

"Colonel." Aaron nodded. "You sent for us."

"The operation is obviously at a critical point. The President has to make the decision to sign Nemesis day after tomorrow."

It was David Braun who spoke. "Colonel, do you really think he will?"

"I don't know. The one thing I'm certain of is that I will surely execute his daughter if he does not. My mind is fixed on that." He looked hard, incredibly determined. "Is there anyone here who doubts that?"

He looked from one to another searchingly. "Is there anyone here who doubts the cause we fight for?"

It was Aaron who spoke. "Of course not. We're with you to the end. Whatever it takes."

"Good. So, the next forty-eight hours is critical. How are the women, David?" he asked Braun.

"I took the Bernstein woman back to her own room for the night."

Levy cut in. "Not the Bernstein woman, David. Give her the proper title. Personally, I admire her greatly. They could do with her in the Jerusalem Criminal Investigations Department."

David Braun looked uncomfortable. "I took the Chief Inspector back to her own room for the night. I haven't taken her to join the countess yet because I was leaving breakfast until after this meeting."

"Give them anything they want." He laughed harshly. "A champagne breakfast. Why not?"

"Any further orders, Colonel?" Aaron asked.

"Not that I can think of. Frankly, we have nothing to worry about. As I've told you before, I have eyes and ears everywhere. Navy Seals are not going to attack us, gentlemen, Special Forces are not going to parachute in, and not just because they don't know where we are, but because the President of the United States knows that if he made one move, his daughter would die on the instant. Isn't that so, Aaron?"

"Of course, Colonel."

"So simple it's a work of genius," and Levy threw back his head and laughed. "Come to think of it, I *am* a genius," and his eyes glistened.

They shifted uncomfortably and Aaron said, "We'll get moving then, sir."

"Good. Usual two prowler guards tonight in the grounds. Two hours on, four hours off. Dismissed, gentlemen."

Once outside, Moshe, Raphael, and Arnold moved away, leaving David Braun with Aaron. Braun was agitated, and Aaron said, "Have you got a problem?"

"For the first time, I'm beginning to think he's mad. Maybe some of that Sinai sun got into his brain."

"Let him hear you talk like that and you're dead, you fool. Now pull yourself together and get their breakfast."

. . .

BRAUN GOT HANNAH from her room and took her along the corridor. "I hope you slept well?"

"You don't give a damn whether I slept well or not, so why pretend?"

He unlocked the door to Marie de Brissac's room and ushered Hannah in. "I'll have breakfast ready in a little while."

Marie came out of the bathroom. "What was that?"

"Just Braun. He's gone to get breakfast."

"He's late this morning. I wonder why?"

Hannah went to the window and peered through the bars. There was a fishing boat passing by not too far from the bay. "Now if only it was flying the flag of its country, we'd know where we were. Roughly." Hannah laughed.

Marie gestured to her easel. "What do you think?" The charcoal sketch was fleshed out in color now and was quite excellent. "Watercolors wouldn't have been right, so I had to use crayon."

"It's marvelous," Hannah said. "Can I have it? I'd love to have it framed."

In the same moment, realizing what she'd said, she burst out laughing. "Well, that's optimistic, anyway," Marie told her.

Ten minutes later, the door opened and Braun pushed the trolley in. "Scrambled eggs and sausages this morning."

"Are they kosher?" Hannah asked.

"Oh, we take what we can get." He lifted the cover of a dish. "The bread is locally baked and the honey is local, too. Coffee is in the thermos flask."

"And the champagne?" Marie asked and took the bottle from the ice bucket. "Whose idea is this, Judas's?"

Braun shifted uncomfortably. "Well, yes, he thought it might cheer you up."

"The condemned man ate a hearty breakfast?" Hannah put in.

"Very hearty if he had this to go with it," Marie said. "Louis Roederer Cristal, nineteen eighty-nine. Judas has taste, I'll say that for him. Mad, of course, but tasteful."

"He's a great man," Braun burst out. "In the Yom-Kippur War, when the Egyptians took us by surprise, Judas was in command of some of the most strategic bunkers, with a hundred men under him. They fought like lions in that burning Sinai heat. When they were relieved, there were only eighteen left alive."

"A long time ago," Marie said. "I'd have thought he'd have got over it by now."

Braun was angry. "Got over what? Arab hatred, the constant attacks by terrorist groups like Hamas? What about Lebanon, and the Gulf, when Iraq targeted us with missiles?"

"All right, we hear you," Hannah told him.

"No, you don't, and you a Jew. You should be ashamed. What about Aaron's brother shot down over Syria and tortured? What of my two sisters, blown to pieces in a student bus?"

He was very agitated and Marie said, "David, calm down, just calm down."

"And Judas."

There was a pause and Hannah said softly, "What about him?"

"His mother, his married sister, decent people over from America to spend time with him, killed in a Jerusalem bus station bomb. More than eighty people killed or wounded. This is funny?"

"David, nobody thinks it's funny," Marie told him.

He opened the door and turned. "You think I enjoy this, Countess? I like you. I like you a great deal. Isn't that a huge joke?"

He went out, locking the door, and Hannah said, "Poor boy, I do believe he's in love with you."

"Well, it won't do him any good or me," Marie said. "But let's get on with the scrambled eggs, and we might as well open the champagne."

"Why not?" Hannah said. "You know the story about Louis Roederer Cristal and why it's the only champagne bottle you can see through?"

"No, I don't think so."

"It was designed by Tsar Nicholas of Russia. He said he wanted to be able to look at the champagne."

"And look how he ended up," Marie de Brissac said and popped the cork.

AT THAT MOMENT the *Cretan Lover,* Stavros at the wheel, passed Castle Koenig a few miles off shore. Aleko was also in the wheelhouse, Yanni and Dimitri worked at the draped nets. Aaron, on the battlements with Moshe, focused a pair of Zeiss glasses, bringing the boat into sharp focus. He lowered them.

"Just a fishing boat."

Moshe took the glasses from him and took a look. "The *Cretan Lover.* Yes, I've seen that one tied up in Vitari when I go for supplies."

He handed the glasses back to Aaron, who said, "I'll be glad when it's over, one way or the other, but over."

"I couldn't agree more," Moshe said and walked away, an MI6 slung from his left shoulder.

IN THE WHEELHOUSE, Aleko focused the old binoculars from his navy days, and every line of the castle came into prominence, sharp and clear.

"Two men on the battlements," he said softly, "one of them with a rifle." He ranged across the bay. "Seagoing motor cruiser on one side of the jetty, speedboat on the other and a powerful one from the look of it. I bet that baby does thirty knots." He nodded to Stavros. "I've seen enough. Let's go home."

As they turned out to sea, Stavros said, "You'd need an army to get into a place like that."

"Maybe not. Let's see what Ferguson comes up with."

. . .

When the Gulfstream landed at Corfu Airport, it taxied under instruction to a remote area where there were older hangars and a number of private planes. There was a police car waiting there with a driver, a young captain standing beside it. He came forward as Ferguson led the way down the ladder.

"Brigadier Ferguson?" he said in fair English, and shook hands. "My name is Andreas. Colonel Mikali phoned me from Athens with orders to offer you every facility."

"That's kind of him," Ferguson said.

"Customs and immigration are taken care of, and I have a Range Rover for you. Is there anything else I can do?"

"Help us load our stuff and we'll be off," Ferguson said.

The various cases were manhandled from the cargo hatch into the Range Rover, and Captain Andreas departed.

"Very obliging, this Colonel Mikali in Athens," Dillon said. "Here we are, importing arms into the country. Does he have any idea what we're about?"

"Of course not," Ferguson said, "but he does owe me a few favors." He turned to Vernon and Gaunt, Kersey standing behind them. "Gentlemen, you're probably as intrigued as hell, but there's nothing I can say at this point except that you've never been part of anything so important. If our efforts come to fruition tonight, your next destination will be Washington."

"Then we'd better get on with refueling, Brigadier," Vernon said.

Ferguson got into the rear of the Range Rover, Blake in the passenger seat at the front, and Dillon took the wheel.

"So, this is where it gets interesting, gentlemen," he said and drove away.

When they pulled up outside the taverna at Vitari, Aleko came down the steps to greet Ferguson as he got out of the Range Rover.

"Hey, Brigadier, you look younger." He embraced Ferguson fiercely and kissed him on both cheeks.

"Stop all that Greek nonsense," Ferguson admonished him. "This is Sean Dillon, these days my main enforcer."

Dillon shook hands. "You come well recommended," he said in passable Greek.

"Hey, a man of parts," Aleko said in English.

"And an American friend, Blake Johnson."

Again, Aleko shook hands. "Come this way. I've closed the taverna for the rest of the day so we can have privacy."

Yanni, Dimitri, and Stavros were at the bar and Ferguson greeted them like old friends. As Blake and Dillon watched, Aleko said, "Quite a man, the Brigadier. He got a message to pick up one of his agents from Albania a few years ago. We get to the beach and find six policemen, and the Brigadier slips over the stern with a Sterling submachine gun and takes them from the rear. Shoots two in the back and holds the rest up."

"That's quite a story," Blake said.

Anna appeared with coffee on a tray, put it on the bar, and embraced Ferguson, and more introductions were made. Finally, everyone sat and got down to business.

"We took a run up to the castle this morning," Aleko said. "Using the fishing boat. There were two men on the battlements, one with a rifle slung from his shoulder."

"So?" Ferguson nodded.

"I've been thinking," Aleko said, "that if we are going up there at night, I'll get a few fishing boats to go as well. Good cover."

"An excellent idea."

Aleko nodded. "So what do you really expect of us?"

"My two friends here, armed to the teeth, intend to penetrate the castle and liberate the two women held hostage there. The six men in residence, the opposition, are all former Israeli soldiers."

"Mother of Christ," Yanni said. "It could be a blood bath."

"That's their business," Aleko told him, "and they look as if they know their business to me. So our job is to land them?"

"And without alerting the guards," Dillon said. "Is that possible?"

"Anything is possible, Mr. Dillon. Are you a scuba diver? We've got equipment."

"Yes, I'm a master diver."

"Well, that lets me out," Blake said. "I was blown up a few years ago on an FBI case and my right eardrum was ruptured. Anything underwater is out for me."

"Never mind, we'll come up with something," Aleko told him.

Dimitri said, "What's it pay, Brigadier?"

Ferguson glanced at Blake, who said, "Money is neither here nor there on this one, but let's say a hundred thousand dollars."

There was dead silence, and Yanni said, "And who in the hell do we have to kill?"

"These are bad people," Dillon told him. "And they can handle themselves. They might kill you."

"Well, we'll see about that," Yanni said with the bravado of youth.

Aleko looked serious. "You told me about one of the women being your assistant, this Chief Inspector Bernstein."

"That's right."

"So it's the other woman that's the key, the one who's really important?"

"Not now, Constantine. One day you'll know, but not now," Ferguson told him.

Dillon stood up. "I'd like a look at the boat, if that's possible."

"Sure." Aleko turned to the rest of the crew. "No need for you to come."

"And I've seen it all before," Ferguson said. "Perhaps the boys could unload the equipment we've brought, the weapons and so on."

"Sure thing, Brigadier." Aleko turned to Stavros. "Have everything taken to the barn. Anything the Brigadier wants he gets."

"Sure thing," Stavros said.

Aleko nodded to Dillon and Blake and he led the way out.

. . .

THE *CRETAN LOVER* was still draped with nets drying in the sun and there was the good salt smell of fish mixed with the smell of the sea. Dillon and Blake looked the boat over while Aleko sat on the thwart and smoked a cigarette.

"So, you still fish?" Dillon said.

"Why not? It gives us something to do when we're not engaged in the Albanian trade, and we need the front."

"Are you telling me the customs and the navy people don't know what you're up to?" Dillon was peering down the hatch into the engine room. "You've got enough down there to power a torpedo boat."

"Sure they do. The police sergeant knows, but he's my second cousin and the lieutenant commanding the most important patrol boat, but then I trained him myself when I was in the navy. On the other hand, things have got to look right from the navy's point of view."

"Then everybody can look the other way with a clear conscience?" Blake said.

Aleko smiled. "I'll tell you what. Let's go for a little run and see if we can come up with a solution to your problem."

He went into the wheelhouse and pressed the starter button. As the engines rumbled into life, Dillon cast off the stern line and coiled it and Blake did the same in the prow.

The *Cretan Lover* coasted out of the small harbor and Aleko boosted power, the boat lifting over waves at that point. It was all very pleasant in the hot sun. When they were about four or five hundred yards from the harbor, Aleko cut the engines.

"Let go the anchor."

It was Blake who saw to that and Aleko braced himself against the wheelhouse door, the boat tilting as the water heaved in long swells.

"Let's imagine the fishing boats put their nets out about this far from the castle jetty. It's pretty similar."

"How deep?" Dillon asked.

"Eighty fathoms, sometimes a hundred. Plenty of sardines this time of the year and they don't go deep, so it would all look legitimate."

"It's the getting to the shore without being seen that's the thing," Dillon said.

"Well, underwater's the obvious way."

"But not for me," Blake reminded him.

"Let's give it a try anyway, if only to check the feasibility. What about it, Dillon? I've plenty of gear in the cabin."

"I'm game," Dillon said. "Lead me to it."

They manhandled a couple of tanks on deck and Aleko provided inflatable jackets, masks, and fins. "No need for diving suits. We'll go in at fifteen or twenty feet only and it's warm enough at that level."

They got the gear on, Blake helping out. When they were ready, Aleko opened a box and produced a couple of Marathons, passing one to Dillon.

"What's that?" Blake asked as Dillon switched it on.

"A dive computer. Absolute bloody marvel. Gives you an automatic reading of your depth, elapsed time under water, how much time you've got left."

"Is that necessary?" Blake asked. "I didn't think there were problems when you stick to shallow waters."

"There's always a chance of some kind of decompression sickness at any depth, small, but it's there. Diving's a hazardous sport."

"Okay," Aleko said. "Let's go."

He went backwards over the side. Dillon tightened his weight belt, checked that the air was flowing freely through his mouthpiece, and followed. He swallowed a couple of times to equalize the pressure in his ears and went after Aleko.

The water was very blue and seemed to stretch into infinity, and it was so clear that they could see the white sand of the bottom eighty feet or so below. There were fish everywhere, most of them quite small, and once a motor boat passed overhead and Dillon was rocked in the shockwaves of the turbulence.

He kept on going, just a couple of yards behind Aleko, aware of an off-shore current carrying them in and of the sea bed shelving. As they entered the harbor, it was no more than thirty feet deep. They swam under the keels of numerous fishing boats and surfaced beside stone steps leading from the jetty.

Aleko spat out his mouthpiece and checked his watch. "Fifteen minutes. Not bad, but we had a strong current pushing us along."

"Not too good for the journey back," Dillon said, and at that moment, Yanni appeared on the steps above them.

"What are you doing here?" Aleko asked.

"They didn't really need me up at the barn, so I thought I'd see what you were up to."

"Good lad. Now go and get the inflatable. You can run us back to the boat."

The inflatable was black and powered by a Mercury engine that was incredibly noisy, even when Yanni throttled back. As they drifted in to the *Cretan Lover,* the boy cut the engine and Aleko tossed the line to Blake.

"It wouldn't be possible to approach the castle jetty in this thing under cover of darkness," Dillon said. "Maybe we could row it in."

"Not without difficulty," Aleko told him. "Outside that bay there is a fierce cross current. It can run a good two to three knots, enough to blow you off-target."

"Then how in the hell are we going to do it?"

Blake was leaning over the rail, listening, and Aleko said, "I may have a solution." He turned to Yanni. "The Aquamobile is in the aft cabin. Bring it up. Help him, Mr. Johnson, it's an awkward size."

It was like a large sledge with a framework of aluminium. In the center was a huge battery pack and a triple propeller inside a wire cage.

"How fast will this thing go?" Dillon asked.

"Four knots. Let's go down and you can try it."

Dillon submerged, the Aquamobile descended in a shower of bubbles. Aleko grabbed the bar at the stern and switched on, moving away smoothly. He returned and offered it to Dillon, who took over and circled the boat. He switched off and came up beside the inflatable.

"What are you suggesting?"

"Let's say you and Mr. Johnson ride in the inflatable and I guide the Aquamobile in and tow you."

Dillon nodded. "It's a thought, but it might be too heavy."

"Well, we'll see." Aleko looked up at Blake. "Join Yanni in the inflatable, Mr. Johnson, and we'll try."

Blake dropped over the rail and Yanni tossed a line to Aleko, who fastened it to the handling bar. "Here we go," he called and switched on.

Dillon swam alongside, just under the surface, but was gradually left behind as the Aquamobile and the inflatable forged ahead. After a while, they turned in a circle and moved back to the boat. Dillon followed, and by the time he got there, they were pulling the Aquamobile over the rail.

He and Aleko unzipped their inflatable jackets and tanks, and Blake and Yanni reached over for them. Dillon removed his fins and followed Aleko up the small ladder.

He toweled off on deck and lit a cigarette. "That's it, then."

"So it would appear," Aleko nodded. "We'll go back and tell the Brigadier."

THE BARN WAS built of heavy stone, and whitewashed. There were no windows, but there was electric light. A row of sandbags lay at one end fronted by cardboard cutouts of soldiers.

"So you take it this seriously?" Dillon said.

"Let's say I like to keep my hand in," Aleko told him.

They were all there, including the crew of the *Cretan Lover,* and the equipment Ferguson had ordered from Harley at the Ministry was laid out on trestle tables, the black jump suits and flak jackets, the silenced Brownings and Uzis, the night-vision goggles, the stun grenades, and the Semtex blocks and timers.

"Mother Mary, we're going to war," Yanni said.

Aleko picked up the pair of night-vision binoculars. "Hey, I could do with these. Beautiful."

"You can have the lot afterwards if this thing works," Ferguson told him and turned to Dillon. "Anything else?"

"Yes, I'd like a decent rope. Let's say a hundred feet long and knotted every two feet." He looked at Aleko. "Can you manage that?"

"I'll put the boys right on to it." He picked up one of the Brownings and weighed it in his hand. "May I?" he asked Ferguson.

"Be my guest."

Aleko took deliberate aim and fired three times at the end target. He hit it in the chest, widely spaced. "I never was much good." He gave it to Blake, butt first. "Your turn."

"It's been a while. Too busy to practice these days." Blake held it in both hands in the approved stance and fired three times, the result, a tight grouping in the heart area.

He handed the weapon to Dillon. "Now you."

Dillon turned to Ferguson. "Do I have to?"

"Come off it, Dillon, you Irish are all the same. You love showing off."

"Is that a fact, now?"

Dillon turned, his hand swung up, two dull thuds as he double-tapped, shooting out the eyes of the first target. There was total silence and then Dimitri whispered, "Jesus, Mary."

Dillon weighed the Browning. "A nice weapon, but I still prefer the Walther," and he laid it down on the table.

"Well, after that, I'd say the only thing to do is go and eat," Aleko said and led the way out.

RAIN SWEPT IN ACROSS THE HARBOR AND THERE WAS A WIND off the sea. Stavros was in the wheelhouse, the two boys on the deck sheltering under the canvas canopy they had rigged earlier when the rain had started.

The other four were in the main saloon, the weapons laid out on the table. Aleko was wearing a black nylon dive suit and Dillon and Blake had already put on the jump suits and flak jackets.

"You didn't mention rain," Blake said.

"Because the weathermen got it wrong as usual. This little lot was due mid-morning tomorrow." Aleko shrugged. "On the other hand, good cover as long as you don't mind getting wet."

"A fair point," Dillon said. "What about the other fishing boats?"

"They've gone up in stages, which will look nice and normal, and it's usual to work together with the bigger nets in the sardine season. If they check them from the castle, they'll only see working fishermen."

"Excellent," Ferguson said.

Aleko lit a cigarette. "So, we go in, I drop you on the beach by the jetty. How long do you think this thing will take?"

"Half an hour," Dillon said. "At the most. It's got to be straight in and hit them hard and out again, or not at all."

"Oh, I don't know. You could always kill them," Aleko said.

"Now there's a possibility," Dillon replied.

"So, this is the way it goes. We join the other fishing boats, move in a little closer to shore. Yanni and Dimitri get the nets out. We'll have the inflatable on the other side of the boat from the shore, load up, and I tow you in." Aleko picked up four signaling flares. "These are mine. Nice and red. You take two each in case of mistakes. Fire one on your way out of the castle and we'll come to the end of the jetty in the *Cretan Lover* to pick you up."

They all sat there thinking about it. It was Ferguson who said, "Your friends in the other boats, what do they know?"

"They think it's some kind of smuggling thing as usual. Once they see us go, they'll leave quietly themselves."

They all sat there quietly and it was Dillon who said to Ferguson, "Do you want to call you-know-who on your mobile?"

Ferguson shook his head. "The only call I want to make to that man now is to tell him we've succeeded."

"Fine," Blake Johnson said. "Then let's do it."

MARIE DE BRISSAC STOOD at the window, peering out into the rain. "There are fishing boats, I can see the lights."

Hannah was just finishing dinner. She reached for a glass of water and drank, then went to join her. "It's a strange feeling, life going on out there, and here we are in durance vile, as they used to say in the historical novels I read as a child."

"I used to like the fairy stories by the Brothers Grimm," Marie said, "and it's the same feeling. They were always locking young women up in towers. Wasn't there one about a girl whose hair was so long, she let it down from the window for her rescuer to climb up?"

"I think that was Rapunzel," Hannah said.

"What a pity," she said quietly. "If Mr. Dillon comes, I wouldn't have long enough hair." She gave a sudden dry sob, turned, and grabbed at Hannah. "Suddenly, I'm afraid. It's so close now."

"He'll come." Hannah embraced her fiercely. "He's never let me down, not ever. You must believe that."

She held Marie close, and looked out at the falling rain and in her head she was saying, *Oh Sean, you bastard, where are you? Don't fail me now.*

RAPHAEL WAS ON the battlements, his MI6 slung from one shoulder, examining the fishing fleet through night glasses. Their red and green riding lights were plain and each had a pool of light in the stern from a deck light. There were footsteps and he turned and found Aaron and Levy approaching.

"Nothing to report, Colonel," Raphael said. "The fishing fleet, but everything else quiet."

Levy was holding a golfing umbrella against the rain. He handed it to Aaron. "Give me those," he said and took the night glasses from Raphael.

He adjusted them, bringing the images of the boats into sharp focus, the fishermen at their nets. It was the same with the *Cretan Lover,* Yanni and Dimitri working away in the rain. What he didn't see were Blake Johnson and Aleko on the starboard side facing out to sea, slipping the Aquamobile over to float, half-submerged, beside the inflatable.

He handed the glasses back to Raphael. "Stay alert," then turned, walked to the end of the battlements, and re-entered the castle on the third floor level. Aaron put down the umbrella and followed him and, at that moment, David Braun came out of Marie de Brissac's room with the dining trolley.

"So, they've eaten?" Levy said.

"Yes, Colonel."

Levy assumed his Judas identity again, pulled on the hood, and stepped into the room. The two women were seated opposite each other at the table by the window.

"There you are," he said. "The clock ticks faster and faster, but then, as Einstein said, all time is relative." He laughed. "Especially when you don't have too much to play with."

"How kind of you to remind us," Marie de Brissac told him.

"Always a pleasure to do business with a real lady, Countess." He made a mock bow and turned to Braun. "Lock them up tight for the night, David," and he went out followed by Aaron.

There was a moment's silence, then David Braun said, "I'm sorry, but you'll have to return to your own room, Chief Inspector."

Hannah kissed the other woman on the cheek. "Good night. I'll see you in the morning."

She walked past Braun into the corridor, and he said to Marie, "I can do nothing—nothing."

"Of course you can't, David. Wasn't it Kennedy who said for evil to triumph, all that is necessary is for good men to do nothing."

He winced, then went out, locking the door behind him, and took Hannah down the corridor to her own room.

ON THE *CRETAN LOVER,* they had just finished getting ready in the cabin. Dillon and Blake were in the black jump suits, festooned with stun grenades and black packs containing extra ammunition and the Semtex door charges and a couple of quarter-pound blocks for emergencies. Each had a holstered Browning and wore night goggles pushed up on the forehead. An Uzi slung around the neck completed the picture.

Aleko fastened a weight belt around his waist, and Stavros clipped an air tank to his jacket. "Anything else?" he asked.

Aleko nodded. "Pass me that dive bag. I'm going to take them a surprise present. You said you'd be half an hour?" he said to Dillon.

"That's right."

"Then I'll drop a little Semtex in the motor cruiser and the speedboat with forty-minute timing pencils. That way they can't come after us."

He put some Semtex and timers in the dive bag and hung it around his neck. Ferguson picked up the heavy coil of rope the boys had prepared and draped it around Dillon's neck diagonally to his waist.

Dillon smiled. "Don't forget to put the other flak jacket on, you old sod, just in case it gets a little warm later."

"Mind your back, Sean," Ferguson told him.

"There you go, on first-name terms," Dillon said. "I mean, where's it all going to end?" and he turned and followed Blake and Aleko out through the starboard sliding panel in the cabin wall.

Aleko adjusted his air and went over the rail backwards. He surfaced and fastened the line to the Aquamobile. Stavros hauled in the inflatable, and Blake went over and then Dillon. They crouched there together, keeping low. A moment later, there was a tug as the Aquamobile took the slack and they moved away.

The rain was relentless and the waves broke over the side, so that they were soon soaked. There was no light on the jetty, but lights up in the castle. When Dillon pulled down the night goggles, he could see the jetty clearly. They coasted in and beached, getting out and pulling the inflatable and the Aquamobile up on the sand.

"Good luck!" Aleko whispered, and Blake and Dillon moved away.

Aleko slipped off his jacket, tank and fins, swam alongside the jetty, then went up the short ladder to the motor cruiser. He took a block of Semtex from his dive bag, found a forty timing pencil, broke the end, and thrust it into the block. He opened the hatch to the engine room and dropped it inside.

He slipped across the jetty to the speedboat, repeated the operation, then lowered himself into the water, swam to the beach to retrieve his jacket, tank and fins, and pulled them on quickly. A few moments later and he was making his way back to the *Cretan Lover,* hanging on to the Aquamobile.

ARNOLD, PATROLLING THE garden, was miserable and wet, so he went up the steps to the terrace and stood in the shelter of the portico. He managed to light a cigarette and stood with the MI6 slung from his shoulder, the cigarette cupped in his hand.

Dillon and Blake, approaching the frontage, paused to take stock, their night goggles giving them a remarkably clear picture. Dillon, looking up, saw Raphael on the battlements leaning over. He crouched down and pulled Blake with him.

"Hey, Arnold, are you there?" Raphael called in Hebrew.

"Yes, I'm under the portico."

"And smoking a cigarette, I can smell it from here. Don't let the colonel catch you. I'm going inside to do the corridor rounds."

"Okay."

Arnold stepped back into the portico and Dillon whispered, "I'll go left and attract his attention and you take him from the rear. Don't kill him. He's too useful."

He slipped away, pulled himself up over an ornamental flower bed, and reached the terrace. He walked towards the portico, Arnold very clear in the night goggles.

"Hey, Arnold," he called in Hebrew. "Where are you?"

"Who's that?" Arnold called, taking a step forward, and Blake had him in the same moment, an arm around his neck, the other hand over his mouth.

In the jump suit and the goggles, Dillon presented a terrifying spectacle. He took out his Browning, cocked it, and touched Arnold under the chin. When he spoke, it was in English.

"This is silenced, so I can put one in your heart, kill you instantly, and no one will hear a thing. Now you're going to answer some questions, and if you don't, I will kill you and we'll go and find your friend, the one we saw on the battlements. Do you understand?"

Arnold tried to nod and Blake took his hand from the young man's mouth. "I'd do as he says if I were you."

"Who are you?" Arnold asked.

"I've come back to haunt you. It's me, Dillon."

"Oh, my God, but it can't be. The colonel told us you were dead."

"The colonel, is it now? Well, he'll always be Judas to me. Now, answers. The countess, is she still in the same room on the third floor?"

"Yes."

"And Chief Inspector Bernstein?"

"She's on the same corridor in the room you were in."

"How many are you? The same number?"

Arnold hesitated and Dillon jabbed the Browning into his side painfully. "Come on. Judas and five of you. Is that it?"

"Yes."

"Who was on the battlements?"

"Raphael."

"We heard him talking to you."

"You couldn't, he spoke Hebrew."

"So do I, in a manner of speaking, something Judas didn't know. Raphael said he was doing the corridor rounds. What's that mean?"

"What it sounds like. He patrols corridors and stairs."

"And the others, where are they?"

"Braun is usually in the kitchen on the ground floor. He does all the cooking. There's a small lift to serve the other floors. That's how he gets food to the women."

"And the rest?"

"The colonel is usually in his study."

"Which leaves Aaron and Moshe."

Arnold hesitated. "Aaron and Moshe?"

Dillon screwed the silencer on the end of the Browning into Arnold's neck.

"I'm not sure. There's a billiards room by the library, that's off the main hall. Sometimes they play."

"Anywhere else?"

"The recreation room on the first floor. Satellite television, that kind of thing."

Dillon nodded. "All right, so to get to the stairs up to each floor, we need the main hall?"

"Yes, you take the stairs from there."

"Good." Dillon turned him round. "Then show us the way."

They moved along the terrace through the rain and Arnold opened an iron-studded door leading the way into a corridor. There was a light on, another oaken door at the end.

Dillon pushed up his goggles. "Where are we?"

"The entrance hall is through there."

"Then lead on."

Arnold reached the door, turned the iron-ringed handle and opened it, revealing a massive hall beyond. There was a flagged floor, a log fire in an open fireplace, an array of flags hanging from poles above the fireplace, the ceiling vaulted. Why he did what he did next was probably a mystery to himself as much as anyone, for he swung the door back behind him and ran across the hall.

"Colonel!" he screamed. "Intruders! Dillon!"

Dillon pulled back the door and shot him in the spine. A moment later, a door opened on the opposite side of the hall, and Aaron and Moshe appeared carrying handguns. Dillon was aware of the billiard table in the room behind them and fired twice to keep their heads down. Blake backed him with a quick burst from his Uzi that sent them into the billiard room, slamming the door.

"Here we go!" Dillon cried and started up the great stone stairway fast, Blake following.

They reached the first landing and began to climb further. As they came out on the second landing, Raphael appeared at the far end, clutching his M16. He raised it to fire and Blake loosed off another wild burst that drove Raphael diving for cover.

"Come on!" Dillon said and made for the third floor and Blake went after him.

In his study, reading a book and drinking cognac, Daniel Levy was instantly alert at the first sound of gunfire. He opened his desk drawer, took out a Beretta which he put in the pocket of his jump suit, and picked up an M16 that was leaning against the wall. His study was on the first floor, and as he emerged, Aaron and Moshe appeared at the end of the corridor, having come up the back stairs. They were each holding AK assault rifles.

"What is it?" Levy demanded.

"We heard Arnold shouting in the hall. He called: Intruders. Dillon. Then we heard gunfire in the hall, went out and saw him dying, two men in black jump suits, night goggles, just like the SAS on a bad night in Belfast," Aaron said.

"Dillon?" Levy stood there staring at them. "It can't be. Dillon's dead." And then some kind of comprehension dawned. "Berger, knocked down in London. Dillon—it must have been." There was gunfire on the next floor. "Come on!" he said. "The bastard's going for the women," and he ran for the back stairs.

Dillon and Blake hit the third floor fast and moved headlong, pausing at the door to the room in which Dillon had been prisoner. He kicked it again and again.

"Hannah, it's Sean." He turned to Blake. "The countess is two doors down. Do it, Blake."

He heard Hannah call, "Sean, is that you?"

"Stand back, I'm blowing the door."

He took a door charge from one of his packs, pushing it into the keyhole of the oak door, Blake doing the same further along the corridor. Dillon twisted the timer cap and stood to one side. Four seconds was all it took. The door rocked and splintered and he was into the room.

Hannah ran to meet him and actually flung her arms about his neck. "I've never been so glad to see anyone in my life." The second door charge exploded and she said, "What's that?"

"Blake Johnson getting to Marie de Brissac." He took his Browning from its holster. "Take this, we're not out of the woods yet and there's only the two of us."

DAVID BRAUN HAD been sleeping in the small bedroom at the end of the third-floor corridor. He awoke, confused and frightened at the first sounds of gunfire, and dressed hurriedly. He picked up an Armalite which he kept by the bed, opened the door, and stepped out.

The first thing he saw was Blake leading Marie out of her room, Dillon and Hannah Bernstein beyond. He raised the Armalite and hesitated, aware of the danger to Marie. Dillon saw him, cried a warning, and pulled the pin on a stun grenade and rolled it down the corridor. Braun jumped into a nearby alcove, and the stun grenade went straight through the archway at the end of the corridor and fell down the stairwell, exploding.

At the same moment, Levy, Aaron, and Moshe appeared at the other end of the corridor and started firing. Dillon pushed Hannah back into her room and Blake and Marie de Brissac followed.

There was silence, then Raphael appeared at the stairhead behind Braun. He called, "Raphael here, Colonel, with David."

"Good," Levy shouted back. "I've got Aaron and Moshe here. There's only two of them and they aren't going anywhere. You hear that, Dillon?"

"If you say so," Dillon replied. "I wasn't going anywhere in Washington, but here I am." He rolled another stun grenade along the corridor and jumped back.

Levy had already opened the door of the last room in the corridor and shouted, "Inside!" to Aaron and Moshe. They made the shelter of the room, and as he slammed the door the stun grenade exploded on the landing.

Levy opened the door. "Not too good, old buddy. Like I said, you aren't going anywhere. Hey, when you get time you've got to tell me about Washington. That must have been real slick."

He fired several bursts from his M16, clipping the wall by the broken door of what had been Hannah's room. Dillon poked the Uzi out one-handed, sprayed along the corridor one way and then the other.

He turned to Blake, who said, "Now what do we do?"

Dillon put down his Uzi and pulled the coil of rope over his head. "A good job I brought this along, it's our one chance. Everybody get in the bathroom." Marie de Brissac looked dazed and Dillon said, "Move it, for God's sake. Hannah, we're running out of time."

Hannah urged Marie before her into the bathroom. Blake followed. Dillon fired another burst from his Uzi into the corridor, then put it down again, took a quarter block of Semtex from one of his pouches, jammed it on the windowsill against the bars, and rammed in a two-second pencil timer.

He ran and flung himself flat on his face on the floor beside the bed. The sound of the explosion seemed to make the room sway, and when he looked up through drifting smoke the window, the bars, and some of the surrounding stonework had disappeared, leaving a jagged hole.

Dillon ran to peer out and Blake joined him, the two women at his shoulder. "Forty feet down to the terrace," Dillon said. "You lower the countess and Hannah one by one, then tie one end to the bed and go down yourself. I'll hold the fort and follow when I can."

Blake didn't hesitate, simply uncoiled the rope and tied a large loop in the end. As Dillon picked up his Uzi and reloaded, Hannah grabbed his arm.

"Sean, you wouldn't do anything stupid like going down with the ship or something?"

He grinned. "Hey, genuine concern, and at this stage of our relationship?"

"Damn you!" she said.

"Already taken care of." He ran to the door, poked the Uzi out again, and fired toward Braun and Raphael, who fired back instantly.

ON THE *CRETAN LOVER,* they saw the explosion blossom in the night up there in the castle, and a second or so later, there was the hollow boom as it echoed across the water.

"What in the hell is happening?" Ferguson said as he stood at the rail wearing the third flak jacket, a Browning in one hand.

"Whatever it is, I'm going to be ready," Aleko said. "We'll move in close, a hundred yards from the jetty. Dump the nets, just cut them loose, and everyone make sure they're armed."

He went into the wheelhouse and took over from Stavros. A moment later, the engines rumbled into life, and as the nets slipped away the *Cretan Lover* moved toward the jetty.

HANNAH WENT FIRST, finding it surprisingly easy with the loop under her shoulder and the rough stone walls of the castle providing good footholds. She reached the terrace, pulled the loop over her head, tugged, and Blake pulled it up.

He turned to Marie de Brissac. "How about it? You'll be safe in my hands, I promise you. Just don't look down."

"And we haven't even been introduced."

"Johnson—Blake Johnson. I'm your father's special security man."

"Well, it's nice to know you, Mr. Johnson, but I've no problem with heights. The general climbed in the Swiss Alps every year. I was ten when he first took me with him." She pulled the loop over her head. "Thank you, Mr. Dillon. I thought you looked like the sort of man who always comes back for the girl."

"In the last chapter only, Countess, and this isn't the last chapter.

On your way," and Dillon crouched back as a storm of firing erupted in the corridor.

MARIE DE BRISSAC ARRIVED safely on the terrace. This time, Blake left the rope hanging and did as Dillon had suggested, tying the end securely to one of the massive legs of the old bed. There was silence for a moment, and Blake said, "What now?"

"Give me your Uzi, then get the hell down the rope and start for the jetty with the girls."

"And you?"

"I'll lay down a suitable field of fire, then I'll be down that rope myself doing my celebrated imitation of Tarzan of the Apes." He shoved a fresh clip into his own Uzi and stood there, one in each hand. "Go on, Blake, get moving."

Blake couldn't think of a damn thing to say, turned, took the rope in both hands, and went down backwards, and Dillon crossed the room, leaned out, and watched him go, for the rain had stopped, the clouds clearing enough to expose a full moon. In its light, he could see Blake descending and the two women looking up.

Levy called, "Hey, Dillon, listen to me."

"Why, it's my old chum Judas or Colonel Dan Levy or whatever you call yourself. Ready to surrender, are you?"

Levy seemed to crack then, rage erupting as he called, "We'll rush him now."

Dillon took a deep breath and stepped into the corridor. Raphael had appeared at the far end, his M16 ready, David Braun behind him. Moshe had moved into the open at the other end. Dillon fired the Uzis in sustained bursts, left- and right-handed, pushing Raphael back against Braun and slamming Moshe against the wall, four or five bullets in him.

The Uzis emptied, Dillon dropped them to the floor, ran for that jagged hole, got a grip on the rope, and started down, knot by knot.

. . .

As Moshe fell backwards, kicking in death, Levy looked down at that bloodstained body and something happened to him. It was as if it confirmed the fact that he had lost, everything he had worked for down the sewer, and all because of Dillon.

He erupted then, crying, "Dillon, you bastard! Face me!"

He went up the corridor on the run, spraying the walls with his M16, and paused in the entrance of the room, confronted by the gaping hole, the rope. The shock seemed to make him speechless for the moment. Aaron, coming up behind, pushed him to one side and went to the hole and peered out.

Levy pulled himself together and crossed the room in two quick strides. "Can you see them?"

David Braun entered the room and stood just inside the door, the Armalite in his hands, as Aaron said, "Down there on the other side of the garden. The two women and the other man are making for the beach."

"Stand back," Levy said and raised his M16. "I can still get that bitch."

"No, Colonel, enough is enough." David Braun held the Armalite to his shoulder. "Just put your rifles down and let her go."

"Why, David, this is a surprise."

Levy put the M16 down on the table, at the same time putting both hands in his pockets, the right one finding the butt of the Beretta. As he turned, he fired twice. Braun was thrown back in the corridor, dropping the Armalite, and lay there groaning. Levy picked up the M16.

"Come on," he said to Aaron. "We're going after them," and as he walked past Braun, he finished him with a headshot.

Running through the ornamental garden, Dillon pulled out one of the signal flares and pulled the string. The small rocket curved up into the air, exploding into a scarlet bloom, clear not only to the *Cretan Lover* but the entire fishing fleet.

Aleko switched on and the engines rumbled into life. "Everybody ready? We're going in."

As Blake and the two women reached the jetty, Dillon ran down the path behind them, the *Cretan Lover* roaring in out of the darkness.

As Dillon joined them, Hannah reached for his arm. "Thank God."

"Yes, I must live right," Dillon laughed excitedly and crushed her in his arms. "We did it, girl dear, we beat that son of a bitch."

The *Cretan Lover* came to almost a dead stop, drifting against the jetty, engines throbbing. Yanni and Dimitri were over the side in an instant, helping the two women, Ferguson and Stavros reaching for them, and Aleko looked out of the wheelhouse.

"Hey, you two wonderful bastards, you won the war, eh?"

There was a burst of firing from somewhere and a bullet ricocheted from the stonework of the jetty.

"Not yet, we haven't," Dillon replied as he and Blake dropped to the deck. "Let's get out of here," and Aleko did just that.

Levy and Aaron arrived on the run as the *Cretan Lover* sped toward the fishing fleet, where most of the boats were already hauling in their nets.

"We've lost them, Colonel," Aaron said.

"Not with the speedboat, you fool. It can do thirty knots. I doubt if they can match that. You take the wheel."

He dropped down into the stern and Aaron slid behind the wheel and found the ignition key under the rubber mat, where he usually concealed it. He switched on and the massive engines sprang into life.

Levy said, "Now run them down!"

. . .

STAVROS SAID, "HE'S coming."

"Don't worry," Aleko said. "We'll be into the fleet soon, but get the women below."

Ferguson took them down to the cabin, then came back and joined Dillon and Blake, the third Uzi in his hands. Yanni and Dimitri and Stavros all had revolvers. Ferguson handed Dillon his Browning.

"The Chief Inspector thought you might need it."

The speedboat roared out of the night, clear because of the moon, Levy crouched in the rear. Ferguson triggered the Uzi, the crew fired single shots, but Aaron weaved from side-to-side, first one way, then the other, and suddenly, Levy stood up and sprayed the *Cretan Lover* with an entire M16 magazine at close quarters.

The wheelhouse shattered, a round took Ferguson in his flak jacket, knocking him down, and another punched Dimitri in the shoulder.

Dillon loosed off a couple of shots, but the speedboat swerved, came in again, and they all ducked as Levy raked the deck.

"We're sitting ducks," Blake cried.

"Not quite," Aleko told him, and back at the jetty, fire blossomed in the night as the motor cruiser exploded.

"Number one," Aleko said.

The speedboat came in again and Levy stood up, black against the distant flames. He raised the M16. "I've got you now, Dillon," he cried, his voice echoing across the water.

And then the speedboat blew up, disintegrating before their eyes into a fireball, pieces flying through the air, some rattling against the hull of the *Cretan Lover.* There was a hissing of steam, and what was left disappeared under the surface of the sea.

"And that was number two," Aleko said. "Now we go home."

Stavros was checking Dimitri's shoulder and Ferguson was sitting down. He plucked the round from his flak jacket. "I feel as if I've been kicked by a mule."

Hannah and Marie appeared cautiously from the cabin. "Is it over?" Marie de Brissac asked.

"I think we might say that," Ferguson said, "but first I'd better speak to your father."

Cazalet was hosting a reception at the White House for a Russian delegation. He'd done well, kept his end up remarkably, his mind understandably on other things. He was deep in conversation with the Russian Ambassador when Teddy approached.

"Sorry to intrude, Mr. President, but there's a call of the utmost urgency."

Cazalet excused himself and followed Teddy to a small anteroom. Teddy closed the door and handed him the special mobile.

"It's Brigadier Ferguson, Mr. President."

Cazalet took the phone, his face pale. "Yes, Brigadier, this is the President."

He listened, and it was as if ten years slipped from him. "God bless you, Brigadier, God bless all of you. Washington next stop. We'll expect you tomorrow."

He switched off the phone. Teddy said, "Mr. President?"

"You know what, Teddy?" Jake Cazalet smiled his famous smile. "What I'd appreciate more than anything right now is a glass of champagne and I'd like you to join me."

WASHINGTON

EPILOGUE

When the Gulfstream landed at Andrews, the bad weather had switched to that side of the Atlantic and, under instructions, they taxied through rain to a remote area of the base, right into an empty hangar. Two limousines waited and Teddy Grant stood beside one of them.

Kersey opened the door and Ferguson led the way down, followed by Dillon and Blake. Teddy hurried forward and took Blake's hand. "I can't believe it and neither can the President." He turned to the others. "Brigadier—Mr. Dillon. A great day."

"Well, in the end it worked, and very much thanks to you." Ferguson shook his hand warmly.

Kersey had followed and was standing at the bottom of the ladder and Vernon and Gaunt joined him. A moment later, Marie de Brissac and Hannah Bernstein came down.

Teddy took Marie's hand briefly, then Hannah's. "I can't tell you what a pleasure it is to see you here. Please follow me."

He walked toward the limousines, and Ferguson said, "A moment, if you please." He turned to the crew. "My thanks, gentlemen. As I've already said, you've never been involved in anything more important."

He shook hands with each of them, then walked to the limousines where the others were waiting.

"The countess is expected at the White House with Blake," Teddy said. "I'm taking her there now. The rest of you go to the Ritz-Carlton, where three suites have been booked. Time for you to freshen up and so on, and then the President will send for you."

"Of course," Ferguson said. "We'll see you later, then."

Marie looked tired and a little bewildered. "Yes," she said. "Later. I must see you again."

She drove off with Teddy and Blake, and Dillon and Ferguson stood back to allow Hannah to get in the limousine first. As they drove away, Ferguson pressed the button to raise the glass divider.

"That all seemed a bit formal under the circumstances."

"You're missing the point, Brigadier," Hannah said. "The President simply wants to be alone with his daughter at this moment in time."

"Yes, I see what you mean, I suppose," he said.

Hannah shook her head. "Men, all the same, no idea of sentiment," and she leaned back.

IN THE WHITE HOUSE, Jake Cazalet was sitting beside the fire, a prey to conflicting emotion. What would it be like? How would she react? There was a tap on the door, it opened, and Teddy entered.

"Mr. President, your daughter," he said and stood to one side.

Cazalet got to his feet, found himself shaking, and then Marie de Brissac moved into the room and stood looking at him, but only for a moment.

"Father," she said.

Cazalet, filled with more emotion than at any time in his life, opened his arms and she ran to him.

IT WAS THREE hours later that the limousine from the White House picked up Ferguson, Dillon, and Hannah Bernstein.

"A nice trouser suit you're wearing," Dillon told her. "Armani, isn't it?"

"They do have a rather splendid boutique at the hotel," she said. "Got to look right for the White House."

"I noticed from the functions board in the foyer that the President is entertaining the Russian Prime Minister at dinner at the Ritz-Carlton tonight," Ferguson commented.

"Well, that's good," Dillon said. "Now that we've got her back, he can enjoy it."

IT WAS RAINING hard as the limousine moved along Constitution Avenue toward the White House, but in spite of the weather, there were TV cameras and tourists on Pennsylvania Avenue.

Ferguson lowered the glass screen. "I'm surprised, considering the rain."

The chauffeur said, "A lot of activity with the Russian delegation. I was told to bring you to the East Entrance."

Ferguson put the screen up again. "They would, I suppose. They use the East Entrance for special visitors who want to avoid media attention."

The limousine drove up East Executive Avenue and stopped at the gates, where the driver spoke to the guard, who waved them through. They finally stopped and the chauffeur got out and opened the door.

"This way."

He indicated the door, which opened at once, and Ferguson led the way in. Inside was a Marine Lieutenant in dress uniform, who snapped to attention and saluted.

"Brigadier."

There was also Teddy Grant, who came forward smiling. "Wonderful to see you all again. If you'd follow me, the President is waiting."

IN THE OVAL Office, Cazalet sat behind his desk and Marie was standing beside the window with Blake Johnson. She made the first move, running to Hannah and embracing her.

Cazalet came round the desk and shook hands with the three of them. "Impossible to thank you. Blake has given me the whole story. If this was Buckingham Palace, you'd be lining up for awards, but it's America."

"And thank God for it," Dillon said.

The President smiled and shook Dillon's hand again. "You always come through, my fine Irish friend." He turned to Ferguson. "I've spoken to the Prime Minister at Number Ten, given him a résumé of what happened, apologized for using you in such a cavalier way but stressed the unusual circumstances."

"Oh dear, that could be awkward," Ferguson said.

"Not at all. He was most understanding and looks forward to hearing about it from your own lips. Now, is there anything else I can do for you?"

"Nemesis, Mr. President?"

Cazalet shrugged. "There's got to be a better way."

"I agree," Ferguson said. "So one last favor. I think we should be getting back to London as soon as possible. If we could borrow the Gulfstream?"

"Of course. No problem, is there, Teddy?"

"Not really," Teddy said. "We'll probably need a new crew is all. A question of them exceeding their hours in the air."

"Take care of it." Cazalet turned to them again. "Our sincere thanks."

Marie kissed the Brigadier on the cheek, hugged Hannah, and

stood looking at Dillon, strangely shy and apparently unable to speak but she managed.

"You are a remarkable man, Mr. Dillon."

"It's been said before, Countess." He laughed out loud and Teddy opened the door for them.

TWO HOURS LATER, they climbed up from Andrews out to the Atlantic and leveled off at fifty thousand. Dillon pressed the buzzer and the flight attendant came from the galley. This one was white and called Roscoe.

"I'll have a Bushmills," Dillon said, "a large one."

"Coming right up, sir."

Dillon grinned at Ferguson and Hannah. "I've earned it."

For once, Hannah agreed. "Yes, I think you have, Dillon."

Roscoe brought the Bushmills, and Dillon said, "Yes, happy endings is what I like, and I suspect Jake Cazalet is a happy-endings man at heart."

"What on earth are you babbling about?" Ferguson demanded.

"It's just that deep down inside, I'm an incurable romantic."

"You?" Hannah said. "Romantic about what?"

"Oh, you know what they say. Read all about it in the papers. The great Dillon is never wrong," and he settled back and drank his whiskey.

AT THE RITZ-CARLTON in Washington on Massachusetts Avenue, the great and the good and the Russian Prime Minister awaited the appearance of the President of the United States. When he arrived at the front entrance, got out of the limousine and waved to the crowds, the Comtesse Marie de Brissac was at his side, wearing a simple black evening dress, a gold cross at her throat. Teddy got out of the next limousine with two Secret Service men, and ran ahead.

Cazalet smiled. "Countess?" She took his arm and they walked through the foyer and paused at the entrance to the dining room.

Teddy moved just inside. "Mr. Prime Minister, ladies and gentlemen, may I have your attention."

There was a flurry of movement as everyone rose. Teddy took a deep breath and announced in ringing tones, "The President and the President's daughter."